Sparkslingers
Cloud City

Julie Christen

Print ISBNs
Amazon Print 9780228625216
BWL Print 9780228625223
LSI Print 9780228625230
B&N Print 9780228625247

Copyright 2024 by Julie Christen
Cover art by Pandora Designs

All rights reserved. Without limiting the rights under copyright reserved above, no part of this publication may be reproduced, stored in or introduced into a retrieval system, or transmitted, in any form, or by any means (electronic, mechanical, photocopying, recording, or otherwise) without the prior written permission of both the copyright owner and the publisher of this book

Dedication

*To the little girl who so long ago asked me which cloud I live on.
Thank you for planting this seed.*

Table of Contents

Helpful Terms to Know 7
Prologue 9
Chapter 1 11
Chapter 2 19
Chapter 3 24
Chapter 4 35
Chapter 5 38
Chapter 6 45
Chapter 7 47
Chapter 8 54
Chapter 9 56
Chapter 10 65
Chapter 11 70
Chapter 12 77
Chapter 13 87
Chapter 14 97
Chapter 15 110
Chapter 16 132
Chapter 17 137
Chapter 18 147
Chapter 19 164
Chapter 20 168
Chapter 21 183

Chapter 22 195
Chapter 23 213
Chapter 24 219
Chapter 25 235
Chapter 26 241
Chapter 27 259
Chapter 28 274

Helpful Terms to Know

Spark: The vital force that nourishes and propels life; the inner element within all living things which initiates drive, desire, longing; that which makes one *want*.

Cloud City: Weather-making city in the sky, organized into three major atmospheric planes comprised of ten sectors. (See Figure A.)

Cloud Master: Ruler of each sector. Works with a precise set of checks and balances to maintain the intricate workings of Earth's climate. (See Figure A.)

Skybounds: Beings that live in the sky.

Earthbounds: Humans and creatures on Earth. They do not see or know of what goes on in Cloud City. Their instinctual desire for *more* is boundless, to the point of self-destruction.

Sludge: Sentient, but non-discerning fog created by Skybounds to travel Earth's surface in order to dampen and regulate excessive spark levels.

Catalyst: Unique and highly uncommon Earthbounds with a spark-slinging genetic blueprint. Their kind traces back to before Skybounds began regulating spark with sludge. Catalysts are sympathetic, reasonable, and passionate. Once trained by Skybound experts to share (or sling) their spark with others, Catalysts are assigned a section of Earth. There, they fix spark level imbalances left by the sludge on living entities. They work under the guidance of an assigned Skybound supervisor called a Kindred.

Sky Levels and the Skybounds Who Govern Them

(Figure A)

Plane		Sector	Cloud Master	Resident Types	Cloud Depiction
Troposphere	Illustrial	Cirrus	CM Tendril	**Crystalines** Seers	Ice crystals; feathery
		Cirrocumulus	CM Makryl	**Crystalines** watchers, messengers, nursery, shard school	Fish scale-like cotton ball rows
		Cirrostratus	CM Shreddard	**Crystalines** Kindreds and the Ice Crystal Guard	Fibrous, nearly transparent veil
	Mezzo	Altocumulus	CM Castella	**Mezzanines** body guards, mercenaries, bouncers	Tufted, globular masses in layers
		Altostratus	CM Virgus	**Mezzanines** peace seekers	Opaque, mostly stable, invisible water vapor
	Basal	Cumulus	CM Bumble	**Stormbuds** transporters, cloud steed keepers	Puffy cotton ball mounds
		Cumulonimbus	CM Loom	**Stormhulks** storm makers	Hot, humid, towering thunderheads
		Stratocumulus	CM Drizzo	**Stormlins** Drizzle Fields Workers	Low, lumpy, dark, suppressed waves
		Nimbostratus	CM Shroud	**Nebuls** rainmakers	Dense, thick stratus
		Stratus	CM Murkemer	**Nebuls** drizzle fields, sludge makers	Low, spread-out gray fog and mist

~ Introductory excerpt from *Catalyst Academy 101*

Prologue

Creeping along the quiet forest floor, it comes. The sludge reaches its long tentacles up saplings. It stunts them. It oozes through shadowy ferns and wilts all in its path. Sludge shadows cling to the trunk of a sequoia tree and creep up, up, up to a nest. Black-mist claws reach in and find two owlets waiting, mouths open. Dark vapors fold around the babies until their beaks close. Their tiny bodies slump. They no longer want. For anything. That's what the sludge does. It takes away the spark.

When done feeding on the owlets, it slithers down the tree and around boulders upheaved from the mossy forest floor. There is no spark to suck from a rock, for rocks want nothing. The sludge glides over decaying sticks and twigs. There is nothing to leech from these things either, for the dead has no spark. The dead cannot want.

It seeks. It always seeks. It is in a constant search for that thing it cannot create and cannot hold. For that is the nature of Want. And so, the shadow sludge continues through the forest on its hunt. Every sense tuned, peering, listening.

Suddenly, it hears footfalls approach, quick with intent. The sludge twists in the sound's direction. Its vapor tentacles prickle with anticipation at the possibility of a spark feast approaching. Then it glimpses a streak darting into the owl tree, and it hears the babies squawk for their mother once again. Happily, even! Their spark has been reignited. Verdant green foliage flows in the streak's wake down the sequoia and through the woods, bright and alive. This is not a feast after all, the sludge knows. It is time to leave this part of the forest.

Silently, before the streak slows enough to notice it, the sludge sinks into the shadows and sets a new course, for now, to find more spark to sap. It knows it is no match for who is coming – Catalyst Wayfare Day.

Chapter 1

WISPs and Ribbons

Bursting through the chest of a colossal teddy bear, the WISP squad cuts and weaves in perfect formation like crystalized fighter jets. Their mission this time: Prevent development of a potentially unstable and unauthorized weather mass in Cumulus Sector of the Mezzo Plane. That's cloudspeak for: Make sure two idiot cloud brothers don't accidentally demolish a section of the western coastline with another one of their cloud animal wrestling matches – what Skybounds call a trumble.

Young Squad Leader Breeslin sounds her sharp whistle and shouts back to her agents as they zip in line, "Snippet! Tuft!" She twirls a crystal finger in the air then slices her entire ice-encrusted arm to the left. The two agents break off in that direction. "Jink! Tygr! With me!"

Off they all shoot at blinding speed toward two skyscraper-high clouds. Arms pressed hard at their sides, crystal-spike hair laid flat, their sleek little bodies slice the air. Snippet and Tuft start flying a close ring around the quickly re-shaping cloud teddy bear. Breeslin, Jink, and Tygr zoom around the other, which happens to look like a partially formed rearing unicorn.

Pixie-like Breeslin juts her chin forward and an ice megaphone made of crystal shards slides out from around her neck. Her voice rings clear with authority. "This is Weather Investigation and Sky Patrol Squad Leader Breeslin. By command of the Ice Crystal Guard, you are both ordered to cease your cloud formations immediately. Repeat. Cease your cloud formations immediately."

A booming jolly voice echoes from the almost-unicorn mass of clouds. "WISP? Who ratted? Oh, come on, Bree. I've almost got this."

Ever-watchful, Snippet's long crystal-spike bangs dangle over her prism cylinders protruding from her eyes. She scans the shoreline far below, checking for any damage the Fairweather brothers may have caused already. She sees a cruise ship rocking from the wild gusts from above every time a new cloud limb is shifted. Snippet reports, "That ship's pier is busting up. Not good!"

Breeslin signals Jink, their fastest, to take care of the situation. "Jink, Recovery Op – Centrifuge and Stabilize."

Jink gives a sharp nod, making his shaggy, crystal hair tinkle. He lights the jets under his feet and veers downward. He pumps his arms and legs in place so ice chips tinkle off his uniform and says, "ROCS it is. My specialty," and flashes Breeslin a wildly charming, blue-lip smile.

She sighs, "Thank you," and tries to force down the flush in her cheeks as she shifts her demeanor to a serious-business face at the brothers. "Cottin Fairweather! I said IMMEDIATELY," she orders. "Jeez, it's like you two don't even remember last time."

Another reply comes from the teddy bear cloud mass. "What's a little accidental hurricane gonna hurt out here? Let him finish his sculpture!"

"No siree, Puffin! Absolutely not," Breeslin says. Little shards of ice sprinkle from her clenched fists. "You guys have no control once you get going. If these two masses fuse, there's no guessing what kind of storm might erupt!"

The unicorn keeps shaping. "Almost done!" says Cottin from somewhere deep inside it. By the sound of his straining voice, he's clearly not intending to cease immediately.

Jink chimes in on the sapphire comm in each team member's ear, "For fogsake! Get them to knock it off already! I know I'm good and all, but those blasts ..." He grunts with the effort it costs him to generate the centrifugal force required to shove the incoming gusts away from the ship.

Breeslin's Crystaline face creases into severe, iridescent angles. The Fairweather brothers may be immensely huge, but, as a self-respecting WISP, she is determined to fulfill her mission. She retracts the megaphone into her neck and speaks coolly into the sapphire comm link hooked over one of her sharp ears. "WISP squad, Initiate Operation Swirly."

Within seconds, both teams start to fly around and around their assigned cloud mass. As they pick up speed, their icy uniforms turn into a blurred blue stream. Their wake starts to pull at the cloud fibers, one layer at a time, smoothing out the bumps and lumps piled on top of each other. They continue to circle and circle until both cloud forms look like pyramids of cotton candy.

Popping out at the top of both swirly peaks are the cumulus brothers Cottin and Puffin. They bicker back and forth about who's animal would have been the coolest and should have won the wrestling match. The WISP squad lines up military-style between the two, their iridescent uniforms glistening in the sunshine. Compared to the immense cloud brothers, the WISPs are tiny twinkles to the unaided eye below.

Breeslin flies out with command. "Eh hem," she clears her throat and stands straight as an icicle.

Cottin and Puffin totally ignore her.

Rotund and dimpled like a head of cauliflower, Cottin stomps his foot. "If I'd finished those hind legs before Miss Buzzkill and her gang of ice pixies got here, my unicorn would've kicked the stuffing out of your teddy bear's face."

Puffin scoffs, "Whatever. Nothing can stop my Fluffinator." He stuffs his roly-poly arms across his chest.

Breeslin bristles at "ice pixie" then shakes it off and rolls her eyes. She lets loose a piercing whistle that could slice a glacier in half. That works. The whistle always works.

"That's ENOUGH, you two." Her voice booms with authority, which in no way matches her dainty frame. "Do not make me come back here. Do you understand me?"

The brothers simultaneously plop onto billowing cloud chairs with a harrumph.

Cottin says, "Fine." He looks pathetic.

Puffin, if possible, looks more pathetic as he says, "Can't even have a little fun."

Breeslin softens. These two boys are harmless. They just don't understand the consequences of their actions. She glances at Snippet, her right-hand girl, who gives a mildly sympathetic look behind her dangling crystal bangs. Breeslin knows Snippet is also thinking of all their own trouble-making when they were young shards, all in the name of "a little fun."

Snippet tilts her head at Breeslin, squints her shiny eyes and nods ever so slightly.

Breeslin sighs then squares her shoulders to Cottin and Puffin again. "I'm not saying you can't ever have your contests, boys."

Their heads perk up with a hint of hope.

"I'm just saying you need to wait for proper authorization from Cumulus Cloud Master Bumble, and get away from shorelines, that's all. I'll put in a request for an Only-Over-Ocean storm for you this one time. But you have to wait for approval AND put in your own Triple O requests from here on. Otherwise, you'll both have to deal with the consequences like everyone else, and serve community time in the Basal Plane working in the Drizzle Fields." She thumps her hands on her tiny hips. Sparkles of ice chips sprinkle away. "Understand?"

The brothers shudder at the words Drizzle Fields, but their eyes light up at the break she's throwing them.

They cheer in unison, "We will! We will." Then they drift toward each other to give a high five that poofs cloud stuffing everywhere.

"WISPs!" Breeslin calls to her team. "We're done here. Let's move." She flattens her ice-bladed arms to her sides and zooms off. Her team follows in jet stream formation, glinting complex prisms in the sunlight. They slice through the thick clouds up and out of the Cumulus Sector.

At the upper edge of the Basal Plane, the squad adjust their thrusters in preparation to jet into the Mezzo Plane. Just then, they're blasted by a rogue cold front that scatters the squad like dandelion tufts.

"Holy ozone!" shouts Tuft over the gale as the team strains to gather again. Her crystal-spikes ponytail flaps and chinks behind her head. "Where'd that come from?"

Finding her balance, Breeslin shouts back, "Probably from the instability the Fairweather brothers generated with their ridiculous cloud manipulation." She buffets against another icy blast then rallies her squad. "WISPs, let's reroute to a lower level. This thing will blow itself out eventually. We'll give it some space."

They give a wobbly salute and dive back down into the Cumulus Sector. But the nasty cold front, with the attitude that only a cold front can summon, veers at them with such force they lose all flight control and plummet helter-skelter down, down, down.

They sink like rocks through all the Basal Plane sectors. First, the Cumulus Sector, then the Cumulonimbus Sector, and then the Stratocumulus Sector. Their cranial prisms flash like a dance party through their hair as they keep up the necessary atmospheric adjustments. But once they reach the thick haze of the Stratus Sector, they lose sight of each other. The hard ground, they know, is racing toward them at blistering speed, but they can't see it.

Tygr is the first to use his sheer strength to regain control. He splays out his bladed arms and flicks his elbows to unfurl his ice-glide wings, which at least help him soar steadily enough to get his bearings and look for the others. His buddy Jink comes into view first, so he glides over and grabs him, steadying him just long enough for Jink to engage his own ice-glide wings. A flicker of piercing blue light bounces off their wings' reflective panels. They both look at each other in surprise.

The clouds are so thick that Breeslin and Tuft knock into each other. Somehow Tuft's crystal-spiked shoulder gets hooked into Breeslin's ankle shards. As they do a lunch-hurling pinwheel twirl, more electric blue flashes strobe before their eyes.

"What the heck *IS* that?" Tuft shouts while she spins. "Did you see it?"

Breeslin, struggling to unhook Tuft from her ankle, shouts back, "I'm not sure. Just help me get this so we can get out of here!"

When they finally get loose, they clasp hands, and engage their ice-glide wings. The blue lights flicker through the fog as they gain flight control.

Breeslin, her voice revealing the worry a WISP captain is not supposed to show, says, "Zephyr Almighty, what is happening?"

Tuft, in shock, points up ahead and hollers, "Look! Tyg's coming!"

Breeslin squints. "He's got Jink!"

All four WISPs clasp together as they look for their last officer.

Breeslin speaks into her sapphire earpiece trying to smooth the worried edge in her voice. "Agent Snippet, what is your location?"

Snippet comes through with crackling static, "I'm o--ay. Flight ---trol managed. Send beac-- immedi—ly."

"You heard her, Tuft. Light it up," Breeslin commands into the wind.

Tygr and Jink drop tinted ice shields from their spiky eyebrow dendrites as Tuft gives a single nod and removes the tie holding her crystal hair. Instead of falling over her shoulders like Snippet's, every strand floats as though full of static electricity. She closes her eyes and bows her head so her hair forms a sort of half globe. Inside her iridescent skull, prisms pulse a light, a bright-white-as-the-sun light, that grows and grows with intensity and punches out each crystal strand. The light slices through the murk and mist.

Tygr says to Jink, "That girl's got a beacon like none other."

Tuft gives him a coy look, not hiding her pride in the least. "My best feature, wouldn't you say, boys?" She bobs her head and bumps the beacon up a notch.

Jink and Tygr just smile and nod coolly.

Breeslin grins and chuckles at her team. But she needs to get Snippet. "Agent Snippet, do you see the beacon? Repeat. Do you see the beacon?"

A crackly voice comes through. "I s-- it! On --y w-- now.

The squad breathes a collective sigh of relief and waits for her to burst through the fog.

"Wait..." Snippet says through the static when a ripping CRACK blasts in their sapphire comms. "Oh Great Zephyr, th--ts --mpossi--!" Then another crack sounds, but not in their earpieces.

"What? What's impossible, Snippet?" Breeslin asks.

Only static.

"Agent Snippet, answer me. That's an order!" Breeslin holds up a fist signaling her squad to halt and hover. She asks again, doing her best to stay calm despite her racing heart and frantic thoughts, "Come in, Agent Snippet. Do you hear me? Come IN."

Through a hiss of static, barely audible, they hear Snippet say, "RIBBON! Lightning!" Her voice is fraught with disbelief, but the words are crystal clear.

The WISP squad just looks at each other.

"Not possible," says Tyg. "Stratus Sector can't make lightning. Cloud Master Murkemer is not allowed."

The explosion sounds again, closer this time.

Breeslin looks at her squad all looking back at her. She is supposed to know what to do. All the time. Any situation. And even on her worst days, though she is not only the newest but youngest leader, this is never a question. But lightning? In the Stratus Sector? Something is very wrong.

Breeslin touches her sapphire earpiece. "Get out of there NOW, Snip!"

Just then, the air is charged with electricity. They all feel it prickle in their dendrites. Tuft squeezes her eyes shut as the current tries to douse her beacon right out from her insides. The clouds behind them thicken.

Jink says out loud what everyone else already knows, "We have to bolt."

The light show in the clouds grows frantic. A massive surge of voltage is imminent, just like inside one of Cumulonimbus Cloud Master Loom's thunderheads. And though it shouldn't be possible here, it is happening nonetheless.

"WISP squad," Breeslin says shakily, "ignite ice-jets."

Unable to grasp the fact that Snippet is still missing, they all flick their feet. Cone-shaped ice-pipes snap out the bottom and glow red-orange.

"On my mark..." She looks one last time for her friend. "FLARE IT!"

Right on command, bursting through the strobe lights of the roiling clouds, blasts Snippet in full jet mode. Her face is fierce as she streaks to her spot next to her squad leader. "Agent Snippet, reporting for duty."

They scream into the clouds above.

Chapter 2

The Days

Warm morning light shines through Demeara Day's glass bluebirds on the kitchen windowsill. No. That's not quite right. Something soft and glowing refracts slightly through the figurines, yes, but to call it "light" and to say that it is "shining" would be exaggeration. But she knows the muddy glow is *supposed* to be light, so she sees it shining in her mind no matter the reality.

The reality is she has not seen actual sunshine since she was a very young child. Which, by the looks of her, one would assume is somewhere around 30 years ago. Her body is lithe and tawny. Her skin smooth and firm. Her hair full and shiny. She appears to be in her prime.

But, she is not 30 years old. In fact, she has kind of lost track of how old she is.

A blonde lock dangles in her eye as she sips at a steaming mug. Outside the kitchen window, her husband and son chop the last of the rotten tree that finally gave up and toppled over yesterday. Garrin, too, is strong and sturdy like he's in his prime, but she forgets how old he is as well.

Spark slinging does that. Stifles age. Maintains cell structure. Keeps a body from breaking down. Until ... well ... until you stop slinging it. Then the slow decay of mortality resumes but at an unnaturally quiet pace.

The life of a Catalyst is long.

She watches her husband gather and stack the wood. The old, massive barn on the hill once housed milking cows, and now stands like a sentinel, watching over the farm.

Deret, their son, swings his axe with swift, precise blows. Their youngest son. He has grown so fast. Deret is different than their first boy, Wayfare. He's now grown and gone away – one of the greatest Catalysts of the ages. Sparkslinger extraordinaire. And, yes, she is fully aware of the fact that every parent probably thinks their children are special, but in the case of her eldest son, it really is true.

But Deret is different than Wayfare, just as all brothers are alike yet different. While Wayfare had learned (masterfully, mind you) to generate and sling spark, Deret is ... full of it. Full of spark, that is. Head to toe. Inside and out. He is spark and spark is him. And it spills freely to all around him.

Plus, Deret stands out. It's not his lanky stature like his big brother, or his freckly face and stick-straight red hair. Something about him reminds her of the long-lost word she hasn't heard spoken or seen written since the days before the gloom settled in over Median decades ago. When the sludge seeped in to "regulate" spark levels.

Sun.

Through the window she sees Deret lean sturdily on his axe as he takes in a deep breath. He sees his mother watching, waves, and swipes his arms to showcase all the wood he's whacked to pieces. He beams at her. A bright shining smile like the ...

Sun. Her youngest son is most definitely sunny.

She smiles. It is sad that the two brothers have never met – or that Deret even knows the other exists. She sips her drink. A wistful sadness weighs heavy on her. That will change today. This is, after all, the day Deret will be taken. Losing your children to the greater call of spark slinging duties is a hazard of having spark run long and strong in the family. She, as well as Garrin, had left home to heed the call so many, many years. Now Deret will following their footsteps.

The little bluebird figurines on her windowsill twinkle for her. She sighs at them, wondering if she'll ever get to see the sun shine through them again. Shrugging and smoothing her loosely pinned bun, she folds down the top of the paper lunch bag in front of her. A fresh mug for Garrin in her other hand, she deftly uses her elbow and toe to open the heavy, carved door.

As she nears them, she sees Garrin is leaning on one knee next to a tree trunk. She slows to let her husband have this teaching moment with Deret.

"You see this rotten wood here? It's all blackened and hollow in some spots all the way up and down this piece."

Deret stoops to look at the end of the log. It's got swirls of black and powdery fibers all around the base. "Looks pretty bad, Dad. Nothing good left to it."

Garrin waggles a finger at his son. "Uh uh." His green eyes give off a light that Deret only sees when his dad is feeling particularly clever. "That is where you're wrong."

Deret tweaks a skeptical eyebrow, but he's listening. He always listens to his father.

"When I run this rotten old log through the mill," Garrin sweeps his hand in a slow, slicing motion, then pats the tree like he might have patted the back of a dear old friend, "we'll find something special." His eyes glimmer at Deret. "Something really beautiful."

Deret is not convinced and screws up his face. "Beautiful? That? It looks like a ruined hunk of wood." He knows he should take his dad's word for it, but this seems pretty obvious.

Garrin nods. "On the outside. Yes. But sometimes, Deret, you have to search deep inside to find the good stuff and coax it out of hiding."

Demeara decides this is her time to chime in. "And if ever there was a man who can coax the beauty out of something ugly," her own eyes twinkle a brilliant blue just like every other time Deret sees his mom compliment his dad, "it's your father. Just you wait and see, Deret. He'll make something amazing out of this 'throwaway' log, as you would have it." She offers her goodies to both of them. "Hey, you two lumberjacks."

Garrin grins softly, stands up and stretches his back. "You've rescued me just in time." He takes the mug and slurps. Then he tips his head at Deret. "I'm afraid he won't stop 'til I'm kaput." This is followed by the usual hair-mussing.

Deret ducks and tries to straighten at least his bangs. "Hey, we could've quit any time, Dad. I've just been trying to keep up with you." He laughs and slaps his arm around his father's narrow but sturdy shoulders.

"Spare me that," says Garrin chuckling and shaking his head. "I don't know where you get the energy."

Garrin and Demeara give each other a knowing glance. They know exactly where he gets the energy – his spark. But Cloud Code states that no underage Sparkslinger is allowed to know anything about their abilities, or the entire Cloud City megalopolis, until they've absorbed the Cloud City text. Naturally, the Cloud Council couldn't have individuals flinging their spark any which way without strict supervision. Without rules, who knows what could happen if people used spark any which way they liked. Rogue entities. Chaos, to be sure. Demeara and Garrin and Wayfare went through the academy, and so will Deret.

Deret just shrugs and brushes his hands off on his jeans. "Good genes," he says with a crooked grin.

Demeara pipes in, "Or good food like Widow Shay's." She lifts the lunch bag for Deret to take. "That woman knows her way around a garden, that's for sure. She's promised to fill me in on her secret for growing eggplants this summer. Mine never turn out like hers."

Deret peeks inside and inhales dramatically, "Cold eggplant lasagna, mmm. Just what I wanted for my last meal."

She shoves him a little and scoffs. "Eat it and like it, Mister. Now scoot. Or you'll be late for your last day of school." She knows he loves her no-nonsense, but today she can't keep herself from pulling him in for a long hug.

After she kisses the top of his head, Deret simply looks into her eyes and says, "Will do, Ma." He takes his lunch and heads for his bike leaning against a tree at the end of the driveway.

Garrin wraps his arm around his wife, squeezes her shoulder for comfort, and calls to their son, "And we've put a little something in there if you want to stop at the book store on your way home today."

Deret turns in surprise, his eyes all lit up. "No joke?!"

Garrin chuckles, "Get yourself something …" he looks a little shiftily at Demeara, "… *fun*, buddy."

That stops Deret in his tracks. He looks at his parents standing arm-in-arm. "*Fun?*"

They tip their heads toward each other and nod with gentle smiles.

Deret hops on his bike, "Will do!" he hollers and speeds off down the road.

As soon as his red hair disappears behind the crest of the hill leading down to the Median, Demeara Day lets loose a heavy sigh. Resting her head on Garrin's plaid flannel shoulder, she asks, "Do you think he's onto us?"

Garrin lovingly pats her shoulder and says matter-of-factly, "Doesn't matter. Widow will make sure he gets the book today."

"I just don't understand what's the rush." She squints to stave off the moisture building in her eyes. "He's still just a boy."

Garrin says, "Something's brewing. Widow says they need him. Says Wayfare needs him. Look at it this way, he'll finally get to meet his brother."

Chapter 3

Rumblings

The wind whips Wayfare's long coattails as he slides to a stop. His arms and legs splay, steady and confident, skidding across the needle-coated forest floor. A whoosh of wind billows past him flopping his hair over his forehead, but it bounces back into its usual lazy mohawk. He puffs. His unimpressive chest and knobby shoulders pump up and down. A bead of sweat trickles past his ear. He flicks it with his thumb, blinks, and takes a settling breath. The sludge is getting stronger. Faster. Hungrier. It never used to be like this.

Or am I getting slower? he wonders.

No matter. Tight-browed, he looks behind him at the lush green that just moments ago had been a crispy puce-colored mat of leaves and grass, thanks to that miserable spark sucking villain. Wayfare checks the device strapped to his wrist. It had read a dangerously low "External Spark Load: 9%" for the forest. Now it reads a relatively strong 89%. His body relaxes a little, and he nods as he looks around, satisfied with his work. That's what a Catalyst does. He restores the spark when he finds imbalance. But something is bugging him, and it has been for a while now. A little perturbed, he taps his SparkBit.

"Only 89%?" he asks out loud.

"Hoo hoo hoo hoooo," Father Owl hoots from his high perch. He contorts his head down so Wayfare can see his moony eyes. Then the owl flaps his wings and leaps soundlessly off into the sky.

Wayfare's sky blue eyes twinkle. "Glad to help," he says with an easy wave. But he's still worried. The owlets had taken quite some effort to get back up to an "Adjacent Body Spark Load: 95%" reading. Maybe his SparkBit is glitching. He draws in another settling breath, leans on his knees, and forcibly blows it out as measured as he can. A half a second's rest is all he needs.

Maybe a *whole* second.

Just as he sits on a log, a familiar prismatic halo forms before him in mid-air. He stands up straight, fruitlessly runs his fingers through his floppy blonde hair, and rubs his face with his hands, blinking hard and shaking his head. "Snap to," he says to himself. "Can't be caught slacking on the job now, can I."

A Catalyst's work is often lonely. After all, no one can keep up with his effortless speed. And of course, there's the unfortunate necessity to keep the perpetual sludge struggle under wraps. (If people ever found out that their spark was getting sucked out of them on a daily basis ... holy ozone, that'd be bad.) Therefore, it is not uncommon to find most Cats talking to themselves. This Cat, Wayfare, is quite okay with that. He likes working alone. Prefers it, even.

But on occasion – a very lucky occasion – a visitor from *up there* effaports down to Earth.

The halo pulses to the rhythm of his heart. It swirls and refracts light and colors in every direction. It pulses more and more rapidly swirling so fast it becomes a blur. Then, with a volt of magnificently controlled energy, an elegant shape surges forth like a butterfly. A very prickly butterfly.

The Crystaline Skybound stands before him. His Kindred from the Ice Crystal Guard has come to check up on him. Her slender limbs with razor sharp edges and pinprick points glisten and sparkle from a light that comes from within. Fractured patterns cast tiny beams across every inch of her sleek body as she moves fluidly toward Wayfare. Her skin-tight, sleeveless and oh-so-very-short dress is made of feathery snowflakes with sparkling, raw edges at the hem. She drifts as if on a cloud, her knife-like feet skimming the dirt.

"Ah Cirissa," he says cheekily, "beautiful beyond the meager words found inside this poor sap's skull."

Cirissa narrows her silvery eyes, not to be flattered. In a flash her bladed hand slices toward his head stopping an impossible fraction from the warm blood pulsing behind that paper-thin skin on his exposed neck. He stands frozen, but unabashed. She lifts her chin and tips her sleek crystal head just enough to look down her thin nose at him. Her finger blades glint with the slightest movement.

Wayfare gulps. "And *dangerous*. Nice." He flashes his most dashing smile and peaks an eyebrow.

Her icy resolve breaks only enough to smooth her hard, thin lips into a warm smile. "Wayfare," she says, and the sound of his name tinkles on the frozen air surrounding her, "you look terrible. Eat a sandwich or something. Your skin's all …" She searches for a word that won't hurt *too* much. "… loose."

Wayfare merely closes his eyes, exhausted and not quite prepared for the insult. But he rallies and shakes it off. "Cirissa, my dear, only you could send such a barb that makes me love you all the more."

"Love? Oh my. Haven't *we* gotten serious now." But she says *we* in a way that does not mean *we* in the slightest.

"Aw," he says, "it's just a matter of time," and wields an irresistible grin. He looks around and asks, "Where's my pretty little princess?"

Cirissa smiles as she flicks two finger blades together making a *ting* sound that resonates throughout the entire woods. Instantly, soaring down through the treetops like a swarm of fireflies, comes another glowing entity. It swims and swirls around Cirissa's legs. Then the flickering lights shimmer together until they merge to form a pure white Frost Fox at her side. A plume tail curls around her.

Wayfare scrunches down on his haunches and pats his knees. "There's my best girl!" he says.

The Frost Fox wags her fluffy tail, sending delicate sparks flying. She opens her petite muzzle into an adorable pant-smile then bounds over to Wayfare.

Love, she speaks to his mind.

He ruffles her ears and holds her face in his hand as he makes smoochy faces at her. "Who's a pretty little princess? You are, that's who."

She dabs the end of his nose with the tip of her tongue. *Love, love.*

Cirissa looks on warmly. He does have a certain charm about him. "Sheena," she calls to her Frost Fox, "good girl, darling. You can go play."

Sheena looks to Cirissa then back to Wayfare. She pant-smiles again and shakes her entire body. Sparks fling and flicker off her fur into a little cloud that floats and clings to Wayfare's coat. It scampers all over him until his whole body is sparkling.

Gift, she says.

He glances at his SparkBit. Internal Spark Load: 100%. "Awww..." he sighs. "Thank you for that."

Sheena tips her head, sneezes and wags her tail at him. Then she takes off like a shot into the woods leaving a trail of sparkles that sprout little white flowers everywhere.

Cirissa says with genuine awe as she shakes her head, "You do have a way with her."

He flashes his loveable grin. "See? She's got good taste, that one." He puffs out his scrawny chest.

Though Cirissa completely agrees, her ice-crusted lashes level with gravity. "No matter," she says. She has come with business. No time to trifle about. "We have a problem."

That sobers him. And that is just one more thing she admires about this Catalyst. He knows how to get serious when need be.

Wayfare is at her side in an instant. "I know," he says. "I've felt it too." His sky-blue eyes bear no sign of levity.

He always seems to know exactly what she's thinking.

"The sludge is stronger, isn't it? It's taking all I've got to keep up." He motions to his physique. "It's running me ragged." He holds up a hand. "Not that I can't handle it."

"Of *course,* you can," she says.

"Dang straight." He pulls up his jeans and shoves his sleeves to his elbows giving the illusion of bulk.

Cirissa tilts her head, and her eyes soften with the gentle smile his antics always coax from her. "No one doubts your abilities, Wayfare. Quite the contrary. The Crystaline Sect, in fact, believes it's time you take on an apprentice."

"Another one? What about Breeslin? Doesn't your council think I deserve a bit of a break after that Shard?"

A tiny scold flickers within Cirissa's crystal features.

He stays his point. "Nope. I'm all apprenticed out."

"I know she was quite a handful at times. Weren't we all? She's turning out so beautifully. Did you know she's leading her own WISP team? Besides, she wasn't exactly an apprentice, simply a Shard earning her dendrites. I remember earning mine long, long ago." Nostalgic, Cirissa looks at the crystal formations elegantly adorning her body. "I got this one," she says and strokes a jagged peak on her upper arm, making knife-sharpening sounds, "for creating the first snowfall Median had ever seen. I'll never forget the spark I lit that day. Children playing and laughing and running in the snow." She smiles sadly. "That seems so long ago." Her gaze is far away, deep within the crevices of her frosty complexion.

Wayfare is quiet. He knows her position in the Ice Crystal Guard is wearying work, keeping all the weather in line, from monstrous hurricanes to the lightest sprinkle. And now, on top of it all, this stirring of sludge. He understands her stress load. Deep down, it's why she chooses to use him as her Kindred instead of any of the other Catalysts chasing after sludge around the globe. He indulges her wistful moments without judgement. He has always been one to find reason for pause.

Regrouping her thoughts and purpose, Cirissa says, "Anyway…" and gives her entire body a shivery shake. Tiny ice slivers and droplets spray from her pointy spikes and edges as they all melt to reveal her appearance as a human. Wayfare shields his eyes, just enough to protect from nicks, but she knows he loves this point of their meetings. She can feel his eyes on her as she transforms. Though her skin remains glossy and somewhat iridescent, this form, she knows, is far less intimidating. Touchable even.

Wayfare gulps. Then blinks.

Cirissa hardly tries to hide her smile as she smooths the wrinkles on her oh-so-short iceberg-blue, glittery dress. Her snow-white ponytail high on her head drapes along her neck and folds in an elegant S accentuating her curves.

His voice cracks, "Tell …" He clears his throat. "Please, Cirissa, tell me what you know about the sludge. Signs of its strengthening?"

She smooths her ponytail with both hands, but her eyes are direct. "Rumors and rumblings, really. But enough to make the entire Cloud Council take notice."

"Lay it on me," he says.

"Three things. First of all, just last week, our Cirrostratus Branch had been called to look into yet another trumble between the Fairweather brothers in the Cumulus Sector."

Wayfare rolls his eyes. "When are those two ever going to grow up?"

Cirissa's laugh tinkles on the air. She shakes her head, "I know, I know. You'd think by now Cottin and

Puffin would learn. But the Cloud Council hadn't approved a thunderhead formation in that area, so they called on our WISPs to check out the situation, intervene if necessary, and report back. Something about making animals for cloud wrestling. Well, it turns out, Breeslin's team was able to get Cottin and Puffin to work it out. Whatever. But, on their way back, the WISPs ran into a nasty rogue cold front that shoved them off course, which is quite uncharacteristic for our WISPs. Usually, they have no trouble slicing through those dense masses, but it collided with our team and bulldozed them down into the Stratus Sector."

"Holy ozone!" says Wayfare as though her words had poked him in the gut.

"They're all okay," she says to ease his worry. "Though by the sounds of it, they did have quite a time getting out. But that's not the kicker. All five WISPs reported flashes and flickers of unauthorized lightning."

"You don't say?"

"Mmhm. And Snippet. You remember her. Breeslin's little friend?"

"Yes, of course. I had to pull those two up by the ear all the time. Little Shards."

Cirissa gives a loving laugh as she fondly remembers the two trainees always off giggling and causing mischief. "Well, Snippet swears on her particles that a ribbon cut through the Stratus Sector murk and nearly launched her into oblivion."

"A ribbon," Wayfare says thoughtfully, "of actual lightning?"

Cirissa repeats, "A ribbon of lightning."

"And you're sure they hadn't just zipped back into the Cumulus Sector? They're so quick, maybe they'd gone farther than they realized."

Cirissa closed her eyes and shook her head definitively. "She's certain it came from Murkemer's level, Wayfare."

They both sit in hard thought for a moment.

"Second?" he asks.

"Second?" she repeats. "Oh yes. The second sign came to us from Drift."

"Drift! I haven't seen that Cat for ages."

"Exactly," she says. "Drift told Prism – she's his Kindred – that he'd been trying to come visit you, catch up on old times, for a few months now, but The Rim won't let him through. Median's entire perimeter seems impenetrable. Prism looked into it herself, as will I soon as we're done here. She says the underbrush is thicker than naturally possible. Prism was able to get through of course, after a lot of slashing and slicing, but the sludge is thick as soup throughout most of it. She says Drift gave up after a while and came to her, worried about you and your little town. I am too."

Wayfare works his jaw. He cannot deny the probability of any of this. He's felt it for some time now, but when one is so close to a situation, sometimes he can't see it for what it is.

"Third?" he says.

She takes a deep breath. "There has been a sighting, more of a sensing really, of an ..." she pauses as though the words she's about to speak cause her insides to tumble, "... absolute extraction in your city."

Wayfare knee jerk reacts to this charge. "Impossible! I've ignited every sludge-induced slack spark in this city since the day I started. Never, *never* have I lost one."

"I'm told it was a chipmunk," Cirissa tries to minimize, even though she knows better. "And it was old. Very, very old."

His face drains of color and is replaced with sad realization. "Grampa Chap," he says. "When I left him yesterday, he was fine." He sits down on his log, face downcast in near disbelief. "He'd been sapped pretty badly, mind you, but I revived him." Wayfare looks up in earnest with glossy eyes. "He even scampered up his tree with a nut and chattered at me, probably embarrassed I'd touched his little belly."

A heartfelt "Oh" is all Cirissa can offer. She could touch his shoulder but decides against it.

"It must have come back." He spats it out as though the words are rank. "The scummuck sludge must have come back to finish its work."

Her voice is soft. "I suppose it did."

Then he looked at the device on his wrist. "Or my SparkBit might be malfunctioning. Could you test it quick for me, yeah?"

"Of course," she says and touches the clear disk with the tip of her slender finger. Subtle green waves pulse back and forth from the disk to her finger until she breaks the connection. "It seems to be fully functional, Wayfare. I ran a full diagnostic."

They sit in quiet for another moment. "Sheena will do a thorough check on the woodland. Its spark levels will be 100% by the time she's done playing." That doesn't seem to brighten his gloom, so Cirissa shifts the topic in hopes of getting his mind off Grampa Chap's death. "I visited with Widow Shay this morning."

That did sort of lift his spirit. "Oh? How's our ancient retiree?"

"Feisty as ever. You should see the eggplant she's grown. Spark still runs strong in her veins."

Wayfare shakes his head. "She is one tough Cat."

"Absolutely, and she's been keeping her eye on your little brother. She says he is strong and getting stronger. But here's what I found most interesting. Widow believes he is able to ignite others. *Naturally*. No training or anything!"

"You don't say," says Wayfare, skeptical. "I've been wondering how he's doing. I really need to check in at home. It's just hard, you know, when he can't know anything about," he wiggles his fingers over his head, "all this yet."

Cirissa says, "Well, he will get to meet you soon enough. Plus, Widow Shay says she thinks he might be the key to teaching others how to ignite their own spark." She looks him straight in the eye. "Counter the sludge on their own."

"*Counter* it? Cirissa, do you hear yourself?"

"I know it may seem a bizarre concept now, but with our limited number of Catalysts, and the sludge strengthening, I'm thrilled at the thought. Let me show you something."

She steps close to him, so close he can feel the coolness of her aura on his bare skin making his heart skip a beat.

"Show away," he says.

She gives him a look then holds her arms out to make a loop. Within the circle, a glassy surface warps into view like a rippling pool. As he peers into it, images appear.

"A vision glass," he says, impressed. "Cirissa, you've been holding out on me."

"Just look," she says and nods her head at the scene forming.

People of their beloved Median ripple into view. He doesn't recognize any of them, but there is something vaguely familiar about each of their faces. And they're all acting weird, nothing like typical Medians at least. These people have a spring in their step. They have sunny faces. They're driving fancy cars and wearing fancy clothes. They're shopping and carrying on with each other. Energy emanates from their interactions. Robust laughter and conversation fill the air.

Cirissa breaks into his thoughts, "There was a time, a long while ago, before you even existed, my dear Wayfare, when the people of Median generated so much of their own spark, they naturally resisted the sludge without even knowing it. There was a balance."

Wayfare keeps staring into the vision glass. "Holy ozone."

She disconnects the circle. "Earthbounds have it in them. But over the ages, the sludge has taken over." She shapes the vision glass again with her arms. "This is what will eventually happen to all Earthbounds if we don't do something to get the sludge under control."

This time, it's a dismal scene. Wayfare sees Median's people turning into zombies, the town deteriorating, living organisms withering away into nothingness. Mold, rot, decay. It covers everything, including people who have no will to even move anymore.

Fight the sludge, Wayfare thinks with a glimmer of belief. "My own little brother."

Cirissa re-adorns herself with icy armor. The sound of swords clashing stings the air. She *tings* for Sheena who comes darting in, tongue lolling happily, a stream of flowers in her wake.

Beginning to effaport back to the Illustrial Plane, her particles begin to separate and rise like champagne bubbles toward the treetops. "Yes. Deret Day, your brother." She lets that sink in.

Then she blows him a kiss that looks like fireflies darting into his skin, and he feels the surge radiate through his whole body straightening his shoulders and clearing his mind to crystal sharpness. His SparkBit, he sees, reads "Internal Spark Load: Off Chart."

And then she is gone.

Chapter 4

Want

Deret Day knows exactly what to do. Yes, he *knows* how big a deal it is. But he will do it nonetheless. He grips his money, tugs his flannel shirt down firmly, and drifts like a shark into the flow of people down the aisles and aisles of books at Skylane Tomes.

Deret is indeed, this very first day of summer, going to ... Buy. A. Book. Oh yeah. And not some dingy copy of *Median Times* either. No new and "improved" version (though the last four "versions" were suspiciously similar) of *Potato Grower's Guide* for his father. Nope. This day is all about him. Something "fun" as his dad had put it. He'll know it when he sees it. And he will get it.

He sneers past books about trees and books about dirt and books about linens and wellness and meditation and ... *Oh my clouds, the boredom!*

He shakes his head. Each of the customers will pick up a book, stare at the cover, fan the pages, put it back, and glide to the next. Deret knows this, for he'd been one of them since he was little. It's like everyone in Median is always searching – not very emphatically, mind you – for something, but they never find it. Worse yet, Deret wonders if they really *want* to find it at all. He used to feel the same. But today, he feels different. Today, it all *looks* different. It's been building inside him. Want.

* * *

Soundless, the sludge shreds itself into gossamer strands that spider web imperceptibly along the floorboards. Skylane Tomes is a restored warehouse spanning three city blocks. Inside the main entrance, stands a map station where one might attempt to make sense of the maze. Shelves are stacked high into aging rafters. Ladders roll from one section to another. Bare light bulbs, many burnt out, dangle from the ceiling leaving the place dimly lit.

A girl tugs at her mother's coat. She begs for a cup of cocoa. The sludge snags her loose shoelace.

"Mommy," she whines. "I want some. I *want* some!"

The mother's tired gray eyes somehow droop even more. "You don't need it."

The sludge stitches itself into the little girl's stocking and reaches the hem of her skirt. It trickles along up muslin fabric and sneaks into hiding underneath her mousy hair. It latches onto the back of her neck, spiderwebs over half of her scalp and painlessly sucks her spark out through the pores of her skin.

The girl's hand drops. Her eyes go dull and droop much like her mother's.

Only a meager taste in that one, the sludge muses. *Child spark. Humph.*

The sludge moves on hoping for richer, more satisfying slurps in the next person. And the next. And the next. Spark sips at Skylane Tomes. None of it is very satisfying.

The shadowy mist slips soundlessly through the crowd toward the door.

On its way, it brushes the bottom of Deret's dragging jeans and red sneakers. Deret stops midstride. Like he's felt something. A small something, but a cold something that makes him want to sit and stare at a wall. He looks around and sees nothing, but he hears a faint, high-pitched shrill that sets his teeth on edge. The bookstore wanderers continue their soft murmuring, oblivious.

Deret narrows his eyes and takes a curious breath in and out. It's fading. It must have been a draft from someone opening the door.

The tip of the sludge's tail is singed to a crisp. It continues to whimper and screech as it slips outside.

Deret happens upon the girl and her mother. "Hey, Mrs. T!" He crouches down. "How's little Water Lily doing?" He holds up his hand for a high five.

Lily's eyes blink hard. She focuses on Deret, quick as a wink, and giggles.

"Put her there, Water Lily," he says as he waves his hand at her, and she smacks it a good one. "Ouch!" Deret yanks it away. Shaking it out, he says, "You trying to beat me up?" He flashes a half-wink and a crooked smile.

Lily blurts, "I'm five!"

"Whaaat!" he says, which makes her giggle. "Like five whole years old? No wonder that high five hurt so much." He stands up straight and says to her mother, "Mrs. T, what are you feeding this kid that makes her so tough?"

Mrs. Temprum blinks hard. She shakes her head and smiles. "I – I guess it must be all that ..." She seems a little confused, looks at the coffee and cocoa stand next to them, and finishes, "hot chocolate." Lily's eyes light up. "How would you like to share a cup with me, Lily?"

Deret nods, impressed. "Drink of champions. Enjoy." As he walks away, he hears several other voices say, "That looks good" and "I'll take one too" and "They serve cocoa here?"

Chapter 5

The Cloud Council

Cirissa stands poised before the Cloud Council in the Sky Room. Though being the subject of their attention is always unnerving, she is confident in her purpose.

"Cloud Masters, I've seen it for myself. The Rim in Median is nearly impenetrable. Something has made it – unnatural. And I tell you, several in the Ice Crystal Guard believe it is connected to the sludge. It is our suspicion that Murkemer is experimenting with elements unauthorized to him." She narrows her icy eyes. "We believe he is up to something."

The Cloud Masters continue their casual murmuring with each other at the crescent-shaped glass table that spans the length of the Sky Room. The opaque floor beneath their feet shows the ocean gently rolling far below. Cloud columns lining the room roil within their pillar shapes.

Cirissa sighs with frustration. This topic has been avoided too long now. She takes a deep breath and says, "Cloud Masters, I must insist the matter of Murkemer's suspicious activity be discussed."

She looks to the lovely Cloud Master Tendril for help. Even though Master Tendril is the representative for the highest sector of the highest cloud plane, her kind manner is a comfort to Cirissa. Besides, when Tendril speaks – rare as it may be – Skybounds listen.

Tendril meets Cirissa's eyes then rises from her seat at the farthest end of the table. Iridescent, gossamer strands flow from every inch of her wispy body. Her steps, light as air, carry her forward. The delicate strands drift in her wake, then float independently around her as she stops next to Cirissa. The other Cloud Masters hush.

"Gracious Cloud Masters, our esteemed Ice Crystal Guard agent here brings a disturbing point to our attention."

Cirissa can't be sure, but she swears she hears a "harrumph" escape in the guise of a cough from the center of the crescent table. Master Bumble of the Cumulus Sector is suspiciously rubbing his bulbous nose with his white-sausage fingers.

"Truly, Masters." Tendril turns her head to address the full council from one end of the table to the other. Her rainbow strands of hair swish with the slightest movement. "Though few of my fellow Crystalines in the Cirrus Sector are willing to acknowledge it, I cannot deny what we have sensed brewing far below in the Stratus Sector."

Cirissa breathes relief. Finally, someone will support her.

Master Bumble clears a gooey gurgle from his throat and says, "*Blurble.* Why should we care what Murkemer is up to?" He sweeps a pillowy arm toward an empty seat – a plush, gray gamer's recliner complete with cup holder – at the end of the crescent table. "He never bothers to show up for meetings, *gurrup.*"

"I have to agree with Master Bumble," says Cloud Master Shreddard of Cirissa's own Cirrostratus Sector. In his smoothly arrogant way, he says, "That kid's got issues, sure, but why make him our problem?" The sound of sharpening blades echoes through the Sky Room as he leans his stick-straight, crystal-encrusted form back in his ice spiked chair. A smug grin curls the corners of his mouth as he crosses his arms.

Cloud Master Makryl of the Cirrocumulus Sector, sitting to Shreddard's right, strikes her scepter on the clear floor. Her long, white ringlets bounce, but her round face remains serene. Very Bo Peep. Everyone seems to sit up a bit straighter. She closes her lavender eyes slowly. When she opens them, her icy lashes now adorn blazing red-orange eyes, as though the sun itself shone from inside them.

Shreddard watches her in awe. His eyes flicker with deep violet.

Master Makryl's voice is lulling, almost too calm, when she says, "I believe the most efficient way to deal with our problem council member would be a swift volting. That will snap him out of whatever sad, little issues he's got in that sad, little head of his."

Murmurs of ascent grumble throughout the room. Even Cloud Master Loom, who typically tries to stay silent, nods her enormous head, and the wind generated from her flying saucer-sized sunhat blows down upon the council members. They all steady their goblets. Her floral Mumu flutters dangerously with miniature lightning strikes.

Bumble reaches up and pats her gargantuan knee. "There, there, my little Loomikins. It's alright."

Jagged hairlines of lightning flitters underneath Loom's brim.

The wind has spun Tendril's ethereal strands into a rat's nest over every inch of her. She sighs, does a shiver shake, and all the strands loosen in a flourish from the tangled mass and go back to floating.

"My dear esteemed Cloud Master Makryl," Tendril says in attempt to calm the energy in the Sky Room. "I am sure your tactics work marvellously with your little charges. I am certain I am not the only one here who has a deep appreciation for your service with our Cloudlings and Shards. And I can't even imagine how you work your miracles with all those darling puffs." She chuckles lovingly and tsk tsks. "You are a wonder, dear Makryl."

Cloud Master Makryl's shoulders straighten even more, though Cirissa can hardly see how that's possible. Her face beams with pride as she continues to look serenely upon the others. Shreddard eyes her lustily.

Tendril continues delicately, "I'm just wondering if there might be a slightly less, um, severe strategy for dealing with Cloud Master Murkemer. Especially considering he is rather young and somewhat new to our council. After all, losing his parents not so long ago has been difficult for him, no doubt. And absorbing all the Stratus Sector responsibilities, as we all know, is no simple matter."

The council members remain reverent as they recall Murkemer's predecessor.

Cloud Master Drizzo of the Stratocumulus Sector puts down her fingernail polish, carefully raises her goblet and says, "To Cloud Master Slurry." All members raise their glasses. "May his journey through the Great Beyond be sweet and peaceful, just like he was." Drizzo carefully sweeps her out-of-control frizzy hair from her face and takes the first sip.

They all take a sip. Cirissa notices a few tears and sniffles. But when Loom goes to blow her nose with the tissue she has stuffed in her stocking, everyone braces again.

Bumble frantically reaches over his head and pats her knee like he's trying to put out a fire. "There, there little Loomy Poomy. Everything is alright. It's okay!"

Loom thankfully sucks in her emotion with a shudder. It pulls up everyone's hair then drops it back down as she lets out a quivering breath.

Cirissa can't hold back. "But it's NOT alright." She has never spoken so sharply to the council. "It is NOT okay!"

Tendril raises an eyebrow with a look that shows she might be a little impressed. Then Cirissa notices her casting a glance at Cloud Master Virgus of the Altostratus Sector. Virgus returns Tendril's look with a tiny smile as he lounges back in his zero-gravity lawn chair, all tan and summery, with Bermuda shorts and flip-flops. He runs a hand through his luscious, blonde locks, his biceps bulging under his *Hang Loose* t-shirt. Tendril's cheeks flush. He nods at her, apparently also a little impressed with Cirissa's more direct approach with the council.

Bolstered by Tendril's look of approval, Cirissa continues. "Please, esteemed Cloud Masters, "I'm not saying anyone has to become his new best friend, or anything of the like. I'm simply wondering if one of you might be willing to check in on him."

No one seems to be able to make eye contact with her. They've all become suspiciously interested in their goblet.

Then Cloud Master Castella of the Altocumulus Sector pipes up bright-eyed, like she just got a dynamite idea. Her hot pink wind suit crinkles as she slaps her hands on the table. "Could it be considered a super-secret mission?" The tawny old Cloud Master whips her gray hair into a bun on the top of her head, pops out of her wheely chair into ninja stance, flips her dentures with her tongue, then snaps them back in.

Shreddard says, "Gross."

Castella winks at him.

Cirissa blinks. "Well, I guess I don't think it has gotten to that point just yet. I was imagining just a friendly visit. See how he is doing. See if he is in need of a little guidance, say."

Castella deflates, yanks her bun out and crumples back into her seat.

Shreddard rolls his eyes and says, "Why don't we send Drizzo." He leans forward to look at the ashen-faced, frizzy-haired Cloud Master down the table. "Weren't you two like a thing?"

Drizzo nearly chokes on a swig of her drink. Then she dabs her mouth with the sleeve of her dingy housecoat. "No way. I mean, yes, we were, but that was a ridiculously long time ago." She blows on her freshly painted gray nails.

Shreddard notes, "You just broke up like a month ago."

"I know," she says, unperturbed, and shrugs him off. This matter is closed.

The council members awkwardly eye each other for a painful amount of time. Cirissa is about to lose hope and start working out another way to help her dear, dear Wayfare and the sweet little town of Median.

Then a raspy voice echoes softly from the far end of the table next to Murkemer's empty chair. "I'll go to him." Cloud Master Shroud's quiet words barely escape from underneath the hood that covers most of his face.

The council members all lean in to hear better, but Shroud offers nothing else. A gloomy aura floats about him that's always made most of them feel uncomfortable, to some degree, but Drizzo seems unaffected by it.

"Well," Drizzo chirps, "there you have it." She reaches down rather indelicately to pull out the cotton balls stuck between her toes now that their polish is dry.

Tendril and Cirissa look at each other then back to Shroud. It's not common for the Nimbostratus Cloud Master to speak, much less volunteer for anything. This is indeed unexpected.

Tendril says, "Thank you, Cloud Master Shroud. I believe I speak for all of us in saying we appreciate your willingness to help."

Shreddard says under his breath toward Makryl, "Taking one for the team."

Master Makryl swishes some of her long ringlet locks aside and returns his comment with a knowing glance.

Cirissa isn't sure on the details, but Shroud and Slurry had been like brothers. Perhaps this will provide the perfect opportunity for Shroud and Murkemer to get to know each other.

Shroud rises from his weathered, wooden armchair. He folds his hands and nods so low that his entire face disappears within his hood. Then he effaports into a fog that whips upward, and he's gone.

Cirissa isn't sure what to do or say. It had happened so suddenly.

Shreddard takes no time. "Well, that does it." He begins to get up. The knife blade scratching of his innumerable dendrites signals the end of this meeting. "Shall we adjourn?"

A general murmur of agreement rumbles across the crescent table as the meeting breaks up. Cirissa stands forlorn with Tendril. Virgus strolls over.

Virgus, his hands in his Bermuda shorts pockets, says, "Well, we'll see what happens." He shrugs and knocks Tendril playfully with his shoulder. "Shroud's an odd duck, but he knows what he's doing. Right, Ten?"

Tendril smiles almost girlishly as her gossamer strands still wave from his bump. She composes herself enough to say with reassuring confidence, "Of course he is. Now, Cirissa, go to your Kindred Wayfare. I know you worry about him. What does he think of having his little brother as his new apprentice? The book has been planted and our little WISP commander, Breeslin, reports Deret is on the way to discovering it."

Cirissa smiles, but it's forced. She feels her face flush at the mention of Wayfare's name. "He's managing just fine. I think he'll warm to the idea. He seems ..." she looks inward for the right word, "... tired." The look on her face betrays her attempt to minimize her feelings for him.

Virgus tilts his head and grins warmly. "He's a good dude, that Wayfare. They don't make 'em like him anymore."

"I know," says Cirissa looking down through the clear floor. "I know."

Chapter 6

Get Lost

"Alright," Deret says, resolute, "this is *not* working for me." It has been nearly an hour of fruitless searching. Standing at an intersection with books about "Rocks and Other Lifeless Objects" going one way, and books about "Socks and other Modest Outdoor Work Apparel" going the other, Deret knows exactly what he has to do.

He has to get lost.

There's no way around it. He has to venture deep into this century-old store, which spans *three* city blocks, and find the forgotten places.

Yeah. His green eyes spark with the prospect of exploration.

Wandering. Turning. Checking behind his back often to see fewer and fewer people.

This is more like it!

Up a few stairs, down a few. Narrow aisles, wide aisles. The wooden floorboards creak beneath his feet. Cobwebs cling to the rafters. Around a corner, through a doorway, around another corner, through another doorway. Finally. Finally! He is not entirely certain he knows the way back.

Yeah. He flicks his red bangs and rubs his hands together.

Most kids his age would be all nervous and whining at this point. But Deret? He eyes his next move.

At the very far end of a very long row, he squints to see a very steep staircase.

Jogging toward it, he can see the boards are worn and narrow and half the depth of his feet. True, he's on the taller side for his age, and his feet do seem to be growing faster than everything else, but he's got this.

He uses the jiggly railing to help him on the severe incline. His breaths come quick, and he wipes a sweat bead from his face, but he's in good shape. All that running or biking into town from his family's farm makes him "sturdy and capable," as his father says.

On a landing he looks out a dirty window into soupy mist. Typical day in Median.

Step by step he continues to climb. When he reaches the top, his legs burn, and he bends over puffing. The very air around him weighs him down.

"Clouds above..." he says raggedly.

An intricately carved wooden door looms before him. It reminds him of his home's front door his father made. Deret's fingers barely touch the brass knob when it swings open with a breeze so fresh it lifts him up. He stands tall, sturdy, and strong again. His green eyes sparkle, wide and inquisitive.

It's more of a hallway with a wall of windows lining one side. Dense fog clings to the glass. For a second, Deret thinks he sees a figure swoosh by in the haze. He stares intently waiting to catch a glimpse of whatever made the movement, but the swirling mist outside settles and goes back to pattern-less undulation.

Hm, he thinks. *Maybe a bird.*

He slowly peels his gaze from the window panes to the other side of the room which is a floor-to-ceiling wall of bookshelves.

And only one book.

Deret squinches one eye and smiles his crooked grin.

Silvery rays shoot from the letters on the spine that reads *Cloud City*.

Now this looks fun.

Chapter 7

The Rim

He's slicing! He's slashing! He's whacking and batting! Wayfare, mightiest of Catalysts, is – getting nowhere.

His lanky arms and legs whirl and fling like rubber bands inside his protective cloak. His floppy Mohawk sags over his eyes, blonde strands sticking with sweat.

Though he may not have the physical prowess of some of the other Cats out there, his SparkSword crackles and snaps with all the strength of anyone twice his size. It obliterates anything in its way inch by inch. But the thickets and underbrush keep growing. It's out of control. No wonder his old buddy Drift couldn't get to him. Something is so wrong with his forest.

"Clouds almighty!" he hollers to no one. Standing in the small opening he's managed, his SparkSword pulses and glows in the ever-darkening gloom of The Rim surrounding Median. If it hadn't been for Cirissa's and Sheena's spark boost earlier, there's no way he would have made it this far.

"Sweet Saint Medard! What is *happening*?" he says to the treetops. He's exhausted, which is annoying, but he's way more frustrated about the quaver he hears in his voice. His shaky muscles are no picnic either.

The Rim has always been a natural boundary around the town and its rural homes. A thick barrier of trees lining Median's borders. One simple road comes in from the outside, and even that entrance is blocked by thorny bramble poking through and crumbling the asphalt. He's been so busy undoing the sludge's sapping lately, that he hasn't made time to maintain the perimeter or the road. It's safe to say, things have gotten away on him.

But it is not in the nature of a Catalyst to despair. He simply needs to whip it. That's all.

He sniffs in hard and raises his SparkSword high over his head. Just as he is about to dive back into the bramble, he hears, or rather feels, a whooshing wind rushing toward him.

"Oh, for fogsake, what now?" He lowers his SparkSword into two-handed, assailant attack mode, and cracks his neck.

In the brush swirls a tornadic orb of earthy hues. Sage-green, mud-brown, rust-orange and misty-gray colors spin straight through the thickets and leave nothing but a vibrant, grassy path in its wake. Wayfare frowns in confusion. There's only one thing he's ever heard of that contains enough spark to undo this kind of sludge work, and he's never actually seen one. Most people call them legends, myths.

The mass reaches him but stays put just feet away now. It sends a gentle wave out around them which clears the area, making it open and cheery like it should be. Wayfare lowers his SparkSword and slouches to one side. The air is filled with positive energy that whirls around him, fluttering his long coattails. His features melt into awe as the thing materializes, much like Cirissa's Frost Fox.

"Shadow Cat," he whispers. Tingling goosebumps wash over his entire body, making him open-mouth smile like a star-struck teenager. "Holy ozone."

Before him stands a cat. A largish cat, more like a lynx or bobcat of the mountains. Its fur is a blotchy calico, but the colors seem to shift and morph with movement. Its face, however, remains a gray mask revealing glittering emerald eyes.

The Shadow Cat sits and licks its paw twice then gazes right into the heart of the Catalyst standing dumbly in front of him. *I am,* he says in Wayfare's mind. *And you are a Catalyst.*

"I am," says Wayfare. He blinks and shakes his head. "I'm sorry. I'm so ... uh ... I don't know ... I just ..."

The Shadow Cat stares at him, unimpressed.

Wayfare tries again, "I didn't think there were any of your kind left. This is such an honor." He swipes a hand through his hair, then gets down on one knee to meet the Shadow Cat at eye level rather than looking down on him. "Wayfare Day. Catalyst for the Ice Crystal Guard, Kindred to the Crystaline Cirissa." He bows his head.

The Shadow Cat returns the gesture and says, *I assure you, there are many of my kind still. I am called* – Here, the Shadow Cat makes a purring sound with a few painfully elongated hairball coughs and then ends with a *phst* sneeze.

Wayfare stares dumbfounded. "Uh, yeah ... it is so totally a pleasure to meet you." He begins an honest-as-the-sun, whole-hearted attempt to repeat the Shadow Cat's name.

The Shadow Cat, interested as he is that the Catalyst is even willing to give it a try, puts up a halting paw to put the poor man out of his misery and says, "Please. Just call me Fillip."

Sheer relief washes over Wayfare's face. "Fillip it is."

This man's infectious smile indeed makes Fillip take notice. *Spark runs strong in this one,* he thinks to himself.

"I remember learning about Shadow Cats in Cat Academy, *Myths and Legends 101,*" Wayfare recalls. "I kind of wondered if you ever actually existed."

The Shadow Cat breathes in and out sort of sadly. *I know this. There was a time, so very long ago, when my kind thrived. But clearly, they do not teach of this in your academy.*

"Well," Wayfare offers, "I know you're the strongest natural spark generating Earthbound ever. And how you can run so fast, you virtually disappear." He has to think for just a moment. "And how you prefer rainy days! Which is, like, every day in Median."

Hm. Yes, Fillip says, again unimpressed. *I see your Cat Academy has provided you with a quality education, indeed.*

Wayfare slumps. "Okay, maybe I could have paid a little more attention in class, but seriously, I have nothing but respect for you. I mean the way you ignited spark in my woods here? I've been hacking for hours with this SparkSword and have barely made a dent!"

The Shadow Cat looks at the SparkSword curiously. He raises an eyebrow, and out of one emerald eye shoots a green lightning strip that blazes up and down the blade. Wayfare startles at the electricity popping and cracking in his hand. He swings it at a dark thicket and vaporizes everything within ten feet. Then lush green flourishes the ground and fresh buds pop up and leaf out.

"Holy Cats!" Wayfare exclaims.

The Shadow Cat smiles a bit smugly.

"Whoa. Thank you." In awe, Wayfare wands the SparkSword around. "Just listen to it." He moves with slow, practiced dance-like steps as he wields it at an imaginary foe.

You are most welcome, says the Shadow Cat as he watches the Catalyst. It feels good to engage his powers for this man. Appreciation is a feeling the Shadow Cats of the world long for most. It is their greatest Want.

"You know," says Wayfare, "the Cloud Council keeps nagging on about how I need an apprentice, but man," he slices his imaginary foe in half, "I don't see what they're so hung up on." He twirls with the SparkSword in the air above his head; his duster coattails twirl with him. "I'm pretty awesome on my own."

Fillip chuckles. The Catalyst's confidence is endearing. *Perhaps you learned in your lessons how we Shadow Cats used to be the spark keepers.*

"Well," Wayfare says as he continues to practice swordplay, "a little. I mean, not exactly. Your chapter was only two pages."

Well, the Shadow Cat mimics a little perturbed, not at Wayfare, but at the poor representation of his kind in the history books, *perhaps you will allow me to enrich your education on the matter.*

Wayfare stops mid-stride. "You'd do that? For me?" He douses his SparkSword. With a sharp lever action, it folds and retracts into its holster inside his long cloak sleeve. "I am *so* all ears, Fillip."

The Shadow Cat sits, closes his eyes, and begins the lesson. *We maintained all the wild kingdoms of the world. That was back when the people were capable of managing their own spark – a time you know nothing about.*

Fillip pauses to stare at a spot in the dirt. Both his emerald eyes emit a green glow that streams into a vision pool on the ground. Images ripple into view. But Wayfare does know something about this time Fillip is talking about. He's looking at some of the very same images Cirissa showed him earlier. A bright, shining sun casts shadows everywhere. People move with purpose. Their faces are lit with drive and delight. *Want* runs rampant within these people of old. Spark comes and goes freely and naturally. And though the sludge is still visible, its effects are countered and parried effortlessly by each person individually. Wayfare can't help but feel the immense sensation of balance within the vision pool's images. He gazes in awe, unable to look away.

Fillip continues as he shifts the images to those of other Shadow Cats in their various environments. *You must understand that my kind did not die out, but rather phased out once the Skybounds took over and started training you Catalysts to do the work not only for the people, but the animals, flora, and fauna as well.* Fillip sighs. *Skybounds do like control. And they do love to regulate all aspects of spark to a very precise degree.* Here Fillip notes Wayfare's SparkBit.

Wayfare looks at the SparkBit wrapped around his wrist as though he's seeing it for the first time. "It's so true, Fillip. The control is intense."

Fillip shakes his head and goes on. *We Shadow Cats were deemed "inconsistent" by the Skybounds' standards. One by one, therefore, we receded to the comfort of our caves where we have watched for ages now.*

"What brought you out, if you don't mind me asking?"

Fillip pauses and looks at Wayfare with a direct expression. *If you don't mind me saying,* you *did.*

"Me? How did I manage that?"

Fillip straightens his posture resolutely then provides his honest answer. *I couldn't stand by and watch our forest sink into ruin any longer, Wayfare. Something is dreadfully wrong with the energy in the woodlands here. I heard about your conversation with the Ice Crystal Guard agent this morning from a chipmunk friend of mine – who, sadly, lost his dear grandparent just recently – so I tidied up my cave and struck out to find you.*

"You came to help me?" Wayfare feels both honored and ashamed.

Suddenly, a screeching cry comes soaring in through the treetops. Both Fillip and Wayfare wrench their necks to catch sight of it. Father Owl, flying at top speed, latches onto an elm branch nearly breaking it with his force.

"Hoo hoo, hooooo!"

Wayfare hollers up to his friend, "You have GOT to be kidding me! Again?" This time, he chucks his SparkWhip out in front of him and coils its length around his arm. He readies himself for a sprint and says, "That scummuck sludge will NOT take your family, Father Owl." He lands a hard look at the Shadow Cat now standing alert at his side. "Not on ... *our* watch." He peaks an eyebrow and nods at Fillip.

The Shadow Cat curls one lip into a sly smile and narrows his eyes into emerald slats of delight. *I welcome the challenge,* he says and crouches like a coiled spring.

Father Owl screams with urgency and lifts off.

"I'll warn you, Fillip. I'm pretty fast. The owl nest is on the other side of Median."

The Shadow Cat doesn't let on that it knows Wayfare's spark levels are low. He simply aims an emerald eye at the Catalyst's feet and sends a spark beam into the man's yellow running shoes.

Wayfare, oblivious to the charity boost, juts his chin up a little cocky and says, "Try to keep up."

But the Shadow Cat is off in a flash of light. Nothing but swirling leaves twist in the air.

Chapter 8

Sunny

The whole book sort of glows.

"Whoa," Deret whispers and sits on a lone, wobbly stool.

Fog presses hard against the windowed wall. It swirls in constant motion as though it's trying to seep through the cracks. Deret touches the glass, and the mist roils around the outline of his hand.

"Double whoa." There's still no sign of the figure he thought he saw.

He opens *Cloud City* to the middle. The figures on these pages move. White forms, like cotton, undulate across both sides, in front of a pure, light blue background. The caption at the bottom reads: *Cumulus clouds against clear blue skies on a sunny day.*

Cumulus. Clear. Blue. Sunny.

"Sunny?" That's a word he doesn't hear much. Median's "sun" is a fuzzy orb in the sky, on a good day. He snaps the book shut with one strong hand and stands up. "*Cloud City*," he says, "You're coming with me."

Deret has zero trouble unwinding his crazy path back through the endless halls and doorways until he makes it back to the main entrance. Somehow, at every turn, he knew exactly what he had to do. Just like pretty much everything in his life.

The lady at the check-out, Wanda Winerd, sighs as she takes his book, like it is such a tragedy that she has to do her job. *Weepy Wanda*, Deret thinks to himself. She always looks like she's going to break down and cry herself to sleep right there on the floor behind the check-out counter.

"Cotton City?" she asks scanning his book.

Deret cocks his head. "What's that?"

Wanda over-enunciates not looking at him, "Caww-tuhhnn Ciiiteee," and jams her finger on the book's title - which Deret sees clearly reads *Cloud City* - with one hand as she punches some buttons on the register with the other. Her face is getting blotchy.

Clouds above, Deret does not want to make her cry. "Uh, okay."

"That'll be $19.50."

"Here you go," he hands over his cash.

She goes to take it, but their fingertips touch, and she stops, frozen for a heartbeat, both holding on to the money. They look each other in the eye. Deret holds still and gives a sort of confused smile. She blinks hard and shakes her straight bangs.

Her eyes light up. "Thank you much, young man." Her voice is bright and her cheeks flush with a rosy glow. "Enjoy."

For the first time ever, Weepy Wanda looks wide awake. Not ready to cry one bit.

Sunny.

Chapter 9

Sludge Swarm

Mother Owl savagely pecks and claws at the sludge mercilessly invading her nest high up in the giant sequoia tree. She stands mightily, wings spread to block it from her babies. It hisses back at her when her strike hits its mark, but it is an impossible foe. It shreds itself into strands around her talons then worms its way through the cracks and twigs of the nest. Inky tendrils curl around her legs and try to latch on. Her spark is fiercely strong, as only a mother's protecting her young can be.

The babies huddle together, but a ghostly sludge finger creeps up the back of the nest. Their fear spark is growing by the second. Mother Owl senses it and starts fighting it off from both sides over top her babies' fuzzy heads. Her frantic snaps and scratches start to wane in intensity as the evil mist leeches her spark from her.

Wrought with panic, she wails to the sky in a resounding screech, *Where are you, Father Owl?*

The sludge takes grip of all three owls like an ink slug. Pulsing, it ravenously saps their spark. Mother Owl's eyes roll, sickened and weak. Her wings sag. The babies' heads loll toward one another.

Then, just as the sludge prepares to suck the very last fleck of spark from the limp bodies, a deafening crack of electricity splits the air, zapping the vicious thing loose from its victims. Wayfare slides to a smoking halt at the base of the giant sequoia tree. His arms are outstretched, his SparkWhip sizzles, and his coattails flap like pirate sails behind him.

The Shadow Cat flashes at his side, all fours digging into the forest floor as it too screeches to a halt. Pine needles and leaves litter the air in the tornadic swirls.

Finally, soaring in from on high with an ear-splitting screech, amber-red eyes glowing like hot coals, Father Owl bursts through the clouds above, folds his wings to his sides and plummets like a missile to save his family.

Wayfare's SparkWhip's serpentine tail lies coiled and crackling at his feet, ready to strike the air again. He shouts to the sky, "You WILL NOT get your feast today, you spark sucking scummuck!" He wields his buzzing SparkWhip over his head in great, menacing circles.

The sludge desperately scrambles to regain its hold on one of the owls. But Father Owl attacks, ripping and tearing at its misty tentacles with his hooked beak and razor claws. An unearthly, wheezing scream pierces the air around them as the sludge tries to fight back.

Wayfare, his SparkWhip still sizzling and snapping overhead, looks to Fillip. Their eyes narrow as they nod once in unison.

Wayfare's heart races and he takes a steady breath. Then he flicks his wrist and *SNAPS* his SparkWhip high, striking the popper with surgical precision. In a jagged ribbon of light, it stretches all the way up into the nest.

Fillip growls a deep, dangerous rumble. Then he squeezes one glowing eye to a pinprick that shoots out an emerald laser beam right alongside Wayfare's lash. Both laser and whip hit their mark and *ZAP* the sludge within a hair's breadth of Father Owl and his family. A thunderclap rattles the forest to its core. The sludge disintegrates into shredded ash that flutters down, down from the heights of the giant sequoia tree. Nothing but charred, flakey cinders scatter the woodland floor.

The forest is silent for a beat.

Father Owl hovers protectively over his family.

Wayfare pants, his bony chest pumping. "Oh dear, sweet Saint Medard," puff-puff-huff, "don't let us be too late."

Worry scrunches Fillip's furry gray face tight. He looks up the tree. *Father Owl*, he calls. *Are you okay?*

There is no answer, and no movement.

I'll go, he says to Wayfare.

"Right," says Wayfare. He bends down, hands on knobby knees. "I'll ..." puff pant, "be..." pant puff blow out, "right here." His head spins. His ears ring a single pitch tone. Reluctantly, he glances at his SparkBit.

Internal Spark Load: 17%. He groans with frustration.

Fillip leaps onto the tree's burly trunk. His calico fur shifts to mirror the crags and bumps of the tree's bark. He is completely camouflaged except for a sort of watery outline he still gives off.

"Fading? Shadow Cats can fade?" Wayfare stands up straighter and shakes his head, which sort of dulls the ringing in his ears. His breaths come more regular now. He calls out, "You guys really do deserve more than a couple pages in the textbook."

You have no idea. Besides, I don't want to frighten the babies, Fillip replies.

Swift as a scud cloud, Fillip scales the sequoia and leaps effortlessly from branch to branch, all the way up to the nest. Carefully, without a sound, he climbs onto the nest's edge and sits, looking down upon the lifeless bodies inside. Father Owl only stares at his family with wide, mournful eyes of liquid gold. He doesn't even acknowledge Fillip's presence though he knows he's there. Father Owl's sorrow spark warps the air around him.

They sit, the Shadow Cat and the owl. Fillip reappears at the nest's edge. And though the sight of an owl and a cat sitting so close together might seem unnatural, this moment is not. Father Owl knows what

Shadow Cats are, and how essential their spark source can be for their world. All creatures of the woods do.

But Father Owl also knows that even the magnitude of spark that a Shadow Cat can generate will never bring back the dead. There is no re-igniting doused spark where not even a flicker remains. It's just not how it works.

Wayfare sinks to his knees on the forest floor and buries his face in his hands. Though he can't see inside the nest, he knows. His eyes burn as he presses a button on the side of his SparkBit. With head bowed low, he scrolls shakily through the Adjacent Body Spark Load readings.

Father Owl: 100%. That makes sense. His Want for his family saturates his entire being with spark. The strongest kind an entity can possess.

Fillip: Off Chart. There's no way to measure the spark levels in a Shadow Cat since they have no limit generating it naturally.

And then, with quavering hesitation, Wayfare scrolls to the others.

Mother Owl: 1%
Male Owlet: .65%
Female Owlet: .55%

"Clouds above," his voice is low and tremulous. "They're ..." He springs to his feet and shouts to the treetop, "They're still there!" His throat tightens making his words crack. "They're still there! Fillip! Father Owl! We can save them!"

He's so excited, he doesn't see the charred, flakey remnants of the shadow sludge scatter in the breeze on the forest floor. They drift and flutter in what seems to be a haphazard way, but it's not haphazard at all. They're gravitating toward each other.

High up in the tree, Father Owl and Fillip look at each other. Dare they reveal the whisper of hope the Catalyst's words have struck in their hearts?

Father Owl's brow furrows into a severe, black-line V. He carefully, oh-so-carefully, touches a wing tip to

Mother Owl's breast. He breathes deep and closes his moon eyes. He offers his spark and says, *Love*, as it waves out of him and into her.

Fillip has never known of an Earthbound able to emit spark to save another. This is quite unusual. And fascinating.

A soft flow of warmth comes from Father Owl. And it makes the Shadow Cat's heart swell to witness such love. So Fillip, without letting on to Father Owl, closes his emerald eyes and inhales deep, deep down. Then he opens his mouth ever so slightly and breathes out three tiny opalescent orbs. The orbs drift gently to the owls and land on their brows like cottony fluff.

They wait. A light breeze moves in through the branches and gently ruffles fur and feathers alike. And they wait. Still as statues.

Wayfare finds himself holding his breath. He sees the spark surge from both Father Owl and Fillip on his SparkBit. What he does not see still, however, is the singed remnants of the sludge whirling and collecting into a cluster. It grows just behind him in the shadowy woods.

In the nest, Father Owl sinks a little as he and Fillip continue staring at the lifeless bodies. "Hoo hooo?" he whispers as he looks up at the Shadow Cat. "Hoo hoo hoooo."

Fillip's emerald eyes glitter in response, and a heartfelt smile begins to glide across is furry face. *Shhhh,* he says to Father Owl tenderly. *Wayfare is not wrong. His SparkBit is just fine. Look.*

It's almost imperceptible, and would most certainly be to the common eye. But a father's eye and a Shadow Cat's? They see it. A fraction of a fraction, Mother Owl, then the owlets. Movement. Their chests rise, infinitesimally mind you, but there is life! Little by little, each in turn begins to awaken, as if they've been enduring a deep, heady dream. Father Owl puffs up to double his size and blows out like a boiling tea kettle.

Rapt with joy, and dazed with wonder, he canopies his family with his wide, sheltering wings.

Mother Owl turns her head so that her brightening eyes meet his. *Love,* she murmurs and folds herself into his warmth to look upon their owlets together.

Love, he whispers back.

One owlet manages a fluffy headshake as he blinks himself awake. The other plops backward on her downy rump, stretches her baby wings wide and yawns adorably. Their lazy eyes find their parents, and they cheep and chirp and peep. Fillip tickles their little bellies with the tip of his tail, and they giggle their fright away.

Wayfare drops his faded SparkWhip and flings his hands up in the air. "Wahoo!" he whoops to the sky. His blue eyes shine, and his irresistible smile is like the sun. He rolls his head back letting the relief wash over him. Then his lanky arms fall limp, and he stands there, hands on hips, shaking his head. "Holy ozone, that was WAY to close." He thinks he might puke.

"Hoo hoo hoooo," Father Owl agrees.

Suddenly, Fillip stops playing with the owlets and tunes his ears this way and that. Something is not quite right. He searches the branches. Nothing. But something feels wrong. His body goes tense and the hairs on his back go rigid.

Father and Mother Owl notice.

"Hoo hoo?" Mother Owl asks, worry in her still sleepy eyes.

I'm not quite certain, Fillip replies. *Shhhhh,* he instructs with a paw to his whiskered lips. He slinks flat over the side of the nest and calls to Wayfare's mind, *Catalyst Wayfare, I sense something odd. Can you feel it? What do you see? Something's not right.*

Wayfare freezes at the warning. "Hang on," he says and tunes in his spark senses as he scans the woods around him.

The breeze has vanished. Every leaf lies still. The ambient background of twittering birds and chattering squirrels goes absent. The heavy overcast clouds press a thick silence into the air and saturate it with the damp, earthy smells of pine and moss. He narrows his eyes as he searches without moving. Not one flinch. It's as though the forest is holding its breath. His skin goes tight and tingly.

At that moment, all things burst!

Fillip's hiss sears Wayfare's ears from high above. He jerks his arm forward like cocking a shotgun. Out from his long cloak sleeve slashes his SparkSword, flickering a dull blue. He feels a coldness behind him. Turning slowly, poised for yet another battle, his duster coattails trailing around.

He sees it. The sludge. It's growing and growing as little shredded pieces of itself tumble and drift from the forest floor toward a blob of inky smoke. Like nothing he has ever seen, it warps and roils into an upright position.

Without warning, it shoots out black shards of mist like wild rockets. It takes everything Wayfare's got to deflect them with his SparkSword. It swells as it prepares to fire again. One tentacle latches onto the giant sequoia's trunk and begins to slither its way to the nest.

And Wayfare is afraid. He looks at his meager SparkSword. At his waning Internal Spark Load reading. Then at the oozing figure before him.

Fillip senses Wayfare's spark level and sees the sludge worming toward him. *Maybe, if I move fast enough,* he thinks to himself.

He shouts to Wayfare's mind, *I'm coming!*

But the Catalyst fires his free hand at him and shouts, "NO! Stay with them. Protect *them*!"

Fillip considers arguing this, but he can see, with his sharp feline eyes, the intensity in Wayfare's face. He thinks again as he looks at the helpless owlets gazing up at him with those round eyes. And though a Shadow Cat has many wonderful powers, the ability to be in two places at once is not one of them.

As if in slow motion, Wayfare summons every last fleck of spark within his being to wield his SparkSword. With a mighty warrior cry, he lunges at it. He feels himself leap, suspended in the air, coattails flying, and legs reaching for purchase. With two hands gripping the weapon overhead, he channels his spark into it, igniting it in a fury of light and fire. As he descends on the shadow sludge, he buries his SparkSword deep down into its center and stays there with it as it writhes and screams and hisses at the pain.

Wayfare grits his teeth and snarls, "I said NOT on MY WATCH, you foul creature!"

Then he lets out a yowl of gripping anguish as he stays his SparkSword, and the inky tentacles lock onto his face and neck like leeches.

But Wayfare does not retract. Instead, he closes his eyes, every muscle in his body shaking with strain, and pulls from a source even he does not truly understand. It is deep within him, and as it bubbles up to the surface it brings images of all the good in his world. His woods and the friends who live in it. The good people in the sweet town of Median. And finally, through a haze of consciousness, Cirissa, with her Crystaline glow and that beautiful, tiny smile she tries to hide every time they meet. All the images linger in his mind as he holds fast and begins to twist his SparkSword even further down into the evil spark-sucking scummuck.

Fillip stands braced at the nest's edge, laser-beaming every little slithering snake coming even close. But he keeps one eye on Wayfare and feels the Catalyst's spark deplete to nearly nothing, and he does not know what to do!

Wayfare opens his eyes for what he believes very well will be the last time, takes what just might be his very last breath, and finds a calm inside him so serene and peaceful he wonders if he's dead already. "Complete Spark Extraction" they'll call it in the report, he knows.

But that's not what's happening at all. Instead, emanating from his chest comes a wave of pulsing power. It creates a low, bone-rattling, bass vibration so strong that even the leaves in the sequoia's highest branches quiver from it. And then – it explodes from Wayfare's body in an eruption of warped, liquid matter that lands like acid on the sludge. It sizzles and fizzes down, down, down to the ground until all that remains is inky residue. Simultaneously, because they are a connected entity, every sludge shard lurking in the woodland evaporates in a spit and sputter sort of way.

And it is gone.

Wayfare slumps. Fillip is at his side in an instant, breathing an opalescent orb into him. Then the Shadow Cat puts a paw on the Catalyst's shoulder and nudges him.

In the far reaches of his mind, Wayfare swears he hears a soothing rumble. It's like a motor. No. It's more like a grouse's wings drumming. No. No, it's ... it's purring?

He opens his weighted eyelids to a furry, gray face and sparkling emerald eyes. Fillip is looking down at him, and he is purring.

Fillip says, *THAT was WAY too close. I believe I see a pattern here, Wayfare.*

Wayfare rolls himself to a sitting position. He can barely lift his head. "Ya think?" he manages. "Maybe an apprentice isn't such a bad idea after all."

Chapter 10

Widow Shay

In the front seat right behind the driver, Deret bounces his right leg as the slow town of Median lumps along outside the trolley window. *Cloud City* is tucked under his arm.

Rolling past Sombrine's Department Store and Drabbert's Menswear, he imagines what his mom would look like in the charcoal-colored dress with long sleeves that puff slightly at the shoulders and the burgundy ribbon tied high at the waist. She'd look nice. But Deret knows that for Demera Day, her plain clothes are "just fine." The same goes for the dark wool jacket and mustard button-up shirt that Deret pictures on his father for going to town. Again, Garrin Day would say his plaid shirt is "just fine."

Dimerion Jewelers' *For Sale* sign still hangs in the empty storefront as it has since Deret was little. Shiny stuff just doesn't appeal much to Medians.

Through the top half windows of the dimly lit Lenity Wellness Center, he sees rows of heads bobbing slowly up and down on the treadmills. No one moves very fast here.

Two grown men wearing shabby suits play chess at a table outside the Slate and Stone Law Office. People tend to get along in Median.

Clouds, the boredom! His left leg bounces out a rhythm with his right.

Unnoticed by everyone on the trolley, a trickle of sludge slithers along the ceiling, down a silver pole and into the folds of the driver's jacket. She sits back in her seat and slows the trolley to a roll just outside Market Plaza at the edge of town.

Just beyond the trolley line lie simple, little houses in simple little rows. No need for fences. People tend not to argue; that would require someone to feel passionate about something. Here, families don't even have pets; they require more motivation than anyone in this town has; besides, they don't crave that kind of companionship. A few farmers have some livestock, a horse or two, and maybe some chickens – nothing that isn't useful or required for sustenance.

Deret sees his next stop, Widow Shay's vegetable stand. Bright-red tomatoes and stark-orange carrots catch his eye. Finally, something *alive*.

The sludge latches onto the driver's neck and starts sucking out her spark. She goes dull in the eyes as she rolls the trolley to a stop and opens the door.

Deret pops up and gives her a playful pat on the shoulder. "Thanks for the thrill ride, Londa," he says, not to be mean, just trying to make light of this sad town with its sad, slow people. His hand stays on her shoulder for just a heartbeat. Londa Lane looks up into his green eyes. He flicks his red bangs. She blinks hard and shakes her head just enough to wobble her knotted bun.

The sludge screeches and detaches instantly from Londa's neck. A white-hot, searing pain scorches its misty tentacles, evaporating it until it is nothing.

Deret, still looking at Londa, cocks his head and knits his brow. He hears a faint, high-pitched hissing in his ears, like a poor creature dying. And then it's gone.

"Anytime, Sugar," says Londa Lane. "Anytime."

"Did you ..." he starts to ask if she heard something then shakes it off. He smiles wide at her. "You have a great day, Ms. Lane. You hear me? I mean it." He points at her and grins his crooked smile.

"Oh, I do hear you, indeed, Deret Day. Same to you. Say hi to your folks." She lets out a hearty chuckle, closes the door behind him, and says to the rest of the sleepy passengers, "Okay, you zombies, arms up!" And away they roll.

* * *

"Ah, Deret the Doubtless," calls Widow Shay as she waddles across the cobblestones. "Always knows just what to do. What will you be having today?" Wild curls from under her flowered headscarf loll over her eyes.

"I know exactly what I'll be having," he says as he props his elbow on her stand and crosses a leg smartly. "Those tomatoes and carrots are calling my name, Widow. Just hollering at me."

Leaning in close, she whispers, "I got an eggplant the size of your head." She points a plump finger behind her hand toward the back of her stand. Her thin eyebrows tweak up.

Deret leans inconspicuously. His eyes widen. Sure enough. A giant eggplant, shiny and black as night, peers out from under a floral headscarf.

The widow leans back, hands on her round hips. Her face is lit with pride. "What'd I tell ya?"

"Oh my!" he says, genuinely impressed.

She shushes him and looks around as she shoves a large crate in front of the eggplant. A man trudges by and politely tips his hat to her. "Good day, Anders," she says, but Deret notices how her eyes go dull and her face sags to say it. Then, as soon as Anders Oldon passes on by, her cheeks lift again and her eyes twinkle like they always do during their chats.

She sees Deret's cocked eyebrow. "Now what do you think of my eggplant? Ain't she a doozy?"

Deret nods his head earnestly. "It sure is that, Widow. I have never seen a thing like it. Why such a secret? You should be bragging that baby up."

"And draw undue attention? That's the last thing I need."

"Undue attention?" he says way too loud for Widow Shay's liking.

"Sh sh *shushy uppy*," she scolds and shifts her eyes restlessly about.

He shakes his head and chuckles. Typical odd-duck ways of Widow Shay. He pulls *Cloud City* out from under his arm. "Check out this book I bought at Skylane Tomes. You wouldn't believe where I had to go to find it."

All the wrinkles on Widow Shay's face crease upward as her eyes go wide. She takes the book and chuckles, "Oh my." As she turns it over and inspects it, she whispers to her late husband, "Well, Ray, he's found it. Just like he was supposed to."

Deret is used to his old family friend talking to the late Ray Shay, but he tips his head at her. "Widow, do you know something about this book?"

She hugs the book to her bosom, looks straight at him and says, "Oh, Deret, my boy. Do I ever." Her gray eyes twinkle shining silver sparks.

Deret startles, "Whoa. Widow, your eyes ..."

She herds him to a corner and turns her back to the plaza. "Listen to me." She presses *Cloud City* to his chest. "It is time to fill you in. Cirissa told me it needed to be soon, and don't get me wrong, I am completely confident in your capabilities, but you're just so young, and..." She trails off and worries her fingers as she begins to count off the things she needs to do now.

Deret blinks twice. "Uh, fill me in on what? Who's Cirissa?"

She ignores him and continues muttering under her breath, "Take the elevator draft. No no – no stomach for that anymore. Get Drift to pick us up. Let your folks know." She scoots back to her stand and starts rummaging through boxes and baskets. "Where is that old thing?"

"Wait. My folks? Let my folks know what?"

She ignores him.

He can't take it anymore, so he grabs both her shoulders to make her stand still and look at him. "Widow," his voice is calm, but his green eyes are pleading, "please tell me what's going on."

Widow sticks something that looks like a watch in his face. "Here it is!"

Deret, still holding her shoulders, looks at the tarnished thing. "An old watch?" Exasperated, he drops his hands and runs his fingers through his bangs. *This is it. She's finally lost her nutter.*

"Don't go looking at me like I've lost my nutter," she scolds. "I'm sure that day'll come soon enough, but not this day. No sir, Deret the Doubtless. Today is *your* day."

"*My* day? My day for what?" He can hardly contain his frustration. "Widow, you've been on your feet too much. Come." He offers her his arm. "Let's go back to the farm. You can relax in the chair Dad made you, and Mom can fix you up that tea you love so much."

She looks at him for a second, then says evenly, "Nope." She slaps the "Be back when I get back" sign on the counter, grabs Deret's arm and yanks him down the sidewalk straight toward Skylane Tomes. "Prepare for a crash course into the world of spark. And just you wait until you meet your broth... uh ... mentor, Wayfare."

Baffled, Deret looks at *Cloud City* and follows Widow Shay because, as usual, he is up for anything.

Chapter 11

Murkemer

Cloud Master Murkemer's thin, red lips slurp the last of his pea soup. Some icky green liquid dribbles down his chin.

Cloud Master Shroud, disgusted, says, "That looks delightful," and tries to hide his grimace in the depths of his shadowy hood.

"Mmm," Murkemer sighs in bliss and wipes his mouth with his hoodie sleeve. "Just the way Dad used to make it." He slouches back into his gamer's lounge chair and looks wistfully at the enormous picture of his father, Cloud Master Slurry, hanging on the wall.

Shroud forces patience into his voice, "Yes. Yes. Slurry was a masterful cook." He looks around for a seat, but the youth clearly doesn't prioritize accommodations for the occasional visitor. Unlike his own tidy parlor in the Nimbostratus Sector, complete with a tea serving set and perpetual elevator music. "In fact," he continues with genuine affection, "Your father was mentioned yet again today at the Cloud Council meeting. He was, indeed, well-loved."

Murkemer drags his lanky self over to the chair in front of a wall-sized screen, "Cloud Council. There was another meeting today? Are you sure I'm not supposed to be at those?" He plops down into an elaborate gaming chair. "I mean, I remember Dad always going. I figured I'd have to take his place now that, you know," His eyes dart to a piece of fuzz on his gray hoodie sleeve. "I'm in charge of the sector and all."

Shroud drags a beanbag chair next to Murkemer, plops catawampus onto it, and tugs at his twisted-up robe. "No, no, no," he says, "don't you worry yourself with all that 'grown-up' rhetoric."

Murkemer slides his long, black bangs to one side and gives Shroud an evaluative look before saying, "Okay, man. If you say so. I mean, my dad trusted you more than any other Skybound in Cloud City."

"Exactly, dear boy." Shroud attempts a light and casual switch of topic. "So … how is our little project coming along?"

Murkemer flings off his Crocs and tucks his feet into a cross-legged position to make a sort of crotch tray with his gray sweatpants, onto which he sprinkles potato chips and a handful of Hot Tamales. "What project, Shroud?" he says as he sticks a cherry licorice whip between his lips and grabs for his control pad to fire up his game system.

Shroud lays back his over-sized hood and pinches his brow. The sounds of gunfire and electronic voices shouting and screaming blares at deafening levels. "Do you have to have the volume up so?" he says, only loud enough to be heard.

"Oh! Sure, man. Sorry about that." Murkemer clamps an ear piece and microphone stem behind his amply lobed ear then resumes play.

Shroud tries sticky politeness with gritted teeth. "The secret project I … ehem … *we* devised. Remember? The one where *you* collect the spark, and *I* make you famous? Hmm?"

Murkemer is bouncing and leaning hard in his cushy chair. His greasy hair dangles in his eyes. He sticks his tongue out as he pulverizes the buttons on his controller. Shroud reaches up to steady the soda in the cup holder keeping it from sloshing all over.

"I can see you're terribly busy," Shroud says as he struggles out of the bean bag chair. "Perhaps I could just take a look at the containment vessel in the collection room? I can record some inventory. I wouldn't want to interrupt your activity here."

Unable to tear his eyes from the screen, Murkemer says, "Sure, man. Whatever."

"Very well, Murkemer. I will be on my way."

Shroud glides down a hall, his cloak fluttering like a smoky jellyfish, to a clear tube elevator shaft. He steps in and presses the "Below" button.

Ding. A breathy, feminine voice says, "Approaching *Below* in ten … nine … eight …"

Under the murky protection of thickened stratus clouds, the tube travels the length of the Stratus sector down through the earth's atmosphere, invisible to the human eye thanks to a perpetual veil of night clouds. It plunges deep into the ground, and when it hits bottom, the curved, clear door slides open with a *ding*.

He walks into a cavern lined with a multitude of electronic panels, blinking lights, and keyboards. This room is carved into the side of a vast stadium of raw, earthen walls. He curls his hands over the rail and peers below.

Closing his eyes, he breathes deeply. "Ahhh," he exhales, "Nothing like the sour smell of sludge to get your head straight."

Below, in the belly of the gaping room, swirls a pool of sludge that cracks and flickers and sizzles with stolen spark. An eerie smile peels across Shroud's face as he watches the inky soup go around and around. He assesses numbers on the monitors. Glowing bars bounce up and down on several grids.

Then his glowering eyes track to a hole in the wall on the side of the pit like a sewage drain. Oozing from it is more spark-leaden sludge. Globs of it splunk and splosh down into the swirling pool.

Shroud muses, "Collection rate is slow." A surly *hhmmm* rumbles within the darkness of his hood.

He scrutinizes another monitor, punches a few keys, and taps the screen a couple times. An animated picture of the pool pops up on screen. If you could see the whole thing from the side, you might think it looks like a gargantuan martini glass or a giant funnel.

The animated funnel/martini glass shows spark slithering from the whirlpool, one silver strand at a time, and syphoning through a perforated glass tube. This tube is constructed straight up the center of the pool. At the pool surface, however, the tube is unperforated and continues up to an enormous cauldron suspended from the ceiling by cruise liner-style anchor chains. It's fitted with an expansive lid that looks like it would need a crane to lift. Above the cauldron dangle tree roots that grow back up to the surface. A digital gauge on the computer-generated cauldron graphic says "Containment Vessel: 19%". A line across the bowl's bottom illustrates this.

Shroud screws up his face. "That's it? Two percent progress since last time?"

Shroud clicks and taps back to the funnel graphic of the whirlpool. The neck at the bottom is plugged with solid gray, and a little oval icon with a red exclamation mark blinks urgently next to it.

"For fogsake," he mutters, "that lazy shard. Can't do the simplest ..." Shroud shakes off his hood as he taps the screen, and the image animates to show a manhole cover flop down at the bottom of the funnel. The dark circles under his eyes and bluish blotches on his face reflect back at him in the monitor screen as he watches the sludge slurp into a drain hole which channels it all back out to the earth's surface.

On another big screen, he crosses his arms and studies an animation showing all the exit points in Median. Sludge vapors trickle back up into the woods, the market plaza, Skylane Tomes and countless other spots.

His eyes smolder, yet a flicker of sorrow rifles through him all the same. It is a shame what his plan will do to the town of Median. But it's the only way. He needs their spark for his plan to work.

He recedes into the depths of his hood, takes a last glance around the collection room, and floats like a scud cloud back to the elevator draft.

What he fails to notice, however, is a small screen off to the far end of the control panel. A thin veil of sludge – a night cloud – has webbed over it, hiding the flashing red and yellow alarms silently going off revealing a leak.

On the very tippy top of the containment vessel's gigantic lid, the sludge has loosened, ever so slightly, the enormous nut and bolt that holds the contraption in place on the ceiling. It has cleverly loosened it just enough for silver strands of spark to slip through and escape out the tree roots above. And once these escaped spark strands channel all the way to the top of this particularly tall sequoia tree, they are sucked up into the stratus clouds and suspended there unchecked. Unmonitored. Unapproved. Uncontrolled.

Just the way the sludge wants it. For if it can cause enough havoc up there in the clouds, and distract those Skybounds long enough, it will once and for all be able to overcome the Earthbounds and feast undisturbed forever. It will no longer be under the suppressive control of the Cloud Masters.

* * *

Ding. "Stratus Sector, arrived."

Electronic gunfire echoes through the hallway. Murkemer is still playing his video game in the living room – the room where Shroud and his closest friend, Cloud Master Slurry, spent endless hours playing strategy games and talking in peace and quiet. He misses the fogfish aquarium. And the nebula lamps. Even the cloud mural he'd chided Slurry about endlessly.

He chuckles at the memory of little Murkemer and Slurry painting purple, orange, and blue swishy swirls all over the wall. Now, that wall is covered by a massive screen with perpetual video war games. And Murkemer sits. And sits. And sits there.

It'd be nice to think that the kid would be turning out more respectably if Slurry and his wife – Great Zephyr rest their souls – had survived the lightning incident.

The memory festers in Shroud's mind. *"Accident" is what they want to call it. The Cloud Masters. It was no accident at all. It was a travesty! Those high-and-mighties lounging up there think they're so in control of everything. If that was actually the case, those idiot Fairweather brothers wouldn't get away with their stupidity. What business do they even have crossing sectors anyway? No one takes responsibility anymore. Accident. I think not. Someone will pay. Someone has to take control around here.*

"Murkemer!" Shroud shouts, unable to curb his true emotion anymore. "Shut that thing off!"

Murkemer startles at the barked order. He blinks, wide-eyed. But he shuts the system down immediately.

Shroud instantly regrets his temper. "Forgive me. I ... I just ..." He brings his hands to his lips like he's praying. "I would really appreciate having a conversation with you at the moment."

Cautiously, Murkemer unfolds his legs so he can sit up properly. He brushes the snack remnants from his sweatpants and looks all sheepish and sorry at Shroud.

At this moment, Shroud is reminded so clearly of the boy's father. His long face and that sloped nose. His big, gray eyes with eyelashes that slant like he's always a little sad. No. Empathetic. It reassures him that the good parts of his old friend have indeed been instilled in this youth. But it makes him miss Master Slurry all the more. He also realizes how hard this must be for Murkemer to cope and adapt from losing his parents and assuming the cloud master position so famously filled by his father. His heart goes out to him.

"Master Murkemer," Shroud says, "Do you understand the importance of our secret project?"

The teen's eyes light up, "Ya, man, of course I do."

Shroud waits. And waits. Murkemer just looks back at him. "Can you *tell* me, in your own words, why this secret project is so important?"

"Oh! Ya, man, sure." Murkemer swipes his black bangs to the side and puts on a serious face that matches his equally serious, well-rehearsed response. "The collection of spark is the only way we, of the lowest atmospheric sector, can ensure an end to the irresponsible and flagrant spark expenditure of the higher sector Cloud Masters."

"And what else are we ensuring?" asks Shroud.

"That we will be able to fight back if anything like what happened to my mother and father ever happens again."

"And why are you the most qualified to take such measures?"

Murkemer pauses and softens his rehearsed tone. "As a son of tragedy, it is my responsibility to keep the Skybounds protected and secure. Even though the higher sectors think they're doing that already, they lack the perspective of the lowest Basal Plane sector to truly be able to govern the use of spark."

Shroud straightens his shoulders and nods approval. "Therefore…"

"We need to wield our own spark. And we can only get it from one place."

Shroud raises his head in pride waiting for the last bit.

Murkemer gulps softly. "Median."

"Precisely."

Chapter 12

Silva Starling and the Sky Steeds

"Yeeowwee!" Breeslin screeches as ice-tears stream out of her eyes. "You're crazy, old man!"

The Halo 500 cloud craft rips over the Altostratus water vapor clouds like a rocket-fueled jet ski.

Drift Goodroad's maniacal laugh whips past her. "You ain't seen nothin yet, Breezy Girl!"

Breeslin grips her side bars so hard, chips tinkle off her knuckles. A tiny shard snips Drift's cheek.

The Catalyst blanches and touches the little cut. He throws her a wild-eye but laughs, "You mind melting for the ride, Kiddo?" His salty dark hair whips every which way.

She hollers into the wind, "Oh my clouds! Sorry, Drift." She gives a shimmy shiver shake. The hard edges and razor points of her Crystaline form disintegrate into snow. She sits in the passenger seat in a more human form, holding on for dear life. Drift reaches up and catches a handful of her snow shed before it's blasted into their wake and rubs it over the nick on his cheek. "Thanks, Breezy." He leans into the steering wheel with a crazy grin buried inside his beard. And the cloud craft blazes on.

Breeslin shouts, "I don't think Cloud Master Virgus is gonna be okay with this."

Drift hollers, "Ha! Who do you think lent me this beauty? Ay?"

He cranks the stick shift down and they plummet, piercing the Mezzo Plane mist. Racing at blinding speed through clear blue sky, she sees the bouncy surface of the Cumulus Sector ceiling straight ahead.

A computerized voice from the dash says, "Basal Plane approaching."

"Hang on!" he orders.

Breeslin cries, "What do think I've been doing this whole time?"

Drift yanks a cord and cranks a wheel somewhere down by his knee. The engine whines as they slow to hovering, and the skis on the cloud craft pivot and transform into tuba horn style tires facing down. The pillowy cumulus clouds get closer and closer.

Drift eases himself back. "Easy Baby Girl. Easy now." The Halo 500 purrs back at the sound of his voice.

Breeslin's insides feel like they're about to see her outsides. Flying at rocket speed on a WISP mission, where she has total control is nothing like riding in a cloud craft with her old friend, Uncle Drift. As her stomach settles, and she sits back in the plush seat, she can't help laughing like a kid on a carnival ride.

The engine hums along a slopy, winding road. Cloud mountains and valleys soar and dip all around.

She sighs, "It is so beautiful here," and gazes dreamily off into the distance.

Drift nods and takes it all in. "Sure is."

Suddenly, Breeslin is distracted, taps her earpiece, and says, "You'll have to figure it out without me. Try Cloud Op 43. Snippet, you *have to* cover for me. I'll be back as soon as I can. Out." She sighs.

Drift hears her frustration, "It's tough being in charge, isn't it."

"Ugh. You got that right," she rests her head against the Halo 500's soft cushion. The million thoughts in her head are evident on her face.

"Snippet's a good soldier. She'll get the hang of it." The seasoned Catalyst gives her a sure-as-shootin, bushy eyebrowed wink.

That grisly face always manages to make Breeslin smile.

They ride in a soft, flowy hush for a stretch. When a cotton ball fence line appears ahead with a looming overhead sign that says *Sky Steed Stables*, Breeslin sits up. She works her jaw.

Drift sees her nerves and says, "Boy that Storm Pony of yours is sure going to be happy to see you again." His mustache and beard curl into one furry smile.

She glances at him then stares back down the road. "You think he'll remember me?"

"Honey," he says in his most fatherly way, "I am positive. Windy has loved you with his whole pony heart since the day you two met when you were just a little Shard."

She gives him a grateful smile and takes a deep breath. Uncle Drift always has the right thing to say when she needs a little boost. And he's almost always right. Almost.

The Halo 500 hums down the long driveway all the way up to the stables and cloud paddocks. When they glide to a stop, a woman dressed in sparkly jeans, sparkly boots, a sparkly shirt, and a sparkly hat comes to greet them with a whole-arm wave and smile to match her outfit.

Drift smoothly puts his SparkShades on. They shade his eyes from the blinding human-shaped bling coming at them, but they also give him her spark reading.

Adjacent Body Spark Level: Off Chart.

Breeslin blinks to engage her sun shield visor which delicately forms around her eyes like silver-rimmed glasses.

"Well, my, my, my. If it isn't the dear old Catalyst, Drift Goodroad and my long-lost WISPy wannabe, Breeslin!" The sparkly woman's platinum sheet of hair sways with her long, lean body as she walks.

Drift leaps out of the cloud craft and opens his arms wide to hug Silva Starling, the Sky Steed Master. "Silva," he says as he wraps her in his muscular arms, "aren't you ever a sight for sore eyes." Pinprick rays of spark seep out from under his arms and around his frame against hers as they embrace. The spark boost she gives him lightens the weight of his feet on the cloud surface even more than his own spark levels do. He feels light as air now, barely making a dent in the spongy surface.

Silva pulls away just enough to touch his SparkShades and smiles. "I don't know, Drift." She wiggles the glasses. "I'm afraid I'm the one making sore eyes." Her cute wink and side grin make the gruff old man blush and kick the cloud dust at his feet.

Breeslin floats to their side, and Silva pulls her in close for a heartfelt embrace. "I've missed you, my sweet." She holds her at arms length. "So, did you do it?"

Breeslin's face can't hold in her pride. She busts out a sunshine smile that almost rivals Silva's belt buckle. Her head bobs up and down. "Yes, I did!" She steps back. "You are looking at the youngest Weather Investigation and Sky Patrol captain of all time. Right here."

Full of attitude, Breeslin points to her feet and trails her finger up the length of her body transforming her soft, human form back into her shining WISP uniform. Ice crystals float in a snow globe form around her as she plants her feet in her superhero pose. Silva and Drift clap and hoot for her, so she takes a bow with a little flare of her ice blade arms.

Silva sighs. "Oh, it's so good to see you two. I've got Windy all groomed up for you. He's going to be so excited. I wouldn't tell him what all the fuss was about. Just that it was a surprise."

Breeslin melts inside and says softly, "I have missed him so much. I just hope he's up for the job we're in for."

Silva gives a serious are-you-kidding-me side grin and says, "Breezy Girl, he was born for this. There is no place he'd rather be than by your side – or rather, under your butt!"

Drift pipes in, "Well let's quit yammering about it and go get that little stud already!"

Silva throws up her hands and shrieks. "Yes! Oh – " She puts her hands to her lips like a prayer and her eyes brighten, if that's even possible. "But I thought first you might like to watch a rumble release."

"For real?" Breeslin nearly squeaked with excitement. "I've never seen one before." She swings a blade arm toward Drift. "Drift, have you ever seen a rumble release before?"

He deftly hops back avoiding her razor-sharp edge.

Breeslin gasps at how close she'd come to slicing Drift. "Sorry." She does her shimmy-shiver shake to transform to her softer self again.

Silva Starling bites her lip to keep from laughing. "My clouds, you two are quite a pair."

Drift just chuckles it off and shakes his head. "A long time ago in the academy. And that was just a vision screen."

Just then, the barn door opens and out come a couple of Stormbud stable hands. They raise their hands high with a thumbs-up and wait for her reply.

Silva says, "Cloud Master Bumble has approved a doozy of a thunderstorm over some prairie lands that have been aching for rain. It's darned near drought stage. I swear, I put in the request – filled out all the dumb forms – over a month ago. Sometimes I wonder if he even bothers reading them until there's trouble on the edge."

They stand in concerned silence for a moment, but then she claps her hands and rubs them together. "But, no matter now. It's time to send down the rain and unleash the Thunder Studs!" She yip-haws and flags the Stormbud stable hands with her hat like the start of a drag race.

The door gets shoved wide open and, slowly at first, out come the Thunder Studs, stepping cautiously, heads high, then down low to sniff and puff the cloud dust into little swirling tornadoes around their stamping feet. They are shades of blue and purple and charcoal. Their white manes swirl and float like smoke from a bed of coals. Their eyes glow like embers, flickering and dancing.

Breeslin stands frozen. She can scarcely find words. "They're so..." her breath catches, "... they're so... clouds above ... I've never seen anything so terrifying and beautiful at the same time."

"Dangerous and lovely," whispers Drift as he puts his hand on Breeslin's shoulder. "Like any good thunderstorm can be."

Silva gazes at her Thunder Stud band as though seeing them for the first time, even though she sees them every single day. She says softly, "We must look upon them with awe and respect. That is what will bring them home."

She blows them a kiss filled with sparks that swirl and twirl toward their feet, making them dance in place. The low rumble is even and steady, like a room full of drums being sprinkled with tennis balls.

Then Silva reaches for a gleaming, opalescent, diamond-encrusted electric guitar that one of the Stormbud stable hands has brought her. "Thank you, Sid," she says, then to Drift and Breeslin, "But this is what will send them out."

As she caresses the guitar's long, thin neck and glides her hand along the elegant curves of the instrument, it glows to life. Threads of fibrous lightning run up and down the neck and swirl around the body.

The stallion at the front sees her, as well as the gate ahead, but keeps stamping and snorting and shaking his head.

Silva stands, strong and steady, and wraps the studded strap over her shoulder with rockstar confidence. Their eyes connect. She winks, juts her head toward the gate, and picks intricately along the strings. Notes shimmer with a clear tone that dances in the air.

The steed snorts once and blows out a dark cloud burst.

This makes Silva smile, and she leans into the guitar as she continues to play. The notes become more urgent as the electric rhythm picks up.

The lead stallion responds to the music. He drums the cloud ground with a complex backbeat. The herd gets restless, flinging their heads to the rhythm.

Silva knows they're ready now. She narrows her eyes, still locked with that lead stallion, and slides her fingers up and down the strings. Intense sound sears higher into the sky as she wields the guitar over head and shakes it. The reverberation screams down the fence line and strikes open the gate with a blinding explosion.

The Thunder Stud rears and shrieks a lightning-strike whinny in reply. With blue fire in his eyes, he tears off in a maelstrom of havoc. Sky Steed after Sky Steed, the herd pours through the gate. Like cannon shots, they ripple past and out into the distance.

Drift holds both hands flat to his chest and sees Breeslin do the same. "I feel it. Inside my … my everything."

Breeslin says with a breathy laugh, "Me too," and lets the reverberation of the rumbling wash through her.

As the last one kicks up his heels and disappears with the rest, Silva sends a final hum of the guitar that follows them.

She turns to her guests and says, "And there you have it. A rumble release. It's really something, isn't it."

Drift is grinning ear to ear and shaking his head. "I'd say so. I've never seen anything like it."

Breeslin can't wait a single second longer to see her own horse. She turns back to the barn and calls, "Windy! Windy boy!"

Silva and Drift smile at each other then at Breeslin. They hear a shrill whistle echoing inside the barn. Silva snaps her fingers up high, and a Stormbud undoes the Storm Pony's tether.

Out races Windy with all the fervor and flare of an Earthbound War Pony. He's a swirling mix of sky blue, sunset pink, and stormy gray. His muscles ripple and bulge under his cloudy coat. He is a sheer delight to behold.

Breeslin taps her eyes to retract her sun shield visor and soars toward her horse with wild abandon. Both squeal at the sight of each other, Breeslin's arms outstretched and Windy's ears pressed forward. For a fleeting moment, they stop and look into each others' eyes, then crash together in an embrace that sends cloud puffs rippling away like a belly flop dive into a kiddie pool. She clings to Windy's neck and buries her face in his poofy mane. He nickers and bends his head over her shoulder, closes his eyes and lets out a cloud-puff sigh.

Happy, he says to his girl's mind.

"I'm happy too, boy," she whispers in return. She steps back, holding his face. His forelock flops down, completely covering one of his indigo eyes. "Are you ready for an adventure?" Her own eyes hold both worry and excitement.

Windy dances in place and bobs his head. *Fun!*

She laughs out loud, grateful her Storm Pony's got game, then swings herself, light as air, onto his soft, sturdy back.

Silva and Drift come up, heads tilted in a parental-type "aww." Breeslin leans down to hug Windy's neck.

Drift rubs Windy's face under his thick forelock and says, "Well that was quite a reunion." He squint-smiles at Breeslin. "I'd say he remembers you just fine."

She chuckles and shakes her head. "I don't know why I was worried."

Silva trails her gentle touch all along Windy's side as she continues back to the barn. "Come," she says.

"Let's get your trainee's mount ready. Not that I want to see you leave, but I imagine you are anxious to get about your business."

Drift agrees, "True, true. Widow Shay sounded pretty urgent. Better keep a move on, and go pick up the new recruit." He nods to Breeslin.

"Yep, Deret Day. I've been assigned to watch him for some time now, and I have to admit, the kid's got potential. He's got something, I don't know, kind of special. How he ignites spark with just a glancing touch? I've never seen anything like it in an Earthbound. I have to say, it's pretty cool."

Windy looks back at her, *Curious*.

Silva nods once and says, "Right." They stop in front of a stall. Windy nickers sweetly. "That's what I heard. And that is also why I've chosen Visa for him."

Inside the stall, stands a dull gray horse. Her head hangs low, and she does not raise her head. Her mane is tangled and frizzy. Her tail is knotted and scraggly. She is, in no uncertain terms, in a sad state.

Drift raises his unkempt eyebrows and rubs his beard, thinking. Then he gives Silva a knowing glance and says, "Moon Mare?"

Silva sighs, "I'm afraid so."

Breeslin says, "A Moon Mare. I thought those could only be found in the Illustrial Plane, way up in Cloud Master Tendril's Cirrus Sector."

Silva confirms, "Yes, but somehow Shroud ended up with this girl. I've heard rumors of his Nebulmen rustling them and other sky creatures for working his Drizzle Fields. It's a miserable life. Hard, cold labor. I don't know how the Cloud Council allows it. Again, I wonder how much thought they give anything these days."

Drift grumbles, low and menacing.

"Regardless," Silva continues, "Visa here somehow managed to escape. She won't give me any details, though. In fact, I find she doesn't want to share much at all since she came here all on her own. Doesn't want to leave her stall. Barely eats. Barely drinks."

They all look upon the Moon Mare with sympathetic eyes. Visa closes her eyes and turns her head even further away from them.

Silva holds back the sorrow in her voice and concludes, "She's lost her luster." She slaps her hands on her hips and says, "And I have a hunch this Deret Day, if what I hear of him is true, could be the one to bring her back. I just know there's so much more life in her. My spark boosts aren't cutting it for her. They don't last. She wanes quickly after I initiate one."

Drift takes a deep breath and says with resolve, "Okay then. She comes with us."

Silva and Drift boost Visa's spark until the Moon Mare's adjacent spark load eventually reads 89% on Drift's SparkShades.

"That'll have to do," Silva says as she hands Visa's lead rope to Breeslin still astride Windy. The stable master doesn't let go of it though, and just stares at it in the young WISP's hand.

Breeslin sits straight and confident on her Storm Pony and tells her, "We'll take good care of her. She's in good hands, Silva Starling."

Silva looks up. Sparkles well in her eyes. "I believe this," she says softly. She releases the rope and watches them walk down the driveway.

Drift says, "You sure you don't want to ride with me? Halo comes fully equipped with a tractor beam tether for the horses."

Breeslin laughs and over-exaggerates a thumbs up. "I'm absolutely sure, Drift. My internal organs have finally settled back into their rightful places again. We're good."

"Suit yourself," he says then calls out to the shining Sky Steed Master, "Until next time!"

Silva watches them go until she can no longer see the cloud dust from their trail. She crosses her arms and says a little sadly to no one, "Until next time."

Chapter 13

Sharing Spark

"Come on. *Come on.* Fire up already."

Back in the upper depths of Skylane Tomes, Deret and Widow Shay stand before the floor-to-ceiling window panes looking out into roiling mist and fog. Widow Shay taps a pointy fingernail at her vintage SparkBit. She screws up her face, tips her head to the ceiling, squeezes her eyes tight, and holds her breath. Then, she ever so slightly peeks one eye down at the device on her wrist. Little glitter sparks float from beneath her eyelashes. Nothing else happens.

Deret asks, "Um. Widow? Maybe I can help?"

She fully opens one eye at him. He really is up for anything.

"You said I have a decent 'spark level,' right?"

She opens both eyes. "Land sakes you certainly do, young man."

He puffs up. "Well, based on that crazy crash course you gave on the way back here, it seems all I have to do is touch you to share it."

The kid's a quick study. She smiles and says, "My spark's just not what it used to be. I thought, maybe... But nope. Here." She sticks a meaty finger at him. Gimme a boost."

They touch finger tips and *ZAP!* Mini-fireworks explode right there. Deret's red hair stands on end as something like lightning streaks across the old woman's arm, up through her eyes, and down her other arm to the SparkBit, crackling it to life. The little blue screen smokes and sizzles but does indeed scroll a pixeled "Welcome back, Fay Shay."

Her eyes sparkle with nostalgia.

Deret says to his finger, his eyes wide and hair a mess, "Whoa. Wicked cool."

"Ha!" Widow cackles. "I'd say!" She dives into the screen, tapping it so fast, her fingers are a blur. "Uh huh. Yep. Just what I thought."

Deret says, "So you say we're waiting for a ride. To Cloud City. Like the title of this book here. And this place is actually a city in the clouds."

"Yup." She keeps fiddling with the settings on her SparkBit.

Deret waits for more details. Nothing. Just more tapping. Getting information out of this woman is like squeezing a turnip.

He tries again. "And I'm supposed to become a sort of apprentice, let's say, to a 'Catalyst'. A dude who basically shares his spark to keep people 'wanting' – but not wanting too much – and battles something called 'sludge' from 'sapping' all the 'want' out of every living thing in Median. Does that sum it up?"

Widow Shay stops for a second and looks him in the eye. "Yup."

Deret sighs, but at least he's summed it up properly.

A *TING* sounds from the SparkBit.

Widow Shay exhales, "Finally."

"What? Finally what?" Deret pleads.

"Gimme the book," she demands.

He immediately hands over *Cloud City*. She flops open the book and lays her SparkBit hand down the center and says, "Reveal."

Deret cannot believe (yet somehow, he really does) his eyes as he watches the words and pictures on the page change from the ordinary images of clouds, which he doesn't know much about, to images of a city made of ice crystals and clouds … in … the … sky. As Widow Shay slowly turns the pages and peers eagerly at Deret's face, he sees buildings and byways and people and creatures and mountains and fields and ... *SNAP*!

Widow Shay abruptly snaps the book shut. Deret blinks.

"There," she says, quite satisfied with herself. "That outa show you everything you need to know. Study up!" She shoves the book back into his hands and goes back to her SparkBit settings. "According to this, they should be arriving right ... about ... now."

Momentarily, the roiling fog outside the windows peels away and forms a dense platform that slides straight out from the window wall. The sky opens up to a pure, light blue background. As Deret squints into the brightness, he sees a dot growing larger and larger as it travels toward them. A car – at least he thinks it's a car – but it's flying. Then two more figures follow behind, but these look like animals of sorts. They draw nearer and nearer until he sees they are horses – one with a rider, the other without. The cloud platform expands. The car's tires rotate so that the sides face down and shoot air downward in spurts to let it hover in place. It has a swirly "Halo 500" logo on its side. He sees the horses land light as air a slight distance away and disappear in the fog rolling over them.

Widow Shay taps a setting on her SparkBit then places an open hand on the glass. The pane ripples and dissolves. The car's clear dome rolls back, and a grizzled, hairy man gets out, grinning beneath a peppered beard and mustache.

Widow says, "It's about time you showed up, Drift Goodroad!" She thumps her hands on her ample hips.

Drift shrugs and shakes his head good-naturedly. "Can't expect a guy as popular as me to show up on time, Widow. I gotta be fashionably late so you miss me more." He winks and throws out his arms for a hug.

The old woman's eyes sparkle as she waddles springily to him and bounces into his arms. "You old cur," she says affectionately. "My lands, it's good to see your scruffy face."

Drift closes his eyes tight as they embrace warmly. Then he holds her at arms length and flicks a wayward curl out of Widow's eyes. He says softly, "How are you, my dear friend?"

"Well, I'll tell you what," she says back, "I'm doing just dandy right now, thanks to that young man's spark boost. Lemme tell you, it's got kick!" She chuckles as she motions for Deret to come out onto the cloud platform with them. "Come on out, Deret the Doubtless." She whispers to Drift, "Deret Day. Demeara and Garrin's boy," gives him a wink, and adds, "Wayfare's little brother."

"That's what I hear," says Drift. "He meet Wayfare yet?"

"Not yet. One thing at a time. But soon." She puts a *shhh* finger to her lips.

Drift nods, understanding, to reassure her that the secret is safe with him.

Deret's eyes are still wide, and he's got a sneaking suspicion they might be permanently fixed that way based on what's going on. He steps cautiously onto the cloudy platform, and though his red and white sneakers disappear into the swirls of fluff, his feet stand firmly on a dense, spongy surface. He's tentative to walk out much farther.

Widow Shay chuckles and flings her hand excitedly for him to walk out. "Don't you worry! With your spark levels, you're not plummeting anywhere." Then she says to Drift, "Skies above, check this kid's levels."

Drift slides his SparkShades down and settles them onto the bump-bridge of his nose. He taps the bow once. His shaggy eyebrows shoot up over the frames.

Seeing the man's reaction, Deret stops mid-step. Awkward. "What?"

Widow Shay can't contain her cheeky grin and elbow-nudges her old friend. "See? What'd I tell you?"

Drift taps the bow again and shakes his head in disbelief then shoves the glasses back on top of his head. He says, never taking his astonished eyes off

Deret, "I never thought it possible. 'Off Chart' spark levels?" He turns to Widow Shay. "Fay, this is unheard of! Even for a Catalyst's kid."

Deret just stands there bouncing his fist against his leg.

Widow beams with pride. "Believe it, Drift, you old Cat. Believe it."

Drift closes the gap between him and Deret and grabs the boy's hand in a crushing grip. "Glad to meet you, Deret Day. Boy, am I ever glad to meet you. And does your little town of Median ever need you right now."

That snaps Deret to attention. He looks to Widow Shay. "What does that mean?"

Widow Shay explains, "Son, there's something very unsettling going on in the clouds above Median these days. The people don't know about it because we have strict measures in place to take care no one knows a thing. They just go about their humdrum lives. But, oh, if you could see the workings going on behind the screens the Cloud Masters have developed to keep you clueless, well, let's just say you'd be amazed."

Drift pipes in, "That's right. And we're putting together a special team to investigate and intervene if necessary."

"A special team?" Deret asks. This is strangely sounding pretty cool.

Drift grins and nods. "That's right, my boy."

Deret steps forward grinning ear to ear as he salutes his elders. "Deret Day. At your service. Or reporting for duty. Or whatever. How can I help?" His scrawny shoulders slouch, but he smiles his crooked smile.

A tinkling voice says from the fog, "Oh brother. This ought to be interesting." Out of the haze walks a pony of swirling colors with a sleek-lined young lady astride. Not just any young lady. A pixie, fairy, icy, frosty, sassy sort of young lady. Her skin is iridescent and her eyes shine. She is so pretty that Deret can hardly keep his jaw up. Her glistening uniform reads *WISP*.

Drift and Widow Shay grin. Widow says, "Deret Day, meet, Breeslin. She and Drift will be escorting you."

Breeslin tips her head politely with a sweet smile.

Widow continues, "Breeslin, meet Deret Day,"

Deret maintains his adorable crooked grin and gives a single-hand wave.

Drift announces, "Well, now that introductions are done, let's get outa here. Time's a wasting. Where's his ride?"

Deret's voice cracks as he says, "What ride? Aren't I going to ride in the wicked cool car with you?" He eyes the passenger seat of the Halo 500.

"Sorry, son," Drift lets him down. "That seat's reserved for Wayfare." He gives Widow a quick, knowing wink. "The coolest Cat you'll ever meet. We gotta pick him up next."

Breeslin pulls gently on Visa's lead rope. Then, out from the mistiness behind her, comes the slow, soft horse with kind eyes. Visa's head is slug low. "It's alright, girl. Come on out. Windy and I are here to see you're safe."

Widow Shay says, "Well I'll be. If I didn't know better, I'd say that's a Moon Mare."

"Sure is," replies Breeslin as she tussles the Moon Mare's forelock and says to the horse, "And you're looking for a friend, aren't you Visa?"

Deret can't take his eyes off the somber creature.

Drift mutters to Widow Shay, "She looks a little rough, wouldn't you say?"

"I'd say," she mutters back. Her face creases seriously as she marches over to Visa, signalling Deret to come along. When she reaches to pat the Moon Mare's neck, Visa shies a fraction from her touch. Deep concern floods the old woman's wrinkles. "Easy there, dear," she says softly as she touches Visa's neck with the back of her hand and strokes it gently. "You know," she whispers to the horse, "In my day, I had a friend like you."

Visa turns her head toward Widow Shay, her eyes searching.

"Yes, that's right," Widow continues. "I too rode a Moon Mare. Her name was Etheria, and oh my, was she a delight. Like *all* Moon Mares. You are so special."

Visa sighs and bows her head to the old woman.

Breeslin says, "Somehow, Visa here was caught by Shroud's Nebulmen and forced to work the Drizzle Fields for I don't know how long. It's clear she's lost her luster."

Drift says, "The drizzle fields? Like Nimbostratus, Basal Plane, produce nothing, day in and day out, but mist and murk and sludge?"

Breeslin is pained at the truth of it. "Yes. I don't know how they caught her or if she somehow wandered onto their turf, but that's what Silva Starling said. Her Stormbuds found her wandering stray, I guess. I suppose she was trying to get home."

Visa sighs at the word "home" and gives a sad, muffled whinny.

Deret moves forward with a calm confidence. His eyes seek Visa's.

Drift starts, "Uh, Son. You might want to watch..."

But Drift is cut off by a halting hand from Widow Shay. The old woman looks on with surprise, but also a little awe, and she slowly steps away from the Moon Mare.

Deret walks in. He stops right in front of Visa, and the two simply share space.

"Hello, Miss Visa," he says with the charm of a gentleman. "I hear you've had a rough go for a while. And maybe you aren't sure who to trust anymore. But you're safe now. We're going to make sure of that."

Visa blinks at him. This boy is brave and good. And that is comforting to her.

When he offers his hand, she is looking at him. Really looking at him – like deep into the fiber of his being.

She closes her eyes and presses her forehead to his hand. *Good*, she speaks into his mind.

Deret's breath sort of catches at her pure, clear voice. He melts inside and says back, "I'm one of the good ones."

Widow whispers to Breeslin, "Would you look at that."

"Uh huh," she replies, afraid to move or say anything that will break this special moment.

Deret too closes his eyes and takes a slow, deep breath. Then he exhales almost imperceptibly. Sparkly glitter dances and floats from his lips. Visa inhales it steadily until the air between them is empty.

There is a moment where all is still.

Breeslin's eyes glisten as she whispers, "He shared spark."

"He did indeed," says Widow Shay. "He's a natural."

Drift's shaggy eyebrows scrunch in astonishment. "How in the name of Saint Medard does he know how to do that? Are you *sure* you've only been observing him, young lady, not coaching?"

"Honest, Drift. I told you this kid's got something special. Like nothing we've ever seen."

Widow shushes them. "Oh goodness sakes, I was hoping, but I dared not expect..."

Deret is smiling but focuses hard on Visa as he takes his hand away. He's not exactly sure what to expect now. He's really not even sure why or how he did what he just did. He just knew in his heart that it was right.

Visa takes a step back, shakes her head, her neck, her body, her legs, her tail until she is nothing but a blur before them. And with it, sparks, like the grandest fireworks display, fly from her in a twinkling cloud of light and color splashes. The drab veil is lifted. Her luster glistens and gleams beneath. From the tip of her velvet-soft nose to the end of her luscious tail, Visa stands as a Moon Mare of the Cirrus Sector should. Tall and proud she stands as the Crystalines intended. She whinnies an ear-splitting cry of joy and rears up, sending her mane and tail aloft. Glittering ice crystals dance everywhere.

Drift lets out an enormous guffaw, slaps his hand into his crazy mountain man hair, and says, "Now *that's* not something you see every day. Land sakes, this is quite a day."

They all cluster around Deret and Visa. Patting and praising both horse and boy.

Widow Shay is the first to break the party up. "I suppose this means it's time for you to mount up, Deret the Doubtless." She whips a finger from him up to Visa's back.

He says, "I suppose it is," and swings up onto her back as though he's been doing it all his days.

Breeslin looks at him, impressed. Suddenly, she's distracted by chattering in her earpiece. She turns away and mutters, "Tygr, this isn't a good time. Get Tuft to show you how to fix the clutch in your jet boots. I'll be back as soon as I can. Out."

Drift hops into his Halo 500 and fires up the purring engine. It starts to lift off the platform.

"Wait!" says Deret to Widow Shay. "Aren't you coming?"

"Nope sirree." She tosses the *Cloud City* book into the passenger seat. "That's all the help you'll need from me for now. And you're picking up one more passenger, remember. You learn all you can from Wayfare. He's one of the best there's ever been." She winks. "After me, of course. Besides, I'm too old to go flying around like a kid anymore. It's all I can do to get around on solid ground!"

"You'll explain everything to my folks?"

She says easily, "I will, Hun. I've been prepping them for this day a long time now. I'll head over there this afternoon to get them up to speed. Trust me, they'll be fine."

In that moment, Deret gets the feeling he's the only one who's been in the dark about this whole world that's been surrounding him and everyone else his entire fourteen years on the planet. He asks Widow Shay, "Do they, um, you know, like *know* about all this?"

She smiles until her eyes nearly crinkle shut. "Welcome to the party, my boy!"

"But, how …?" he starts.

The Halo 500 whines and revs as it shifts into flight mode. "Let's move 'em out!" He presses a button that makes the clear dome slide over top.

For the first time since Widow Shay has known Deret, something like uncertainty flickers across his face. She tips her head and grins a proud, grandmotherly grin at him. "You will be wonderful, Deret. Just share who you are, and all will be well."

With that, Breeslin wheels Windy around and takes off like a shot, leaving wispy streams behind. Drift lights the spark thrusters and floors it. The Halo 500 streaks away leaving a trail of cloud dust.

Deret is at a loss for just a moment then rubs Visa's neck with vigor. "Take it away, Miss Visa. Show me how it's done!"

She squeals in sheer delight and shoots into the blue after them.

Widow steps back into the building, fiddles with her SparkBit to retract the platform, and waits for the glass to solidify. Her confidence is sure. But she gazes back out the window as dark fog rolls in again, slowly closing her view of the blue sky.

"Good luck," she clucks. "You're gonna need it."

Chapter 14

Murkemer and Shroud

Descending to the depths of the containment room, Murkemer jams out to the tunes playing in his earpiece. He wrenches on his air guitar down low, then way high – eyes closed, a rope of cherry licorice dangling out the corner of his red lips. The night cloud veil surrounding the clear elevator tube hides him from any human eyes as he plummets past ground level. The feminine elevator voice says, "Approaching 'Below' in three, two…" but he can't hear her. The platform jolts to a stop and he flops, all arms and legs, against the tube wall and splays out like an octopus. The door *DINGS* open.

The air is musty, which he inhales deeply as he chews on his licorice. He nods like a lazy bobble-head as he slouchy-strolls into the control room where blinking panels and screens greet him. His rubbery sandals squeak with each step. A poke at a screen here. A tap at a keyboard there.

"Yep," he says wishing Cloud Master Shroud could see he's doing his job. "It's all good, man." More strolling. More head bobbing. "See, man. I got this under control." Tap tap. Clickety click.

Over the railing he sees the sludge centrifuge swirling as usual, but the tube shooting up from its center, the tube that is *supposed* to siphon the spark from the sludge, isn't showing any action. Just a blip now and then of spark going up into the cauldron.

He shifts his droopy eyes to take a closer look at the data on one of the screens. "Okay, okay. What's goin on here?" He pulls out another strand of licorice and chews nervously. When the screen reveals exactly what he sees, he stands up straighter and quick glances around the room, especially at the door leading to the elevator.

He gulps, sniffs, and says, "Huh. Let me see." He wipes his sticky palms on his sweatpants then laces his bony fingers and cracks his knuckles with a ripple that echoes around the cavern. With an *actual* serious effort, using his *actual* kick-butt computer skills, he scoops his wiry hair out of his eyes into a knot and begins to lock in on each screen along the entire curved railing.

As far as he can tell, it appears that there simply has not been much spark harvested in the last few hours. Something is definitely odd, but nothing seems *wrong*. The sludge levels on the next readout are clearly low, but that just might be a coincidence. The exit ports show slow trickles of sludge leeching back to ground level instead of the steady stream he's expecting.

Murkemer's face tightens as he continues down the line. "Dude, where's the sludge?" he mumbles to no one. Inside his belly, jostling around with chocolate donuts and red licorice, he begins to feel the unfamiliar pang of mild panic. "Aw man, this is not good," he groans. "Where is it?"

When he gets to the end monitor, he does a doubletake. Something's not right about the spark soup cauldron readings either. They're too steady. Too repetitive. And there's hardly any spark actually going in. His own eyes tell him this is wrong. He strains his head toward the cauldron's screen like a curious owl, then he slowly reaches a finger to tap its refresh button. With that mere touch, a night cloud (placed there by the sludge itself to hide the actual data) swirls and poofs away. Murkemer sees, clear as his fingers in front of his face, the spark leaking out the loosened lid and up through the tree roots directly above the ground.

"Ahck!" he squeals. "What the ...? Aw jeez, Shroud's gonna chuck me to the drizzle fields for this." But he types and clicks and pulls a lever then turns a crank, hard. He cannot remember the last time he felt so alert, his senses so tuned. The numbers on the cauldron's seal readout eventually begin to decrease, one painful percent at a time until finally it says zero and he hears a hiss like the release of the airbrakes on Median's trolley.

It's closed tight again. But how long has it been open? And how could he be so stupid? Fooled by the oldest trick in the book – a night cloud. More importantly, Murkemer is baffled at who the heck put that night cloud there.

A-a-a-n-nd ... where the heck is all the sludge?!

He paces back and forth, sandals squeaking up a storm, chewing on licorice after licorice. "Not good, not good, not good." He can feel his eyes welling up as he darts glances every which way, seeing nothing that explains this. He lurches down into a scrunched position and wraps his hands over his head.

Time for a meltdown. A rocking, hair-pulling, fist-pounding, impress-even-a-toddler *meltdown*.

Once *that's* out of his system, the teenaged Cloud Master, sits slumped, exhausted. The air around him feels heavy. He sighs and plops his head in his hands.

"Feel better?" a familiar voice says. He jolts up, assuming Cloud Master Shroud has found him. But it's not Cloud Master Shroud. And there is no one else in the room still. A little shakily, he closes his eyes and says, "Not really."

"Then make it right, Murkemer," the low, soft voice says. "Make this right. As I know you can."

Cloud Master Slurry, his dad, used to tell him this when he was just a cloudling. When he spilled his pea soup or threw night clouds over the furniture to make visitors trip, it was always the same, "Make this right, Murkemer."

Shayd, his mom, would often try to clean up his messes, dismissing them behind his father's back. She meant well. But Murkemer usually felt even more guilty when she did that. Like his penance hadn't been served, or his reward hadn't been earned. Invariably, he would clean up his own mess. He would make a genuine, face-to-face apology. These are the kinds of things he hopes people will remember about him, not the screw-ups.

It's hard hearing that engrained teaching still echoing in his head. It makes him sad. But at the same time, it makes him feel like his father is still, in some very permanent way, with him. And that bolsters him off the floor. Sniffling and swiping away the stray bangs dangling from his hair knot, he blinks hard and says out loud to the echoing room, "I'll fix this." He gulps. "I don't exactly know *how*, but I can fix this."

He pulls out the last, linty rope of cherry licorice from his sweatpants pocket. Letting it dangle from his lips, he eyes the thing he needs. Stuck to a big, round button, which is hidden under a plastic protective flap, is a sticky note that reads: IF YOU NEED *THIS* BUTTON, YOU MUST HAVE REALLY SCREWED UP. It's in his own handwriting. He grimaces at how well he knows himself.

It's the *RALLY* button. The *RALLY* button sends out a subsonic pulse that only the sludge can sense. It's a safety measure installed way back when the entire concept of sludge sapping spark originated. The Skybounds figured, just in case things got out of control (whatever that might look like), this pulse would work like an attractant-on-steroids and bring all the sludge back in from Median for, say, a regroup or some kind of reprogramming. The pulse is irresistible to sludge. Collectively, it should worm its way back to the hall like zombie smoke. The Skybounds, of course, have to have full control over such a thing, or who knows what kind of chaos could happen.

Murkemer just needs to round up the sludge for like ... inventory, so he can reset and restart spark collection. Then he can show Shroud he can maintain control. He can be trusted with important things. He's capable and smart and ...

A twinge of uncertainty makes him doubt this whole plan Cloud Master Shroud has roped him into. It seems shadier than his dad would have approved of, and everyone knows he takes more after his dad than his mother. His mom, of course, would've been all over it, but that's just because it was her nature. Shayd loved a good sneak, a sheisty trick. That's what made her so fun. That and her huge, gray hair. But Cloud Master Slurry, being the fair and gentle cloud master that he had been, usually made sure his wife never went too far. They had been an odd pair but, to Murkemer, a perfect couple.

And those arrogant Skybounds up there in their lofty Cloud Council (He really should get to one of those meetings.) are the ones who have driven him and Cloud Master Shroud to this point of secretive spark collection. They deserve some chaos. It's just going to be a planned chaos that will teach them all a lesson about just exactly how sludge and spark should be wielded.

Cloud Master Shroud's words come to Murkemer's mind, *It must be done in a way that will show them how careless they are with spark. How thoughtless. How irresponsible.*

A fire burns in Murkemer's belly. It might be the habanero nachos. But he knows he needs to set things right in more ways than one. He removes the sticky note warning, lets his hand hover for just a beat, and musters the authority bestowed upon him the day his parents perished in that Fairweather trumble the Cloud Council allowed to get out of control.

The authority of the Cloud Master of the Basal Plane Stratus Sector.

Eyes narrow, jaw set ... he presses the *Rally* button.

A suction sound slurps, a shaft plunges, a clunk opens a valve, and a pulse beats a steady rhythm. The monitor shows the attractant being injected at every exit site and out to the surface all over Median.

Now, he waits.

And he waits.

Little. Very little. Very, very little happens.

A strand here. A slither there. The sludge is not coming in droves like it's supposed to. And the screeching these few do make is ear-scraping. That can mean only one thing. The sludge has been hit. And hit hard ... by Sparkslingers.

Like he doesn't have enough to deal with!

The young cloud master stands there, dumbfounded.

Shayd's voice whispers to him from his memories, "Fix this? How about we fix *them*?"

His mom did have a knack for getting even. It always made him feel better, in a shamefully small way, when she would give him pointers for getting back at any cloudlings who made fun of him. Called him names. Drip Nose. Muck Master. Stupid kid stuff. The more he thinks about how to deal with Shroud, as well as the rest of that arrogant Cloud Council, the more he hears his father's voice warning against it. The conflict within him churns.

It's time to start thinking for yourself, both his parents' voices say in unison.

And there it is. A resolute thought breeches his mind and flows right into the very creases of his long face. Though it makes his heart pound, he goes to the station at the end of the line. Cranks a wheel hard to the left. Pushes a single button that lights up all the other buttons on the console. A little flap door opens, and a cylindrical canister raises steadily from below surrounded by steamy fumes. Murkemer stares at it. Cracks his neck. Grabs it. Twists its top open and pours its black ooze down into a mini-funnel that juts up from the console.

He grips the lever next to it and slowly slides it past green, then yellow, then orange, then he stops at the red-orange level where another sticky note in his own writing says, *Are you 100% sure you want to do this?* He hesitates just a second.

A ghastly grimace takes over his face. He knows he should get Shroud's help before he makes this call. But he also knows, deep down, Shroud totally wants this anyway. Like he's probably just been waiting for *the new kid* to do it, so he won't have to take the rap.

And that thought makes Murkemer mad. He's been a sucker too long. Shroud's little ignorant minion. But this young cloud master's father didn't raise an idiot. And his mother taught him, like only the best can, how to sneak his way through just about anything.

"Here goes nothing," he says. "If I'm gonna do it, I might as well DO it."

He shoves the lever all the way through the red line until it can't move anymore. Clanking and whirring echoes throughout the cave. The giant funnel seals itself and the whirlpool of remaining, screaming sludge speeds up. Injector tubes release a ghostly serum into the pool, thickening it, darkening it ... growing the sludge in there.

Once it's all just a soupy goo, and the funnel is filled within an inch of the top, Murkemer spins the wheel all the way to the right. With a flushing sound that could only be rivaled by a Stormhulk's toilet after a chili fest, the container drains and drains and drains its fresh sludge out to every single one of Median's exit ports.

If Shroud wants spark, Shroud's gonna get spark.

The earth surrounding him groans and creaks like a massive ship holding back the sea. A vibration hums through his core. He sees on the animated screen that he's released so much sludge, it's pushing through cracks and weak spots all over. It's seeping up to the forest floor like fumes through a sieve. This, he has not expected. His Adam's apple bounces up and down once. A flicker of panic flashes across his eyes. But really, what does he care? At this point, he might as well wreak real havoc.

A thought – a super shady thought his mother would have been proud of – slips into the corner of his mind and leads his eyes to the spark containment vessel's screen. The one he'd found was cattywampus but he had sealed up as soon as he saw it leaking spark up through that monster sequoia tree up there.

With a snarky sneer, Murkemer undoes the spark cauldron's lid, just slightly, again. Once he's perfectly reapplied a night cloud to the cauldron's screen – he's still not sure how it had gotten there in the first place – and replaced it with a normal reading, he nods. "Shroud can take the heat for that."

He turns to go then hears the swooshing of the elevator. He squares his shoulders – as square as his perma-slouch allows – smirks, and stretches a night cloud like pizza dough until it envelops his entire body. He is completely invisible.

A twinge of sadness laced with anger and rolled in spite churns his insides. Would his *father* be proud?

He has no time for a moral dilemma. Shroud is coming. Maybe it's just all the junk food anyway.

"Time to catch my first Cloud Council session."

* * *

Shroud floats through the elevator door and glides, dark cloak billowing. He sucks his grimy teeth, perturbed.

"Where is that lump?"

He'd searched the main level, but Murkemer was nowhere to be seen. The entire dwelling had been eerily still. No bloody combat scene playing out on the wall screen. No Murkemer in his gaming recliner. No Murkemer in the kitchen making some disgusting "snack." Only a ripped-open, mostly empty bag of cherry licorice lay on the counter.

But the cavern. It feels ... different. A faint vibration shivers through him from toes to hood. Much like a Stormhulk's hum as it meditates before blistering into a tempest. It's an unnerving sensation. And that puts Shroud on cautious alert as he begins viewing all the screens along the curved panel.

He stops, frozen with suspicion, at the very first display. Cherry red finger-smears dot the glass.

Quickly, he taps into the program's history. What scrolls before his yellow eyes tells him everything. Everything Murkemer has done. And, according to the time stamps, recently! It's a marvel they didn't bump into each other inside the elevator.

He whisks a quick glance toward the elevator. His gaze lingers on it. His face darkens. He swipes his hood off and listens. A faint swoosh betrays the boy's escape.

Instinctively, Shroud goes to chase after the little sneak. Thin strands of hair fall from his balding head to dangle in his eyes. Frustrated, he glosses them back and sets his hood in place.

To think, he was fooled by a child's game of night cloud. He, Shroud, Cloud Master of the Nimbostratus Sector of the Basal Plane! The sneakiest of all sneaks. The slyest. The most devious. Stealthiest of all until this dense, pubescent shard ...

But he stops himself. He'll deal with Murkemer later. Now is the time for more pressing matters.

Damage control.

Swift and adept, he flips up the flap covering the big red RALLY button. He mutters to himself, "Just need a mild draw." Off to the side lies a sticky note that reads IF YOU NEED *THIS* BUTTON, YOU MUST HAVE REALLY SCREWED UP. He picks it up and scrutinizes it. He rolls his eyes and pinches the bridge of his nose. "Why I ever thought he'd be able to handle this ..."

Shroud sucks in a deep, cleansing breath. He almost imperceptibly shakes his head and forces his droopy lips into the semblance of an *it's-fine-everything-is-fine* grin. He turns one last dial and presses the button. Suction sounds, a shaft plunges, a valve clunks, and a pulse beats a steady rhythm. The monitor shows the attractant at 50% potency being injected at every exit site.

Then he waits. And waits. And waits.

He murmurs, "Well this is unusual," and cranks up the attractant to 75%. Nothing happens. Finally, 100%. The sludge is not responding. His wrinkles deepen even more as he tries to sort through this enigma.

* * *

On the surface, the collective voice of the swarming sludge hisses at the attractant's pulse assaulting its senses. It remains static but does not fall for the artificial spark draw. Its only desire is to suck the *living* spark out of every *living* thing inside The Rim. This little town of Median has been providing a very desirable spark buffet for some time. That is the only thing that will satiate its frenzied desire. It will not give up until it has feasted on every last *living* spark fleck.

Eventually, the pulse stops. If one was fluent in sludge-speak, one could make out the vague undertone of two words within the raspy hiss.

Want. More.

* * *

Having shut down the attractant, Shroud sighs and says to no one, "What's done is done. The sludge is not responding. To call that much of it back would be a nightmare to manage anyway, I suppose. Spark collection is just going to have to amp up, like it or not."

A singe of excitement strikes his dark mood. Maybe this is exactly what needed to happen. Maybe it simply is time to bring his plan to fruition. What, after all, has he been waiting for? Subtlety? Ha! If he's going to do this, he might as well DO this. Enough with *gradual* accumulation of spark. Enough with those Catalyst nuisances delaying the inevitable.

Grim determination riddles his darkened face within the depths of his hood. He looks to the mottled spot on the rock face at the back of the cave and goes to it. With a sweep of his bony fingers, he plucks away a night cloud he's set over a safe's door revealing a blue-lit keypad. His hand reaches for the numbers and falters. Is he really ready for this? This isn't the way he planned it. But then, what in life ever *does* go the way one plans it?

Had Slurry, his best friend since they were just little puffs, *planned* to be blown into nothingness by those bumbling idiots Cottin and Puffin Fairweather, making their ILLEGAL cloud wrestling monstrosities? And while on routine sector review business no less? Had Shayd *planned* to pine away for her husband until she became nothing but wandering mist, leaving behind their only son?

He'd grown up with them both and had gone through the rigors of Cloud Master Makryl's Cloudling Care and Shard School up in the Cirrocumulus Sector in the Illustrial Plane. In play, they'd called themselves The Dynamic Trio. Causing mischief and pulling pranks, but nothing harmful. Slurry wouldn't have that. He'd been as good for their little group in childhood as he'd been for the Cloud Council in adulthood. Good at keeping tempers in check. Good at governing overzealous plans.

He was just ... good.

And now he's gone.

And someone should be held accountable for that.

And by *someone*, he means the entire Cloud Council.

He realizes his fingers are twisted into a white-knuckled fist hovering in front of the safe's glowing keypad.

Beep. Beep beep. B-e-e-e-e beep. Beep. Bebeep.

Twist. Clunk.

He inhales, resolute, and pulls on the safe's door. Its seal cracks, and hinges creak as the door swings open. Deep inside, on a triangle mount, sits his secret weapon.

The Bolt Blaster. His own design, which he has painstakingly developed over the course of the last year. He cradles the bazooka-style gun in his arms as he checks it over, loosens its levers, and spins its dials.

"Time to load up," he says to no one. His soft, raspy voice eerily echoes around the cavern. He pauses to listen to his own words whispered back to him from all corners of the cavern. It is somewhat unnerving.

Over at the spark cauldron, he pulls out the siphon tube from the cabinet below and plugs it into the receptacle on the countertop. He locks it in with a click and a twist, then he plugs the other end into the port on the Bolt Blaster's belly. His fingers curl around the siphoning lever. Shroud checks the readings on the screen. All appears normal.

A message scrolls repeatedly across the screen. It says: *Initiate spark transfer*.

"Here goes." He slowly slides the lever upward. A pulsing sound whirs as spark loads into his weapon. An LED screen shows green once it fills up all the way to "Full."

He disconnects the tube and hoists the Bolt Blaster. With a swoop of his cloak, it disappears inside the fabric folds.

A whir of nerves trickles through him. He gulps. Then he strides to the elevator. Inside, he turns to press the button, and as the doors close, he says, "Time to catch a Cloud Council Session."

* * *

What Shroud hasn't seen, behind the night cloud Murkemer so slyly placed, is the continuous spark leak still seeping up into the massive – and still growing – Sequoia tree above. And at the very tippy top of that tree, Shroud has no way of knowing how the spark is streaming up through the perpetual cloud-cover of Murkemer's Stratus Sector and continuing up into his own Nimbostratus Sector. There, lightning crackles wildly. Reaching upward STILL toward Cloud Master Drizzo's Stratocumulus Sector.

And it continues to expand. And no one seems to notice.

Yet.

* * *

In the far-reaching arms of the sequoia tree, all the way up to the highest, swaying branches, lies a nest. An owl's nest. The very same owl's nest that nearly succumbed to the sludge swarm had it not been for the excellent fight given by the owl family themselves and the ever-vigilant Sparkslingers in the forest.

This same tree is experiencing an unnatural surge of continuous spark now. And it's not just the tree itself, but all its inhabitants as well. The young brother and sister owlets are nearly grown already, though they're just days old. Father Owl and Mother Owl are larger, fuller, and sharper than ever.

A nimbus glow surrounds each of them. And though they don't realize it just yet, they are all becoming Sparkslingers themselves.

Chapter 15

Sparkslingers

One sequoia tree at the far edge of Median's Rim stands taller than all the rest. It's so tall, its crown disappears into Murkemer's perpetual cloud layer.

Drift taps his SparkShades com piece, "You remember seeing this?"

Breeslin taps her sapphire com to reply, "I swear I've never seen that tree before, at least it's never been so tall that it disappears into the clouds. How on Earth did a mature tree like that grow so fast, Drift?"

The Halo 500 zooms closer and tours around the tree's entire spread before circling back to Breeslin and Deret on their Sky Steeds. They all float in the air just above Median's cloud deck.

Deret adds, "My skin is tingling. Like *vibrating*." He holds out a hand to see flecks of spark bouncing in place over his skin.

"What was that?" calls Drift on the com. "What'd he say?"

"Ugh," Breeslin says. "We've got to get you a spark device, Deret." She taps her com again. "His skin is vibrating, Drift." She looks at Deret's red hair sticking out in all directions. "I haven't seen this before. But let's land. You got a read on Wayfare yet?"

"Roger that." Drift taps his SparkShades again and sees Wayfare's familiar icon blinking in a clearing not far from the gigantic sequoia. "Got him." He squints at a second, unfamiliar icon next to Wayfare's. "And he's not alone. Spark levels look to be off the charts. Better gear up Breezy. Never know what he's dealing with down there these days."

"On it," she replies instantly. "Deret, you might want to step aside a bit. Windy and I need some space."

Deret needs no explanation. "Okay. Visa, sounds like we need to move."

Visa nickers and dances lightly away from Windy's haunches.

Windy looks back at Breeslin with his bright blue eye peaking under his fluffy forelock. He gives a snort.

"Yep, buddy," she says, "time to suit up."

With a you-got-it-boss look of determination, he flicks his tail and stamps his feet into the cloud dust beneath them. Breeslin levitates above her saddle like they've done this a thousand times. And the Storm Pony transforms. Windy is still Windy, but sheets of clear curved ice slide into armor plates over his chest, then barrel, then rump. His head sprouts an angular, spiked helmet of sorts. A cocoon-type shell ripples over his mane, wrapping it into braids that cling tightly to his neck. His eyes are shielded with protective, clear cups. And his feet and legs are laced with knife-like shards of ice where there once was feathery hair.

Deret says, "Holy ozone ... Storm Pony turned War Pony!"

Visa whinnies and flings her head at the sight. *Handsome.*

Deret laughs, "I suppose even Moon Mares are suckers for steeds in uniform."

She flings her head some more.

Windy stands proud, at attention, and says, *Ready*.

Drift alerts Breeslin, "Hurry it up. I'm reading a lot of commotion down there."

Breeslin replies, "Got it."

To Deret's amazement, she does a shiver-shake with her whole body and transforms from head to toe. Crystals spike from her glistening uniform's shoulders, and razor-sharp blades slide out overtop her fingers. Her ankles, her elbows, even her hips are covered with shards of ice. But perhaps most astonishing is her head. Her pixie haircut crackles, crystalizes, and glows with a soft white pulsing.

Deret is speechless.

Visa says, *Pretty*.

"Uh. Pretty fogging amazing, I'd say." He blinks and closes his gaping jaw only to grin and say to the transformed Breeslin levitating before him, "Warrior Pixie."

Though normally anyone who calls her a "pixie" would end up with an ice blade at their throat, Breeslin finds herself completely smitten at the boyish fascination in his voice, as well as in his eyes. So instead, she laughs – a tinkling of bells – fires her thrusters with a flick of her feet, and does a quick flight-hop right onto Windy's heavily armored back.

"Warrior Pixie ..." her feet suck in the orange flare, and an ice-shield slides over her eyes, "... with *gadgets*."

Deret says, "I gotta get me some of them."

"In due time, recruit. Let's bolt!" Breeslin commands.

"On your tail!" Deret leans over Visa's neck, entwining his fingers in her mane, and they're off.

The Halo 500 revs then zooms ahead of them at a steep angle, swerving through the Rim's trees, blazing a path. Drift reads the monitors on the dash blinking at him to veer this way then dip that way. He's turned on the Void Vacuum which creates a sort of temporary tunnel behind him so that the horses can follow easily all the way down to the ground without having to slice their way through the thick trees.

As soon as the clearing appears, Drift pulls up sharply and hovers slowly to the ground. Breeslin and Deret rein in Windy and Visa until they are trotting side-by-side on solid ground. They slow to a stop next to the cloud craft as its clear dome rolls back and Drift leaps out, SparkPistol ready for action.

But what they see is not a battle, or anything of the sort. It's the great Wayfare and a ... a ... cat ... spark-sparring in the woods. Hiding behind logs, launching, and volleying zaps, leaping out and rolling into superhero stances.

Drift just scratches his head and says, "They're ..." his shoulders relax, "... playing."

Breeslin squints and says, "Is that a ..." Her tinted ice-shield retracts, and prism cylinders protrude around her eyes which make the scene before them clear. "... a Shadow Cat?" She whips around to look at Drift. His face is enormous through her goggles. "Holy ozone!" she squeaks and retracts the cylinders. "Wayfare's found himself a *Shadow Cat*!"

"No shard?!" he squawks and flicks his SparkShades to enhance-vision mode. He shakes his head in disbelief. "Sure enough. Huh. Leave it to him."

Deret interrupts, "Um. Guys? What's a Shadow Cat?"

Drift considers Deret for a moment, not exactly sure how to explain. After some beard rubbing and umming and uhhing, the Catalyst grabs *Cloud City* from the passenger seat and tosses it to Deret. "Better read up, kid," he says and starts walking toward his old friend Wayfare.

Deret looks to Breeslin for an answer, but she just says, "*Myths and Legends 101*. Page 372," and nudges Windy to follow Drift.

Deret shrugs and slides off Visa's silvery back. "I'll read this later," he says.

Visa gently positions herself in front of Deret, blocking him. Curling her sleek neck toward the book in his hands, she says, *Read*. She looks at him softly then touches the book with her nose.

Deret gives her a curious look, rubs her forehead, and says, "If you say so, Miss."

The Moon Mare nods and blinks slowly.

Deret opens the book which immediately fans to page 372. He smacks it shut and eyes it all around.

There's no way this thin book has more than a hundred pages. He squints at it and opens it again. The pages automatically fan in a blur then land on page 372. The top of the page before him reads *Shadow Cats*. The two-page section is covered with the tiniest print Deret has ever seen, but he squints hard at the first paragraph and puts his finger under the first sentence. Try as he might, the words are just too small to make out. He even notices them blurring and wavering.

He blinks to try to focus until he has to close his eyes hard for a break. At this moment, with his finger on the page and his eyes tight shut, he feels a trickle of electricity pulse through his finger, up his arm, and straight into his brain – no, his mind. Images strobe behind his eyes, words flicker and flash, until suddenly, it all stops, and he opens his eyes knowing all the things *Cloud City* has to say about Shadow Cats.

"Clouds above," he says and runs his fingers through his red hair. "Where was this little trick all school year?" He opens to another page about *Sky Levels and the Skybounds Who Govern Them* and does it again. "Oh my clouds," he says and looks up into the overcast, pea soup sky he's grown up with all his life, never imagining – yet somewhere deep down he's *always* wondered – what kind of a world went on *up there*.

While any normal Earthbound would have figured they were losing their nutter, suddenly, Deret's world made more sense.

* * *

Lurking within the dense underbrush, which it's managed to maintain around the clearing regardless of these Catalysts' attempts to hold it back, the sludge works out its next move. Not long ago, it would have been wary of all these spark wielders and probably have slunk back into the safety of shadows, but that is not how it feels now. Not anymore.

Its yearning for spark is never assuaged. It will endure many dangers to get its next fix. Its oneness all over the little town of Median is frenzied to sap spark. The sludge is irrevocably addicted. And *that* controls it now.

It will not stop until every last speck is drawn from every last Earthbound in Median. But what then? Yes, then it will slice through the Rim to the next unsuspecting town.

It heaves in and out, pulses with need. It will get its fix.

* * *

Breeslin's sharp whistle pierces Deret's thoughts, making him snap *Cloud City* shut and stand at attention looking toward the crowd on the other side of the clearing. "Get over here, cadet!"

She and her storm pony have retracted their full-body armor. She's smoothing her iridescent skirt and skin-tight, pearly top. Sparks spray from the long sleeves as she swipes her arms, dusting off any remaining ice chips from her armor. She shakes her pixie hair free of ice armor particles, leaving it all askew in an adorably reckless way.

Deret strides confidently across the pine needle floor toward her, Visa at his heel. Once he's closer, he sees the one that must be this ever-famous Wayfare, and as he takes him in, he can't help but feel he's walking toward a future mirror of himself. This makes him falter ever so slightly, but Visa's silvery shoulder is there to ease him forward. He pats her neck, making opalescent dust poof from her coat, and they approach the group.

Drift's booming voice is buffered in the dense woodland, "Deret the Doubtless, m'boy!" One of his hands is on Wayfare's shoulder as his other extends toward Deret. "Allow me to introduce you to the one and only," he bows slightly, "Wayfare. Catalyst extraordinaire!" His growly laugh echoes up into the treetops.

Breeslin, still sitting astride Windy, keeps looking from Wayfare to Deret then Deret to Wayfare. She notices the striking resemblance too.

Fillip sits amongst the group, his posture proper. He stares at Deret, unimpressed, and licks his paw.

Drift booms a hearty laugh. "Don't take this feline's opinion too seriously, Deret." He leans down close so only Deret can hear what he says next. "Nervy, snooty, and not hypo-allergenic, ya know." He nudges Deret with his elbow and raises his bushy eyebrows to emphasize his smile hidden beneath his beard.

Deret tweaks an eyebrow too and chuckles, but he also takes in the creature's presence with awe.

Fillip sits there, studying the boy.

Wayfare stands strong, his long coattails a dark backdrop for his streamline frame. His arms are crossed, and his head is tipped appraisingly so that his floppy, blonde mohawk dangles to one side. And though everything about his stance says he's tough and judgy, Deret sees the truth in the man's smile, which genuinely reaches his eyes, making them crinkle and spark.

Wayfare's voice is crisp and full. "So, this is the new kid. The greenhorn. The rookie." He's not quite ready to drop the hey-we're-brothers bomb on him just yet.

Drift, who looks like a hulk of a man next to Wayfare, slaps his back which flops Wayfare's hair over one eye and makes him stagger forward a half-step. "Try *apprentice*, my friend. Apprentice."

Wayfare grins a wily smile at Drift. He straightens and swipes his hair out of his face, tiny sparks thread his locks, keeping it place like hair gel. His stance relaxes into a friendly, welcoming posture as he chuckles and reaches for Deret's hand. "Well, young man," his eyes twinkle with sincerity, "whatever we end up calling you, it is indeed our good fortune you are here. I've heard a lot about you and your spark talents. And right now," he lets go of Deret's hand and warily scans the woods all around them, "we can use all the help we can get. So, thank you." Wayfare gives a short, head-down bow.

Deret says, "I don't think I'll ever get used to how you all seem to know more about me than, well, than *I* know about me." He raises *Cloud City* and smiles his up-for-anything grin. "But, hey, turns out I'm a wicked-fast reader, so I'll give whatever you got a shot."

Wayfare, impressed already, says, "You absorbed that whole textbook? Niiiice."

Deret confesses, "No, not the whole thing. Just a couple chapters. I think. It seems," he thumbs through the pages which never seem to stop, "there's more here than meets the eye."

They all laugh. Except Fillip, who's still a little cheesed that the Shadow Cat section is only two pages.

Wayfare musses up Deret's hair and reaches for the book. "That's the understatement of the century. Here, lay it like this, flat out, and place both your hands on the pages." He explains to the group, "If all the hype about you is true," he looks at Deret as though he's about to set off a bunch of fireworks, "I *think* this ought to work."

"Think?" Deret squeaks.

"Well, *I* was never able to do it." He looks to Drift. "And I think it's a pretty good guess that Drift wasn't either."

Drift chuckles and crosses his big arms. "That's a fer sure *NOPE* for me."

"So whaddya say we get this first little *apprentice* test out of the way? Huh?"

Deret looks to Visa who blinks her soft eyes, then Breeslin who crosses her arms and cocks a hip, then

Drift who raises his thundercloud eyebrows and tips his chin down.

The young apprentice lays his hands on the book's pages.

"Good. Now close your eyes, breathe deep, and think *absorb*, you know, like a sponge."

At first, nothing happens.

Wayfare says, "Come on, Buddy. *BE* a sponge."

At that moment, a wave of shimmering, crackling energy infuses Deret's hands and courses up his arms into his mind.

Wayfare steps back, hands up. "Oh! Ha ha! Will you look at that!" He leans in to get a better look at the silver lines of information absorbing into Deret's knowledge-base.

Drift nudges Wayfare and taps the outdated SparkBit on his friend's wrist. "Check it, Buddy."

Wayfare scrolls through the Adjacent Body Spark Load readings to see "Deret Day: Off Chart."

Wayfare startles, "Holy ozone! But he's just a ... a kid!"

Breeslin sing-songs from her mounted position, "Told ya."

Wayfare gives her a you-sure-did head bob but never takes his eyes off Deret.

Windy flings his head up and down, bouncing Breeslin in her seat. His frizzy forelock flops to the rhythm revealing one bright blue eye, then hiding it. *Not bad*, he says. His entire coat excitedly swirls its misty sunset colors.

Deret remains in his absorption state.

They all hear a sophisticated, *Well I'll be ...* in their minds and turn to see Fillip, head cocked, watching Deret too.

Visa stands in awe, glowing for her new rider. *Good*, is all she says. And that is enough.

The last wave flows through Deret and a single strand of spark zips around his head then to his eyes, popping them open. They all look at him anxiously waiting for him to say something.

Finally, he says, "Well. That's interesting."

An effervescent voice comes from behind the group and says, "Deret Day, you just might be our last hope for Median."

Cirissa has joined them. She has melted her Ice Crystal Guard armor away to present her softer, more human form.

Wayfare gulps at the sight of his Kindred and smiles his irresistible grin.

Breeslin squeals with delight, "Cirissa!" and slides to the ground. The little WISP runs to Cirissa and squeezes her in a hug. "I've missed you," she whispers. Then, as abrupt as a static shock, she touches her earpiece and turns away saying, "What? And Thread can't maneuver it?" Pause. "Well, try a strobe beacon, Snippet, then ..."

Cirissa smiles warmly as Breeslin, all grown up now (sort of), attends to matters going on in her absence.

Wayfare coolly gives a chin-up and a sly smile, which teases a tiny smile from the Crystaline. He looks around – not without theatrics. "And where is my pretty little princess?"

Cirissa says with a hint of regret, "I dropped Sheena off at Silva's for the time. Dangerous elements afoot these days."

"Aw come on, Cirissa. You know as well as anyone, that Frost Fox's got game."

"I know," her brow knits, and she lowers her eyes, "but I just couldn't bear it if anything happened to her."

Just then, glittering down in a stream of spark dust comes Sheena. She hits the forest floor yapping and running in circles, tongue lolling like *Isn't everyone just so happy I'm here?* She leaps onto Wayfare, who's kneeling on the ground to catch her and ruffle her up until she looks like a sparkly puffball.

Cirissa crosses her angelic arms and eyes him. But everyone can see the curl on her lips.

He looks up at her with a sheepish grin. "Hey, don't look at me. I don't have a secret Frost Fox whistle or anything of the like." He stands, opens his coat to prove he's got nothing but his SparkSword and SparkWhip. "Honest."

Cirissa sees in his blue eyes that he is, as always, completely honest.

Sheena scuttles to Cirissa and props her front paws imploringly on her. *Honest.*

"Oh?" says the Crystaline. "Then why are you not at the Sky Steed Stables chasing Billow Bunnies? Hm?"

Sheena smartly sits on her rump, chest puffed out, eyes determination. *I go too.*

Cirissa breaks her icy façade and scoops Shenna up into her arms. She whispers to her little friend, "I'm glad you're here."

Sheena dabs her nose with a tiny tongue flick and gives a proud-as-punch pant-smile.

There is a collective *Awww* among the crowd.

Fillip snorts like he's got a hairball and rolls his eyes.

Wayfare notes a possible – though he can't be sure – hint of resentment. He says, "Cirissa, have you had the honor of meeting my friend here, Fillip? He, let me tell you, is one superstar Sparkslinger."

Cirissa looks at Fillip then at Wayfare and catches on instantly. She bows honorably toward the ancient Shadow Cat. Her aura glows as she says, "It is an honor to meet you, Fillip. Your kind is a wonder to all Skybounds. What a privilege." She offers him a gentle stroke overtop his wide, smooth head.

Fillip, try as he might to maintain a semblance of formality and propriety, can't hold back the gurgly vibrations surfacing from him. And he purrs. Cirissa softens even more at the depth of the earnestness she feels emanating from him. She gives him one last pet and then glides on to greet the others.

The horses bow their heads low with a whinny nicker. She returns their bow and delicately touches both their brows. Windy sighs heavily, and his coat swirls like mercury. Visa stands a little taller at the Crystaline's touch.

Drift gives a one-handed wave and says, "Hey," then shoves his hands in his pockets and kicks a few pine needles around with his toe. A pale crimson flushes his cheeks just barely visible above his fuzzy beard.

Her eyes crinkle at the man. "Dear Drift. You are looking," she bobs her head, "well, my friend." When she pats his enormous arm and squeezes, her eyes light up. "Prism, it seems, is taking good care of you."

He presses his fists together to flex his arms until his muscles bulge and squeak under his t-shirt and leather vest. "Or maybe I'm the one taking good care of her." His hairy eyebrows bounce into a wink. The SparkGuitar design on his shirt ripples with electricity.

Cirissa laughs out loud and pats his shoulder.

Breeslin stomps back to the group. "There. The squad oughta be set for a minute at least." She grins and takes the com piece out of her ear to move right in and wrap Cirissa in a full-on hug again.

Cirissa smiles lovingly, always humbled by all their admiration.

Even Deret has enough Cloud City background in his brain now to help himself not look like a doofus in front of this high order magical being, so he sniffs, straightens his flannel shirt, and says, "Deret Day." Exuding his natural confidence, he extends a hand to her. "At your service."

"Charmed," says Cirissa, and she truly is.

Deret isn't quite sure why everyone else is all tongue-tied, so he claps his hands, rubs them together and says, "What do we do now? Did I hear something about ... *gadgets*?"

"I'm so glad you asked," she says with a laugh then looks to Wayfare.

Wayfare steps up closer to Cirissa. "We," he gestures to his Kindred, "have a plan."

"A plan. That's great." Deret prods with an eager grin, "And the plan includes *gadgets*?"

Wayfare and Cirissa eye each other carefully. "The plan is sort of extensive," he says. "And will involve a bit of explanation and teaming up and, yes, a *gadget* for you. Therefore, I suggest, we relocated to a less sludgy place."

A steady mist has begun to filter down through the forest's canopy. A hazy veil darkens their little clearing.

Deret's stomach suddenly clenches slightly. His shoulders press downward as though carrying a burden. He's not sure if he should say anything, but something feels very ... off. Maybe he's just hungry.

Fillip looks intently at the new kid. Squints his eyes. And presses his attention hard toward Deret's thoughts.

Drift raises both hands, "I'd love to join the party, but Prism will have my hide if I don't get back to my side of The Rim soon."

"I've spoken with your Kindred, Drift. She is aware of our plan and our need for you to be a part of it," Cirissa explains. "In fact, she'd rather see us quash whatever is going on in Median before it spreads to Levelin.

Drift's face falls a fraction, not sure he exactly likes the fact that he's already a part of this "plan" and sort of wishing he'd be able to make it back to his place in time for ... well, he doesn't really have to get back to his place for anything in particular, but he hadn't expected to be much more than a taxi service today. Then again, it'd been some time since he'd had much excitement brew up in Levelin.

"What about the Halo 500?" he asks. "I promised Virgus ..."

Cirissa again interrupts with a pleasant, "I already let him know we'll be commandeering his cloud craft a bit longer. He said, and I quote, 'Groovy,' and told me only you, my dear Drift, are allowed to drive it."

Honored, Drift slightly puffs up at the compliment from Altostratus Cloud Master Virgus.

Cirissa and Wayfare share a knowing smile. Drift is in.

"Well," Drift drawls, "if you really need my superior driving services," he looks lovingly at the Halo 500, "I suppose I can help out for a little while."

Fillip slowly detaches his attention from Deret to join this exchange. *In case anyone is wondering, I have zero intention of going up there. Nope. No sirree. I was born an Earthbound, and bound to the earth I shall stay.*

"But you'll miss out on all the *bonding*," says Wayfare, smiling. He is fully aware that there's no way they're going to get the Shadow Cat to visit Cloud City. But he eggs him on just for fun.

Nope.

"There'll be *tuna*."

In that moment, the woods falls still and silent. The mist is thick and drenching. Deret gulps and takes a step closer to his Moon Mare. His breaths quicken and his eyes dart around the woods. Something is not right out there. And it's making him feel something unfamiliar deep inside him. If he's not mistaken, it is fear.

Visa stamps nervously in place, looking out into the thick underbrush. Her mane and tail go dull, and Deret notices her losing her luster. "What is it, Visa?" He doesn't even hesitate to place a hand on her and share his spark until it ripples over her whole body again.

Sludge, she says with urgency to Deret's mind.

He doesn't catch on right away. "Sludge?" he says aloud. Everyone freezes and stares out into the forest. Like a computer virus racing through a maximum-security system, Deret's thoughts travel at lightning speed through synapse after synapse. Chapter after chapter of *Cloud City's* contents. Until ... DING ... it stops at *sludge*. And he knows.

Fillip rumbles a low growl and warns the same thing into the others' minds, *Sludge*.

Everyone's eyes dart back and forth to each other and out into the woods. Then, as though on some subliminal cue that only Sparkslingers can understand, they each generate a spark shield which spreads a nimbus around their bodies keeping them dry. Then they spread out evenly around the full circle of the clearing.

Deret isn't a hundred percent sure what he's looking for, but Visa and Wayfare eye him and nudge their heads toward the base of the bushes that create a border around the clearing from the thick woodland beyond. He peers hard. Finally, he sees the odd, slithery movement in the shadows. Like smoke snakes winding through the roots toward them. Thumpa thump. Thumpa thump. His heartbeat quickens in his ears. He tears his gaze away to look around the circle. He's ready to follow whatever lead he catches onto from whomever makes a move or gives a command.

Drift is the first to speak. "What the haze is this? Never seen sludge so bold before. Right out in the open. What does it think it's gonna do? Take us all down at once?"

Wayfare responds with grit in his voice, "This is the scummuck we've," he nods toward Fillip, "been dealing with lately. Just seeps out of nowhere. Doesn't even hardly try to hide now."

Fillip's sophisticated voice says to all their minds, *This new age of sludge is like no other I recall from all my days. Bending rules. Ignoring boundaries. Fascinating.*

"Fascinating, indeed," says Cirissa, disgust lacing her words. She nods at Breeslin and Windy to suit up into their ice armor with minimal flare. Ice chips flick and fly out into the shrubs, making some of the ghostly vapor retract for a second before continuing its eerie creep toward them.

Breeslin can't take her eyes off it as she recites from her well-studied *Cloud Code* book, "*Cloud Code* clearly states: 'Sludge may utilize its natural ability to dampen spark levels wherever and whenever deemed necessary in order to maintain a healthy stasis of existence that will ensure the planet's longevity.' You guys, *us* all being together. Here. In one contained space? Maybe it sees us as an imbalance. It probably just thinks this area needs to be regulated."

"Yeah," says Drift a little creeped out by the smoke snakes, "but it's supposed to do its thing in secret. Undetected. On the down low. Who's in charge of this stuff, anyway?"

Cirissa says nearly to herself, "Cloud Master Murkemer. He hasn't been ... present much lately. Cloud Master Shroud was supposed to meet with him to make sure he was absorbing his Cloud Master duties." She looks to Wayfare, revealing more concern than she wished within her silver-lined eyes.

Wayfare shakes his head, "Well someone's not *absorbing*," he overemphasized air quotes, "so well these days. Sneaky little scum is everywhere. You never know when it'll latch onto you."

Deret instinctually twists slowly in the opposite direction of his mentor to glance around the circle, taking in their full situation.

The mist edges on rain now, but the inky tentacles leech forward, unaffected. Deret then realizes everyone is slowly inching back, making their circle tighter, as the sludge advances.

Wayfare warns, "It's everywhere. This is no 'regulation' effort."

Cirissa breathes in disbelief, "No, it is not. I can sense its objective." Sheena stands rigid and lowers her head. From somewhere deep, deep inside comes a growl so low it seems impossible that it has come from such a fluffy little furball creature.

Breeslin dares a glance at Cirissa. Her voice is pitched with shock, "Great Zephyr. It's going for absolute extraction!"

Windy whinnies and snorts and stomps at the ground.

A ridge of fur all the way up Fillip's spine spikes on end, and his tail poofs out into a menacing bristle-brush. He growls, "Not this cat! Not this day!" He seethes a nasty, fanged hiss and shoots an arc of spark ribbon from his eyes, singeing the sludge in a swath back and forth until it is nothing but ashy tendrils escaping into the air.

Sheena scrambles to his side and yaps a shockwave of spark barks at the smoke snakes lingering on the outer edges of Fillip's swath. They pop like ink bubbles and dissipate upward as well. Fillip eyes her with more approval than he ever imagined he'd have for such a simple creature. She pant-smiles at him.

Deret's own spark snaps under his skin. He's just not sure what to do with it.

Wayfare flicks out his spark whip and wrenches a wicked *CRACK* of electricity. Deret's hair stands on end. Visa's and Windy's manes and tails dance on the air as though floating in a sea of charged water. A vibrating buzz-wave pulses out into the underbrush around the clearing sending the sludge back into the shadows.

Deret says, "Whoa," to both Wayfare and Fillip. "And tell me again, *why* you think you need me? You two are staggeringly good at this!"

Drift points and hollers, "There! The fogging scummuck! It's sneaking back in already." He rapid-fire shoots at it with his SparkPistol, but there are just too many to keep up.

Wayfare and Fillip look at each other and take a deep, and mildly irritated, breath. Their frustration is palpable.

Cirissa takes one elegant step forward. Her long ponytail drapes gracefully over her shoulder and curves like a winter river over her chest. Ice armor shards scrape like diamonds with her movement.

"ENOUGH!" she commands, silver eyes ablaze. The wormy little clouds still dare to crawl toward her. She flexes her bladed arms across her body then bends to one knee, glowing armored head bowed, and swipes her arms out wide, sending circular spark blades skimming across the pine needles, slicing the sludge vapors into ash.

Windy and Visa snort and stamp the ground. Their forefeet send spark waves through the dirt. The sludge evaporates into burnt ash, but more seeps up from the roots of the shrubs.

Visa says, *Look there*, and points her delicate head toward the spot she sees it coming right up and out of the ground.

The heavy mist has changed to a bone-chilling drizzle. And though the Sparkslingers, big and small, remain protected in their element-blocking auras, the shields are visibly weakening. When at the start, the glow was electric blue, now it has taken on a muted, hazy tone. Sheena's fluffball fur looks heavy and damp, though she seems none the worse for it. Her incessant spark barks keep popping sludge snakes into bubbles. It's Wayfare, however, who notices her shield waning. In one swift motion, he swoops the Frost Fox up into the fold of his long coat and holds her close while he again snaps his SparkWhip.

Windy whinnies and flings his head, forelock flopping. *Urgent, Breeslin! Look there.*

Breeslin sees. "Holy ozone, you guys! These are NOT approved sludge exit ports. It's getting out on its own somehow." Fear disguised as anger rifles through her ice armor and settles deep into her silver eyes. She crunches down slightly, "Murkemer. Shroud. They've got to be behind this. Should've known. Those shady, shifty ..."

The horses prance uneasily. Fillip and Sheena lower their heads and growl. Drift draws back the hammer on his SparkPistol. Wayfare stands strong, whip in one hand, Frost Fox in the other. He'll have to put her down if he needs his SparkSword from his coat too. Sheena spark barks as she peeks out. He'd give her a spark boost himself if he didn't feel his own levels dropping.

Cirissa sees Sheena in Wayfare's arm. Worry shimmers through her facial features and makes her cranial orb pulse crimson. But before she can even flick a finger blade's worth of spark to boost Sheena, a sludge snake slithers a tentacle up her ice blade leg. Again, the Commander of the Ice Crystal Guard advances on the swarm. Breeslin advances with her. Together, they attack head-on with a blasting of SparkDarts from their bladed fingers.

The Shadow Cat sends a spark beam into the Frost Fox. *There*, he says to Wayfare, *now put her down and arm yourself properly!*

Sheena wriggles out of Wayfare's arm and goes right back, element shield glowing full and strong, to spark barking.

And the sludge keeps coming. It is relentless. Unfeeling.

Deret stands there watching the others. He doesn't have a weapon like everyone else. He hasn't even gotten his own SparkBit or gadget or whatever he's supposed to get. Again, he finds himself in unfamiliar territory – he is in a … quandary. He does not know what to do. And … he is afraid.

This realization seeps into his mind and grips him. But the thing about Deret Day, son of Demeara and Garrin Day, is that he has something inside him that is different than anyone else. He's not certain what that "something" really is, but he knows it's there. He's always known it. So the fear lingers but a second before Deret sniffs, cracks his neck, and shoves up his flannel shirtsleeves. Deret blows his stick-straight bangs out of his eyes, puts on his serious-stuff face, and hones in on the creepy sludge with all his senses.

As he narrows his eyes ever-so-slightly more, the world around him fades out of view, like he's being swept down a long, dank tunnel. He *feels* himself stepping forward until he *sees* himself standing inside a cloud of swirling smoke.

Careful, Sheena says in his mind.

"Would ya look at that nervy little guy," says Drift.

Fascinating, Fillip comments.

So brave, says Visa.

Wayfare's voice comes last with a simple, but clearly impressed, "Huh."

Heavy sadness clings to Deret's clothes. Dreariness worms into his pores making his shoulders slump. Apathy caresses his face and trails down his neck until it wraps its vapor tentacles around his skinny neck.

At first, he sucks in a shallow gasp. Doubt forces his eyes closed. What's he gotten into here?

Then, from a far-off place that seems ages away in time and space, comes a sharp, spryer-than-her-age voice trickling into his mind. "Deret the Doubtless! Always knows what to do."

And at that very second, he blinks open his eyes and draws an invigorating breath, sucking in some of the very stink that's trying to take him down. In that moment, in the nanoseconds before the sludge particles inside him are annihilated, he sees, or rather feels something he was not expecting. Not evil. Not calculation. He doesn't even sense hostility.

It's desperation. Even Deret knows *that* is an exceptional foe.

On the exhale, Deret puffs up his chest and lets his arms hang loose. A halo surrounds him, and he steps back to the circle with the others.

All eyes on him, he says, "Hang on," and reaches his arms out to either side.

Visa sidesteps toward him until his palm rests on her shoulder. Wayfare offers his arm, SparkWhip crackling in one hand, SparkSword gripped in the other. Then Wayfare slides a yellow sneaker toe for

Fillip to place a paw on. Sheena, somewhat to Fillip's chagrin (though the feisty little bugger is growing on him), gives Fillip an earnest-eyed, tongue-loll and slides her paw to touch his other foot. All around their little circle of fortitude, they connect with each other.

When Drift holsters his SparkPistol and gently rests a hand on Visa's other shoulder, completing their loop, Deret finally knows exactly what to do. His skin has been popping and sizzling since he got here, and now he understands what his body has been trying to tell him. It's his time.

He sends a crackle of spark rifling around to each of them then commands steadily, once again oozing confidence, "Everyone, take three steps forward ... now."

They do as he says because why not? No one else seems to have a better plan. As they lose their physical connection to each other, they remain connected by a single ribbon of spark looping through them maintaining their circle.

Through the hiss and hum of the heavy drizzle, Deret says, "Ready to sling in three ... two ..." He looks to Wayfare but a second for something he's hoping feels like a we-got-this kind of face.

Wayfare lights a crooked grin and does him one better. "ONE!"

In that instant, their circle becomes a singular, spinning ring of light with flecks of spark dancing around its edges. As they continue to emanate their own spark, the ring begins to pulse until the air can hold it no longer. It explodes outward through the brush, into the ground, and up through the trees. The sludge is pulverized, frying and sizzling and evaporating into nothing but dark mist. Its collective screams pierce their ears. All the birds and creatures flee in a single flourish.

For a fleeting moment, a hole in the cloud canopy straight above them folds back. Blue sky, like nothing Deret has ever seen in his short thirteen years on this earth, pierces through the treetops. It's a color his brain is having a hard time registering, but in the back of his mind, he recognizes it from the little bluebird figurines his mother looks at longingly every morning.

Finally, a beam of light the size of the entire clearing washes down upon them. Breeslin is the first to shut off her element shield. As she looks to the sky and closes her eyes, she lets the warmth stream down to melt away her ice armor and Crystaline form until her softened, pixie self is bathed completely in sunshine.

The others do the same. As well as Deret. This tingling on his skin is a sensation he has ever known.

Even Fillip squinches his eyes tight at the sky and shamelessly purrs – a rattling, guttural, indulgent purr.

Until the sludge is no more. All that remains is the echoing screech of desperation and sorrow dissipating into a fresh breeze that has found its way into the clearing.

The Sparkslingers stand in awe for a moment until Sheena pounces forward on all fours and gives a good-riddance sneeze. She turns and snaps her triangle ears up at the crowd.

"Uhh, what just happened?" Drift speaks everyone's thoughts.

"Ya," says Breeslin, turning slowly toward Deret. "What *was* that?" Oddly, even she hears the slight perturbed, but totally impressed, edge in her voice.

As all eyes turn their gaze on Deret – some with sheer awe, others with scrutiny – he shuffles his red sneakers in the pine needles and says, "Um, well," he clears his throat, "That was a, umm, Spark Loop. Page 743. Emergency Spark Dissemination." He gives an irresistible grin.

Wayfare exhales heavily, swipes his floppy mohawk then drags his hands down his face. He says, exhausted, "I *really* should have studied harder."

Overhead, the clouds roll back into place.

Chapter 16

The Plan

"We need to split up," Breeslin demands.

Cirissa and Wayfare eye each other with a hint of pride at the young WISP's take-charge attitude.

Wayfare straightens his shoulders and replies, "Agreed." He tugs his long coat closed and flips up the collar. "What do you suggest, Squad Leader?"

For an instant, Breeslin thinks she hears the slightest patronizing tone in her former mentor, and she shoots him a resentful eye. But he responds with a single affirming nod. She detects a hint of a wink in his sky-blue eyes and the slightest curl at the corner of one side of his mouth. He is proud of her.

Windy hrr hrrs at her shoulder, *What're you waiting for? Take charge.*

"Eh hem." She hesitates again.

Go ahead, Windy assures her. *You're good at this.*

Eyes sparkling, Breeslin looks around at all the Sparkslingers awaiting her orders. Deret, as green and innocent as they get, stands patting Visa's shoulder, head cocked, ready for anything. Drift crosses his big arms and blinks expectantly behind his bushy eyebrows. Fillip licks his paw as though he doesn't plan to listen to anyone tell him what to do, but Breeslin sees him twitch the ear closest to her, and his emerald eyes keep casually glancing her way. Even little Sheena plops her fluffy butt down and pant-smiles with her little triangle ears snapped at attention. *I. Do,* the Frost Fox says into Breeslin's mind. That little pup's determination makes her smile.

Fists on hips, the WISP leader smiles and nods. *I am good at this.* "Here's what we're going to do. You," she points hard and straight at Deret whose eyes go wide, "You're coming with me."

He gives his crooked grin and nods once. Then he glances at his new mentor and wonders if he should probably stay with him.

But as though reading his mind, Wayfare affirms the order, "That's a good idea. This'll be your first assignment, Deret. Nothing like throwing you into the thick of things to kickstart your training." He winks confidently at Deret.

Deret winks confidently back. Again, it's as though he's looking in a time-warped mirror.

"Yep," Breeslin agrees. "Deret and I are going to fly through all that weirdness happening above the sequoia tree. Something's definitely not right up there. I'll alert my WISP team too. Plus, Windy and Visa will get us safely through any nasty spots."

"Nasty spots?" asks Cirissa. "What do you suppose you're going to find up there?"

Breeslin looks at her evenly and takes another deep breath. "I have a hunch it's the same illegal electrical activity my team got caught up in that day we put a stop to the Puffin brothers' cloud wrestling trumble. And that sequoia tree – something's not right there. Even Deret knows it."

Deret confirms, "There's definitely something going on with that tree. My skin and hair vibrated." He sends a spark wave through his body to mimic for them what had happened at the tree – red hair on end, static snapping through his flannel shirt.

"Exactly," she says. "We'll investigate and figure out what we're dealing with there. Because, guys, there's more going on than just the sludge getting stronger. And we need to get down to the bottom of it. Clear picture, you know."

They all nod thoughtfully. Now she's really got their attention. She presses on.

"Cirissa," Breeslin calls out, "We need you at the next Cloud Council meeting."

Her Crystaline idol nods gracefully. "It's this afternoon. I will be there."

"Good. See if you can get a vibe on what's happening with Murkemer. And that creep Shroud." She shivers. "That dude gives me skin crawlies. He's up to something."

"It is done," says Cirissa.

"And you two," Breeslin whips both hands at Wayfare and Drift whose eyes widen, impressed with her ability to take charge. "You go back to Sky Steed Stables, and tell Silva Starling everything we know. If blows come to blows, we're going to need her."

Drift holds his hands up, "Hang on here, 'blows come to blows'? Just what do you imagine is going to happen? You make it sound like we've got a war on the brink."

Breeslin knows she has to say what the others are afraid to admit out loud. "Guys, look. I think we all know something's brewing. Something big. And I'm not sure the Cloud Council has a clue about any of it."

Cirissa steps forward. "She's right. We all know she is. It's just, well, it's just an uncomfortable scenario to digest. But we must. If we don't, I'm afraid no one will. And then …"

Wayfare's voice comes low and grave, "Chaos."

All eyes are on him. They can all feel each other's spark pulse thrumming heavier than just a moment ago. Sheena grumble-growls to echo their feelings.

Breeslin breaks their nervous hush, "Exactly. And I don't know about the rest of you, but I will not have it. Not on my watch."

Or mine, Windy snorts and stamps his front feet. Breeslin lifts her chin a little.

Or mine, Visa shakes her head so her silvery mane waves and lingers in the air. The Storm Pony and Moon Mare give each other a look of such commitment that it rivals the closest of mates.

"There's one more assignment," says Breeslin squaring up with Fillip.

The Shadow Cat stops licking his paw to regard her dispassionately.

"And it's quite a crucial one, mind you, so I personally wouldn't entrust it to anyone but the very best. The one I know can take care of business without a flinch."

Fillip tips his head, slightly interested now. No one ever said a Shadow Cat is immune to flattery.

Breeslin takes that as a cue to go on. "The people of Median, and the creatures of the woods need protection from the sludge swarms." She waves her hand around the area they had all just blasted with their unified spark. "*That* was not the last of it. You can all feel it in your toes. There's more sludge on the way. And we need to keep Median safe while we figure out how to kick it for good. Once and for all. But we need time. And we need to find a safe haven for everyone to wait this out. We need someone strong enough to protect them from even the worst swarm possible."

Fillip stands at attention on all fours now. Shadow Cats do thrive on appreciation and being needed. *Agreed*, he says and gleams his emerald eyes toward Wayfare and Deret. *And I know just the place.*

Wayfare looks at Fillip like he knows exactly where the Shadow Cat is thinking of. The two are talking to each other's minds without letting everyone else listen in. Finally, Wayfare's eyes go soft, and he looks full-on at Deret. His lips part, like he's about to talk then he chuckles softly.

The others look expectantly to Wayfare.

Fillip says for all to hear, *I'd say it's time Deret knows.*

Deret sees they all know something he doesn't. He glances from Wayfare to Fillip. "What?" Deret asks, a little put out. "Time I know what? Where will he take them?"

Wayfare swipes his mohawk back and lets it slump back into place. One hand on his hip, he leans casually toward Deret and puts his other hand on the youngest Sparkslinger's shoulder. "He's going to get as many people and creatures as he can and take them to ... Mom and Dad's place."

Deret screws up his face. Wayfare hadn't said *your* mom and dad's place. He'd just said *Mom and Dad's* place.

The stillness that follows is palpable while everyone digests this new turn of events. Deret gulps and forces himself to speak. "Mom and Dad's?"

Though Deret's eyes are wide and unbelieving, Wayfare can see the flicker of excitement in them too. "That's right, little brother. The Day Farm. Where spark runs long and deep in our family. Always has," he gestures grandly to Deret, "and apparently still does." Wayfare's sky-blue eyes pop with spark and laughter as he holds Deret at arm's length and musses his hair fondly. "Man, it's been a long time since I've been home." He backs up and puts his hands in the pockets of his long coat. A rueful hint passes over his eyes as he says, "I miss them."

Even for Deret the Doubtless, this is a lot to take in. But he manages himself with confidence and mentally grasps the entire section in *Cloud City* on Catalysts within the synapses of his mind until understanding dawns on his face.

"A Catalyst's life is long," Wayfare says with reverence.

They look at each other for a warm moment. The others mummer their own understanding.

Finally, Breeslin takes over again. "Alright you guys. We can have a happy family reuniting later. You're brothers. Awesome. Figure out the details another time. We gotta move." She taps her spark shield down. "Rendezvous. Sky Steed Stables. Tonight."

Chapter 17

Divide

"Widow Shay!" says Demeara Day wiping her hands with a towel as she beckons their dear friend inside the little house. Outside, a heavy mist drizzles down. "I didn't think we'd see you quite so soon. And supper's ready!"

Shaking off the beads of water from her shawl, Widow shuffles inside. Demeara takes the shawl to dry by the fire. A pot of soup hangs over the flames. Fragrant wisps stream through the air. This home is cozy and full of warmth.

Widow sniffs dreamily and says, "Goodness, Demy Dear, that smells magical!" She grins and winks.

A demure smile peels across Demeara's expression. She goes to the cupboard for some bowls and spoons. "So, how did it go? How did our boy do? I assume he found it. Come. Sit." Demeara peers out the window. "Garrin's on his way in from the barn." She ladles a hearty helping of vegetable soup into a bowl and hands it to Widow Shay. Then she starts filling another.

"I gotta sit." Easing her weary bones into a sturdy wooden chair next to the fire, Widow Shay allows her muscles to soften. "Ahh ugh," she groan-grunts. "All this running about and up and down Skylane Tomes' stairs business." She situates herself, careful not to spill. "Goodness me, yes, he found it right away." She blows gently on a spoonful. "I told you, he's a natural. Truly. First I've seen in so many years. Not since," Widow slurps her soup, "your older boy."

A sigh escapes Demeara's lungs.

The intricately carved door creaks open. A swirl of misty coolness rolls in with Garrin. He takes off his plaid cap and matching jacket. "I thought I saw your scooter outside, Widow." He strides over to give the old woman a peck on the cheek.

She pats his face affectionately, eyes glittering. "You old dog, you, Gary."

He grins at the flush of pink in her wrinkly cheeks.

"Smells good," he says reaching for the bowl his wife offers. "Wood's all stacked. Fixed that leak too."

Demeara helps herself, and they all sit by the crackling fire. "Were you able to salvage anything for carving?"

He blows on a spoonful and says, "Not much. It was mostly rotten from the inside out." With a good-natured expression, he adds, "But *because* of some of that rot, I might be able to coax a few special pieces out once I run it through the mill." He chuckles softly. "Hard to know what you're dealing with until you take a look deep inside. I'm always surprised at what I find."

She looks at him with the same awe she's felt for him the day they met so many, many years ago. "You do work magic, hun."

"Here, here," chimes Widow holding up her wooden bowl and wooden spoon. "Spark still runs strong in *both* of you!" They raise their bowls to *cheers* together. "I mean, look at you. You haven't aged a day, and it's been, what, fifty-some years since you sent Wayfare off to Cat Academy?"

Garrin sets his soup down and inhales deeply, puffing out his slight chest and rubbing his developing paunch. "Oh, I wouldn't say I haven't changed," he chuckles.

A snort and humph come from the old woman. "Just you wait until you're a hundred and whatever like me. That paunch will be the least of your troubles." She rests her bowl in her lap. "Sparkslinging does have its limits." She sighs, "I'm pooped."

Demeara and Garrin smile softly at her then at each other. She's right. They know spark has its limits, but so far, they've been able to foster a steady stream for their family and their farm. It's no accident that Garrin is able to sell his beautiful furniture to a town that always figures what they have is "just fine." And it's not a freak of nature that Demeara is able to grow the vegetables and fruits she gets from this sodden land that hasn't seen a day of sun for decades. Granted, she learned everything she knows about gardening from Widow Shay, but without spark in Median, even she would not be able to coax a single sprout from the dirt.

Demeara clears her throat in that tiny, polite way she has that says it's time to switch topics. "Widow says Deret found the book, no problem." She takes a small sip of soup, but Garrin hears her gulp loudly.

Garrin raises his spoon. "Excellent! That's our boy." He looks at Demeara then at Widow then back at Demeara. She returns his curious look with a sad one. This makes him ask, "What? What's wrong? That's a good thing, right? We all know he's got the gift. Just like his ..." Then it dawns on him, and understanding fills his expression.

Demeara's eyes are glossy, but with some effort, she maintains a positive tone. "Yep." Composed, she smooths her day dress. "He is indeed just as gifted as our Wayfare."

Garrin looks on with empathy. "Hun, I miss him too. But you know as well as I do, that active Catalysts are bound to duty until they retire."

"But it's not against any rule to check in on us once in a while. To pay a short visit. And now Deret?" She sounds like she's pleading, but both Garrin and Widow Shay know the truth.

She simply misses her boys.

The fire crackles and heavy mist thrums the windows like waves on a sandy shore.

Garrin eyes Widow for a little help.

In her practical manner, the old Catalyst empathizes the best she can. "Demy Dear, Life of a Catalyst is indeed long, but no one said it's easy."

"It just would've been nice to give Deret a proper goodbye this morning. It must have come as such a shock to suddenly discover all this then get whisked away in that Halo death trap Griff parades around in all the time."

Garrin pats her knee.

But Widow Shay cackles, "Ha! Are you kidding me? That boy took it all in stride. But, you know, truth be told, he actually seemed *relieved* once the cat was out of the bag." She rocks noisily on the wood floor. "In fact," she goes on, "my goodness gracious, that boy ... how he can generate and share spark without even knowing he's doing it? Truly a gift." She pokes a bony finger at them. "And that might be the only thing that saves us this time."

Eerie silence permeates the room. Out the window, the mist has turned to steady rain as fog folds heavily over the hillside.

Demeara takes Garrin's hand. "The sludge swarms are that bad?"

Widow Shay considers her for a moment. Breathing noisily, she eases her body out of the comfortable chair and moves to the window. They can all see what she points to just out beyond their fence and up into the hazy layers of rolling hills.

"Bad?" Widow says. Her eyes are still keen enough to see the smoky snakes shredding across the landscape. "I honestly don't know how long your spark shield is going to hold it back."

Demeara and Garrin join her at the window. Now the rain falls straight as nails across the landscape. Puddles and rivulets form in low spots and curves.

Garrin puts his arm around Demeara's shoulders and speaks what they're all thinking. "Especially now with Deret gone."

Mist hangs heavily in the trees lining their driveway. It sends a chill – a deep, bone-soaking chill – through the valley, as well as through these retired Catalysts' hearts. They can barely make out the outline of the ancient barn sprawled high on the hill.

"I think we're beyond sludge swarms, kids." Widow's voice is grave. "Things aren't right out there."

They stand in silence and watch the sludge vassals roil up against the perimeter fence. It struggles to break through. An inky finger here and there reaches in then quickly retreats as though recoiling from burning fire.

Suddenly, from a point on the horizon, an orb of light cleaves its way through the fog and rain, leaving a swath of bright green in its wake. Something is traveling toward them in some kind of protective bubble. Widow Shay is the first to see it.

"Look there," she says and points a gnarled finger.

Demeara and Garrin track her line of sight to the object now growing closer and closer to their perimeter fence. It pours itself through their spark shield and continues straight toward the house, still shielded from the rain by a clear protective nimbus. It travels like a sunbeam leaving a trail of tiny flowers. Demeara's breath catches in her throat as she touches her fingertips to her lips. Garrin squeezes her shoulder and lets out, "Well I never in all my days ..."

Fillip zooms to a stop on the doorstep, not in the slightest winded, as Garrin opens the door. All three retired Catalysts stand there, mouths agape.

Wasting no time with formalities or introductions, the Shadow Cat says, "Thank Saint Medard I've got the good fortune to find all three of you in one place."

Garrin can't help himself. "Shadow Cat? Are you a real, live Shadow Cat? On my doorstep?"

"A Shadow Cat, yes. I am. But one that would *prefer*," his dignified inflection hints impatience, "be invited *in* as opposed to being left on the doorstep like a stray awaiting a charitable bowl of cold milk." He sits.

Perfectly straight. And blinks his sparkling emerald eyes at them. Once.

Widow Shay cries, "Fillip!" Shooing Demeara and Garrin aside, she ushers the Shadow Cat inside with flourish. "Make way. Make way." She brushes off her own chair and offers it to him. "Here! Take my seat by the fire. Warm yourself, my dear." She beams at the couple. "It's not every day one gets to host a legend in their home."

Demeara rushes for a bowl to offer her guest some hot soup.

Fillip, however, has no time for social graces. He waves Demeara off with a paw and sits properly, paws together, on the hearth rug. The warm fire does indeed feel good as it warms his backside. For an instant, Fillip has to stifle a purr. "I'm afraid it is with the utmost urgency with which I visit you."

All three make their way to their seats, their attention locked on Fillip.

"And I'm afraid," he says, "that your services are required."

"But," Garrin automatically responds, "We're retired. All of us."

Fillip closes his eyes trying to mask impatience, breathes deeply, opens them again, and says, "I henceforth relinquish your retirement as is protocol akin to that delineated in Cloud Code 211, page 752 of the Emergency Spark Dissemination section. Consider this your official call *back* to duty."

Demeara asks, "Does this have something to do with our ... our boys?" Worry threads her voice, but she stays strong.

Widow Shay sighs and sits at the edge of her chair. "It's starting." She eyes Fillip, a hint of question lines her words. "Feels like a frenzy."

"A frenzy?" asks Demeara. A loose tendril falls from her bun and curves around the soft lines of her face.

Fillip explains the best he can, "Too much spark in the wrong hands creates an effect much like that of a drug. A wicked drug, mind you. Greedy spark has no governing ability while in a frenzied state. It dominates all sense and reason. There is little one can do to combat a frenzy."

Garrin looks out the window again, his brow creased, and says, "There has to be *something* we can do."

Fillip straightens his shoulders. "There is." His eyes glimmer with ferocity.

The people in the room hang on his next words because, though they don't want it to be so, deep in their hearts, they know what he is about to say.

The words come from deep inside the Shadow Cat's growling chest, "Destroy it."

Dread ripples up Demeara's spine. She shivers. Garrin takes her in his arms.

Something that sounds like exhaustion and disgust swirled together sighs out of Widow Shay as she sits back heavily in here chair. "I'm afraid, my dears, the sludge war is starting."

"It is," Fillip confirms. "And I fear it may be worse than we may have imagined."

They take a moment to take in the full gravity of that statement. Fillip sits. Unwavering.

Garrin asks, "What can *we* do?" His words are committed and resolute.

Demeara looks at her husband with such adoration that it bolsters her nerve. "Anything," she says. "Though it's been quite some time since either of us has performed actual Sparkslinger duties. I'm ... I'm afraid we might be a little rusty."

Fillip shakes his head. "No. You are not rusty. Once a Catalyst, always a Sparkslinger." His emerald eyes twinkle. "But, if all goes to plan, you can leave the sparkslinging to me."

"Then ... what do you want us to do?" asks Garrin.

Fillip walks over to the window and looks at the enormous barn standing barely visible now behind the veil of mistiness. They follow him. "We – and by *we*, I mean the people and creatures of *Median* – need you for a very different purpose."

The rain falls steadily, and a slight breeze now bends it in sheets to and fro. Realization dawns across every crease and wrinkle on Widow Shay's face. Her eyes are set with fortitude. "We need to house them."

Fillip looks to the old woman and nods. "As many as we can get to follow us here. I just hope it's not too late."

* * *

"You never told me your baby brother is a Catalyst!" hollers Drift.

The Halo 500's engine hums as it pierces through the billowy clouds of the Cumulus Sector. The top is down and both men have an arm hanging out their window, hair whipping in the wind.

"Ha," Wayfare laughs, but Drift knows his friend well enough to hear a hint of something that is not humor in his voice. "Clouds Almighty, my friend, you and I hardly get to see each other. And it's not like I've spent any time – truth be told – watching over him. He's a stranger to me too, really. Breeslin's spent more time with her eye on him in the past few months than I have since he was born." He thinks for a second then adds with a rueful smile. "I guess that's what I get for never calling home, as they say."

They ride in silence for a moment, watching the cottony fluff peel away before them and swirl behind them like whipped cream.

Drift sort of feels bad for bringing it up now, so he tries to set it right. "Aw come on, buddy." He looks at Wayfare, but his friend just keeps staring straight ahead. He chews the fringe of his beard curling up the corner of his mouth. Then he sighs. "Look, the way I see it, *everyone* knows now, and that's a heck of a good thing, right? Nothing like having one more Sparkslinger in the family." He looks to Wayfare for at least a glance of affirmation here.

Wayfare looks out his window at the peak of a cumulonimbus mountain off in the distance. The life of a Sparkslinger is long and filled with hard work and danger. On duty 24/7, 365. He doesn't know if he would wish it on anyone, much less his little brother.

He looks at Drift, ready to voice these very thoughts to his friend. But when he sees the genuine fuzzy face grinning at him, he is reminded of the fierce dedication all Sparkslingers – the *whole* Sparkslinger family – have for each other. And that is something he is so very glad to have his brother be a part of. This makes his concern simply dissipated like downy fluff on a breeze.

Drift props his SparkShades on top of his head, gives crazy-eyes, and howls to the sky.

Effortless laughter escapes Wayfare's lips as he tosses his head back, gazing into the blue sky, and says, "Yes, Drift, this is indeed a good family to belong to."

"Yes, indeedy!"

Wayfare goes on, "I just feel like I should be with him. Deret, I mean. Like I'm his big brother for cloudsakes, and here I go taking orders from a near-pubescent WISP – no offense to Breeslin, she's rocking that role – "

Drift grins and shakes his head in both disbelief and pride for Breeslin for how she's growing up.

"I just think," Wayfare continues, "I should be looking after him. And not because he's supposed to be my apprentice – that kid's got more raw talent in his pinky toe than I've ever had – "

Drift gives a few big nods at that.

"It'd just be ..." Wayfare pauses to find the right words then blinks softly. "It'd be nice to get to know him."

"There'll be time enough for that. Soon as we sort out this sludgy mess." Drift claps a beefy hand on Wayfare's scrawny shoulder.

It's good to have a friend.

"Look!" Wayfare points off into the distance toward what's left of the cloud mountain's peak. Wispy, long-necked, snow-white birds stream together as though they're brushstrokes on a wet canvas. "A flock of Sky Swans!"

Drift flops down his SparkShades and squints to where Wayfare is pointing. "Would you look at that. Sure enough. Can't say as I've ever seen so many before." He gets a mischievous glint in his eye and says, "Let's swoop 'em!"

Before Wayfare can even choke out an answer, Drift punches the Halo's thrusters, and they tear off straight for the flock of Sky Swans. He lets out a wild whoop and throws his arms in the air.

Maniacal laughter rifles out of Drift's wide-open mouth as he pulls a steep climb up-up-up then forces the steering wheel forward careening the craft into a plunging dive. They swoop right through the Sky Swans, which sort of *poof* apart then reform as soon as the Halo breaks through. They squawk and honk, irritated at the juvenile shenanigans, but they shake it off and get back to the business of gliding and being pretty.

As soon as the Halo 500 breaks through the other side, the scene before them takes their breath away, just like it always does. And they fly toward the glittering fields and fences of Sky Steed Stables.

Chapter 18

Cloud Council

Yap! Yap! Yip yap! Sheena, ever the obstinate child, stomps her tiny paws at Cirissa's feet. Diamond dust floats in the air all around her fluffy white coat. Standing at the base of the steps leading way up to the Cloud Council's pillared platform, Cirissa tries to appeal to her Frost Fox.

"This is not a place for a Frost Fox," Cirissa says firmly.

Sheena, however, will not have it. Her tantrum is a sight. Twisting and turning and jumping up to be carried. Finally, she resorts to standing sturdily on all fours, and she sneezes.

Behind them hums the bustling streets of Cloud City. Every size, shape, and color of Skybound flow to and from the multitude of shops. From the ethereal Crystalines to the burly Stormbuds, Cloud City citizens fly, float, billow, and bounce all along the strip. Cloud furniture, cloud clothes, cloud groceries. Cloud licensing, cloud real estate agents, cloud government buildings. Anything the people of the clouds need can be found here.

If not on this main street, a venture down side streets will lead to the lesser advertised places some may consider a bit unsavory, but everyone knows every Skybound at some point patronizes these stores too. Black market spark devices, super charged fireworks for extravagant parties, or under-the-radar deeds to cloud acreage.

Among the hums and thrums of cloud crafts zooming and fluttering below and overhead are the oohs and aahs from a cluster of cloudlings on a field trip with their teacher. At the Dream Cloud mattress store entrance, a couple squabbles over the price of fluff these days. All around is the general commotion of everyday life in the sky.

Sheena flops down on her side. She wriggles and writhes as though in physical pain, only to flip up on all fours and press her fluffy tail and tiny nose in the air.

I. Go, she demands.

It's all Cirissa can do not to laugh at the scene. What choice does she have? Sheena goes.

The mighty Ice Crystal Guard caves, "Fine."

Sheena's ears snap to. Her eyes sparkle with delight as she starts a smart trot up the steps, sprinkling diamond dust everywhere.

"Don't act so proud of yourself," Cirissa says. "And don't look to me if they decide to send you down to the Drizzle Fields."

Sheena sniffs and bumps her rear in the air at that. Everyone knows a Frost Fox would be useless in the Drizzle Fields. Unless they wanted to manufacture pretty bubbles. Besides, everyone loves her!

Upon entering the Sky Room, they are met with a most unexpected scene. None of the Cloud Masters are sitting at their assigned seats at the crescent glass table. Except Cumulonimbus Cloud Master Loom, who is simply too enormous to move about the space with any ease … or without creating a gale. They seem to be congregating toward the far end.

Cirissa strains to see what – or who – they are crowded around. Sheena raises her nose to the air to sniff the glorious smells wafting from that direction. It takes but a second for the little Frost Fox to start levitating, eyes closed, following her twitching nose.

"Sheena!" Cirissa squelches a cry and ineffectually reaches out to grab her. The only thing to do now is brace for the repercussions.

Altostratus Cloud Master Virgus is the first to notice the floating Frost Fox. Lounging in his zero-gravity lawn chair, he leans forward and waves to Cirissa. "Hey!" holding a gooey wedge of pizza, he hails her, "Cirissa! Grab a slice." He gives a huge, mouth-filled grin and nods to her. Then he tears off a bite-sized piece and offers it to Sheena who lands and bounces at his feet.

Cirrus Cloud Master Tendril, with her iridescent strands swimming about her, lets out an uncharacteristic but delightfully lovely laugh, making each tress ripple with positive energy.

Apparently, no one minds having a Frost Fox here. Sheena does have a way about her.

Mildly flummoxed, Cirissa approaches the group. When she sees young Cloud Master Murkemer, she stops. Her silver eyes narrow, and she goes rigid. At a second's need, she is prepared to flash into her full ice armor. But as she takes inventory of the people in the room, she does not sense any potential danger.

Cirrostratus Cloud Master Shreddard flashes his violet eyes as he stands just a little too close to Cirrocumulus Cloud Master Makryl. Her white ringlets yo-yo as she giggles at whatever he is saying. They are nibbling on pizza and sipping at what looks to be cans of soda.

Altocumulus Cloud Master Castella is whooping and spinning wheelies in her crinkly, hot-pink jogging suit. Her gray bun, nearly undone, leaves wiry strands streaming behind her as she goes. Cirissa can just make out the colorful letters that read *Max Voltage* written on the tall energy drink crunched in her hand. Castella's wired expression could be an energy source of its own.

Cumulus Cloud Master Bumble hustles back and forth from the party platter – consisting primarily of donuts with sprinkles, cheesy curls (spicy and regular) and a multitude of flavored pudding cups – to Loom with a trifle of this and a taste of that. Someone has made her an ice straw that reaches all the way up into the shade of her sun hat so she can sip at some effervescent bubbly stuff from a goblet way down on the crescent table.

Cirissa worries, *Great Saint Medard save us if she works up a burp.*

At that very moment, Loom does this thing like a swallowed hiccup, and every person in the room freezes, wide-eyed.

Bumble reaches up to her stockinged shin and rubs soothingly. "There there, Loomy Poomy. Easy now." His twitchy eye betrays his nerves. But swift as lightning, the round, little Cloud Master whips out a pink jug from his coat, yanks off the cap with his teeth, and shoves the straw into it. "Sippy sippy," he coos to her.

Loom drains it in seconds.

The others release a collective sigh, and they go back to their mingling.

Drizzo, in her dingy housecoat and fuzzy slippers, pats at the curlers helmeting her head. "Well," she scoffs and clings awkwardly to Murkemer's arm, "that was a close one, wasn't it, Murky."

The look of discomfort on the teenager is enough to make Cirissa stifle her own laughter. He must be the one who brought all this junk food to the meeting. His first meeting. And he wants them to like him.

He's ... schmoozing. She has to give him credit. This is clever. He does have some making up to do for not coming to even one Cloud Council meeting yet. He seems harmless, and he's cleaned himself up, sort of. His long hair appears clean and tied back in a neat knot. He's wearing black joggers – a step up from gray sweats. And he's presenting himself with a fair measure of charisma.

But she wasn't a shard just yesterday. Life experience tells her to keep a very close eye on him. After all, he is Shayd's son. And that is one sneaky bloodline. Cirissa recalls how Shayd, though not a

Cloud Master, was a master of disguises and trickery. She hopes Murkemer reflects more of his father's side. Cloud Master Slurry was quiet, kind and a very good Skybound.

Then something makes Cirissa's head tilt. More precisely, the *absence* of something. No. The absence of ... *someone.*

Where is Shroud?

She scans the room with Ice Crystal Guard intensity. Something feels off. She reaches out with her senses. Closes her eyes. And then she feels it. The tiniest prickle at the point of each crystal connection on her body. Her ice armor is alerting her of a threat in close proximity. It is begging to be released from its bondage within her softened form. But where is the threat coming from?

She scans the room again. Jovial conversation. Laughter. Fun.

The Sky Room is filled with positive energy.

Her Ice Crystal Guard training, however, tells her there is *too much* positive energy. It is an unnatural state that requires balance. An unnatural state that draws forth its own remedy – a sludge swarm. Thank the Great Zephyr sludge can only exist far below in the Basal Plane. That would be an awkward mess.

Of course, if there also happened to be a surge of negative energy for some reason now, the remedy to restore a natural balance would be a lightning blast.

An unnerving possibility dawns on her – *Is Murkemer making the Cloud Masters generate a dangerous situation to provoke, like a magnet, some sort of ... negative energy?*

In this flash of understanding, Cirissa discretely blinks her spark lenses into place under her ice encrusted lashes. Then she sees him. Shroud. In the far corner entrance, his hooded cloak stands flickering under the guise of a simple night cloud. And by the way he stands, she can tell he is holding something ominous.

A night cloud? A child's trick?

This is not right. Something is very not right here.

The natural instinct of her ice armor can hold back no longer. In a flash of light and a ripple of slashing *TING TANGS*, Cirissa's true Ice Crystal Guard form appears, startling the Cloud Council momentarily.

Within moments, however, they go back to their merry Murkemer party. Crystalines, after all, tend to shift on a whim quite often. Nervy beings as they are.

Shroud remains still in his darkened corner. He knows he's been spotted, but he does not move. The council members are clueless, at least for a few more moments. He must choose carefully when to make his big appearance. He won't get another chance.

Shreddard also feels his crystal dendrites screaming to escape, and he steps quickly away from Makryl to allow his Crystaline form to make the shift without slicing her to pieces.

Makryl gasps. Her ringlet curls bounce. The Bo Peep puffy layers of her dress flounce and swirl. Shreddard takes a second to give her a wink, then gets serious and strides *CLINK TINGING* toward Cirissa. A hint of a girlish smile curls Makryl's lips as she flushes and fans herself.

Cirissa, discretely as possible, explains just to Shreddard, "There," she half-whispers to her Cirrostratus Cloud Master, "Shroud is hiding under a night cloud. And he has something that is throwing my spark sensors off the charts. I cannot see it. It must be hidden under that cloak of his." She taps a finger to her silvery eye indicating he should slide his spark lenses into place.

As soon as he does this, Shreddard sees the gloomy, warped figure behind the night cloud. Never being one for subtleties, much to Cirissa's chagrin, he calls out across the room loud enough to interrupt the chatting, "Shroud! How good of you to join us!"

Cirissa sucks in a breath. The others all turn to look. They cannot see Shroud under the night cloud veil.

"Please, please," Shreddard continues, waving a crystal spangled arm beckoning the Nimbostratus Cloud Master to come out of the shadows, "you must join us! Come, enjoy some of the spread our fine young Cloud Master Murkemer has brought. I imagine we have you to thank for providing him the mentoring and encouragement necessary to convince him to come to a meeting finally."

At that, Murkemer locks his eyes on the dark corner, takes one huge slurp of his Cherry Coke, and pushes himself out of his cushy gamer's chair. "Yeah man. Dear, dear Cloud Master Shroud," he says, louder than is called for. "Why don't you do that? Come on outa your corner and take credit for *getting* me to come to my first meeting."

Cirissa picks up on the young Cloud Master's sarcastic tone, and by the awkward hush that falls over the room, she gauges the rest of the Cloud Council has too. Sheena scurries to her side.

This dynamic is unexpected. Shroud and Murkemer are at odds.

Cirissa dares, "Perhaps Cloud Master Shroud needs some ..." With a simple whisk of her bladed hand and a quick, high-pitched whistle, she sends Sheena toward Shroud in his dark corner. "... encouragement."

Without hesitation, Sheena bounds over the table and skids to a stop right at the invisible Shroud's feet.

Half not expecting to be discovered, and half not knowing what he actually planned to do once he got here with his Bolt Blaster, Shroud shirks back. After all, a Frost Fox, though fluffy and adorable, is not to be trifled with. Before he can gather his wits to react, Sheena snatches the corner of the night cloud covering the him and whips it off in a single motion. Shroud stands there, aghast, and exposed. Sheena sits and pant-smiles at him.

This is his moment. This is the chance he's longed for since the day his closest friends were obliterated in that freak storm stirred up by those idiots, Cottin and Puffin Fairweather. *These* are the irresponsible governors who have no interest in *governing* the atmospheric treacheries that take place. They don't deserve the title of Cloud Master when they are the master of nothing but their own comforts!

He straightens with resolve.

Sheena stands in front of him asking innocently, *Pat? Good girl?*

He looks down on the Frost Fox with disdain. He's fully aware of the looks everyone is giving him. Particularly, that *beach dude* Virgus, sitting rigid at the edge of his lawn chair. He looks ready to pounce, which is quite a change from his typical slouchy attitude. And that nosy Ice Crystal Guard Cirissa – that righteous poise of hers. Typical Crystaline – thinks she knows everything. The others either look confused or nervous.

Good. Exactly how he wants them.

Now *is* the time. Shroud's heart beats faster. What is his first move?

A vision of his friend Cloud Master Slurry flickers in his mind. Like a horror film, it plays through his mind. Of the *one* Skybound who seemed to care about doing things right. Treating others properly. Trying to stop the ridiculous Fairweather brothers from their stupid games with no thought of consequence or responsibility. Of the blinding "stray" lightning bolt that hurled Slurry into the beyond.

Sheena senses the pulse of negative charge he's emitting. Her ears angle outward. *Party?* she offers Shroud and cocks her head, big-eyed.

Shroud takes a severe breath through his ample nostrils. He swipes back his cloak and hoists the Bolt Blaster onto his shoulder. Then he winds up one leg to kick the little Frost Fox like a soccer ball.

Just as his black boot is about to send Sheena sailing across the glass floor, Cirissa screeches, "No!"

In that same instant, while the rest of the Cloud Council just give a collective gasp, Virgus launches himself at the Frost Fox. He snatches her up in the safety of his arms and skids across the floor.

Cirissa instinctually lets fly a net of mist mesh to catch them.

Cradling Sheena's dazed, shaking body in his arms, Virgus pops up and surfs smoothly, the mist mesh evaporating in his wake, to Cirissa's side. He gives a sure nod.

Cirissa is furious. She sends Shroud an icy glare and commands, "Stop right there, Shroud!" Her authority is indisputable. She gets into fighting stance and weaponizes her ice armor by blowing, with dangerous calm, on the crystals as if enlivening the coals of a fire. Each crystal glows red and pulses in sync with her own heartbeat. She trains her SparkStunner's ominous laser orb on his chest. She's ready to arrest him but looks to Cloud Master Shreddard for approval. She has never, in all her Ice Crystal Guard days, been in a situation like this where a Cloud Master requires arrest.

Shreddard puffs out his Crystaline chest – not to be upstaged – and tries to take charge. Using his most authoritative voice, which doesn't hold a candle to Cirissa's, he says, "Listen here, Shroud. I don't know what you think you're doing, but a highly unregulated, *illegal* Bolt Blaster? Really. What *are* you thinking?" His arrogance forces a scoff past his blue lips. He gives a quick glance and wink at Makryl, who swoons over by the nacho dip.

This does not sit well with Shroud. His negative energy becomes a visible warping of the very air around him. Clashing at the edges of all the positive energy that has filled the room from Murkemer's party, little static shocks and micro lightning bolts crackle and snap. Something like a snarl escapes him.

But before Shroud can get a word out, Murkemer feigns naivety, "Whoa there, Shroud. My main-man mentor." The teenager gets up and acts as though he's trying to talk him down by way of flattery. "Wisest on the wise-o-meter. Whatcha doin', Dude?"

Shroud's eyes glow angrily within the darkness of his hood. The boy has clearly chosen to abandon their cause. He should have known. When he finally decides to speak, Shroud's voice is eerie and raspy. "You know *exactly* what I'm doing, you lazy-lob excuse for a Cloud Master."

Drizzo stands defensively next to the boy. The others murmur their discontent with the insult to their new fully accepted friend.

"Oh, isn't that just typical," Shroud spats with disgust. "All it takes is a junk food buffet and fizzy drinks to win you *high-and-mighties* over."

Castella takes an awkward gulp, rippling her wrinkly neck, and sets down her Cherry Coke. Her crinkly pink wind suit betrays her, and the others all glare at her to be quiet.

"You," Shroud continues, aiming his disgust at Murkemer, "you know full well I have *you* to thank for this little beauty here." He pats the Bolt Blaster. "Ladies and gentlemen!" he formally addresses the room, "had it not been for our new Stratus Cloud Master Murkemer's dedication to the continual sludge dissemination and around-the-clock spark collection from the sad and simple people of pathetic little Median, I would not be able to apply one of the most prestigious of gifts to you all today." He pauses for dramatic effect. "Education!" He throws back his hood to reveal his flaky scalp and thin-lipped, sagging face.

Another collective gasp aerates the room. Tendril, however, drifts forward. Her ethereal presence pushes positive charges along her every strand. The air surrounding her too carries a warped air quality which presses against Shroud's energy.

There is more sizzling and popping where the positive and negative fields dangerously dance at the others' edge.

Tendril looks to Murkemer, disappointed, and asks, "Is this true, young Cloud Master?" She nods for the Ice Crystal Guard to join her.

Murkemer just shrugs.

Cirissa, not failing to notice the smug look on Shroud's face, reinforces Tendril's inquiry. "Cloud Master Murkemer, *are* you responsible for the frenzied sludge wreaking havoc in Median?"

Murmurs of "frenzied" and "havoc" rifle through the room. Though Cirissa has been here before warning them, seeking council from them, the council acts like this is the first time they have heard of such goings on. She takes a deep, frustrated breath.

Murkemer, gauging the best way to respond, meets Shroud's self-satisfied sneer with level calculation. Still staring at Shroud, he answers the Ice Crystal Guard's question with perfect, almost childlike, innocence. "I have no clue what you're talking about. After all," his gaze shifts to Cirissa as he recites his well-rehearsed job description, "my job as the Stratus Sector's Cloud Master is to maintain balance by issuing just the right amount of sludge to curb any excessive, *life-endangering* Want. If the sludge has gotten out of hand, I assure you," he puts his hands in the air, "I had nothing to do with it."

Cirissa doesn't buy it. It is time to lay the facts out plainly for all to hear. "So, you're telling us ..." she sweeps her bladed arms indicating the council, "that you have *no* knowledge as to why or how the sludge is running rampant, unchecked, nearly unstoppable? Our *best* Sparkslingers are at their sparks end fighting it. But, since you are, in fact, 'doing your job,' you must then be fully aware that the sludge is out of control. And we can all rest assured that you have a plan to get it back under control?"

Murkemer has gone genuinely wide-eyed. Because, no, he had not realized it had gotten that bad. He has to schmooze this over, even though he's starting to feel the pang of guilt. "I ... I guess ... that being new at this and all ... I didn't realize things had gotten so ... so bad." It's a partially true statement.

"Didn't *know*?" Cirissa starts to lose her composure. "Great Zephyr, sludge is seeping straight up from the pores of the earth! I saw it *and* battled it myself just hours ago!" She waits. Virgus and Tendril stand strong by her side, but it is obvious this is news to them as well. All eyes on her. No one knows what to say.

Murkemer, with honest sheepishness, says, "I didn't know." His expression darkens just slightly. "I guess I was just always counting on my *mentor*," he gestures to Shroud, "to make sure I didn't make mistakes or miss, you know, really important stuff."

Shroud hisses, "Traitor."

Murkemer gives a quite believable look of shock, hurt, and best of all ... fear at the accusation. He must choose his next words carefully if he's going to get the council on his side. It must be something to confirm his innocence, as well as push Shroud over the edge. And then, he really does need to get back to the containment room and do whatever he can to fix this mess he and Shroud created.

Then, like a scud cloud randomly roving through a clear sky, it comes to him.

"The truth is ..." he takes a steadying breath, "I don't feel safe with Shroud. And I don't think any of you should either." Pause for effect. "He's not right." He points to his own head and tweaks an eyebrow, "Up here, I mean."

Drizzo cracks up at this. Then, realizing she shouldn't have, she clamps a hand over her mouth. She clenches her eyes tight and flops her frizzy bangs over her face.

But Shroud sees the chuckling jerks in her shoulders. He sees all of council members holding back their reactions. It is fascinating how they so quickly believe any little thing this teenager tells them, as though *he's* the one with ages of experience and dependability. He will show them all how to take him seriously. How to appreciate his seniority. But most importantly ... how to show respect!

"ENOUGH!" Shroud roars. Electricity zaps outward from every inch of him as it collides with the positive charges. He flicks a switch on the Bolt Blaster, fully arming it. The weapon glows and pulses as it sucks in the remaining positive energy available from the lingering party atmosphere, as well as from every living entity in the hall.

The Cloud Council, stunned, cannot counter-react in time. They are rendered slumped and helpless. Shreddard's ice armor dulls and softens, as though he is melting. In fact, a glossy puddle forms at his feet. Makryl tries to run to him, but her pudgy legs get bogged down under the weight of her skirt.

Tendril's floating strands fall limp. She tries to roust her spark levels but cannot. Her eyes are pleading.

Even Sheena weighs heavy in Virgus' arms. Her fluffy fur looks as though she has been doused with a bucket of water. He crumbles to the floor with her.

Castella falters to her knees, unable to force her shaking arms to hold herself up with her rolling-walker a moment longer. Mezzo's frizzy hair, now straight and glossy, extends past her knees.

Bumble looks like a glob of melting ice cream as he tries, ineffectually, with all his might to reach a plump arm up to Loom.

Loom, however, appears to be affected very differently than the rest. She is absorbing the electricity. Thin veins of spark stream up her sides. Once they get to the top, they create a strobe light effect under her sun hat, vaguely illuminating her normally dark and indistinct features.

Cirissa can see visible creases and curves showing worry in Loom's flickering expression. Like the worry Loom always has just before she is about to unleash a StormHulk.

And that means danger.

Shroud howls, "Perhaps you all could use a little lesson in spark wielding!" He unleashes a warning blast that sizzles through the hall, frying the air, striking a pillar. The roof hardly gets off balance before a scud cloud flies in to replace the support. But his message is received. Several council members duck under the table in fear. They all look to their Ice Crystal Guard for protection.

Cirissa takes quick inventory of the situation. In doing so, she realizes, with a nagging sense of betrayal, that Murkemer has disappeared. Just *POOF*. Gone. Sneaky bloodline, indeed.

Loom's involuntary rumbling grows and vibrates everything and everyone in the room. This is a welcome surprise to Shroud. A nice bonus. That bolsters his confidence to raise the Bolt Blaster again, this time aiming at Cloud Master Bumble.

Bumble squawks and flails his hands into the air. Terror turns his face blue. "I-I-I- d-didn't do anything!"

"Exactly!" Shroud booms. He tries to regain some mild composure and continues, seething disgust. "You're *all* so very good at doing *nothing*."

Cirissa flashes her full-body SparkShield in front of her and takes a few powerful strides toward Shroud. "That's enough, Cloud Master Shroud."

He jerkily aims the Bolt Blaster at her as she comes toward him.

Cirissa's trained eye, however, sees the weapon shake slightly in his hands. *He is nervous. As he should be. There's no way I can let him get away with this behavior. I'm going to have to take him down to take him in.*

She slows her steps, but her body is coiled for action. She says steadily, "Cloud Master Shroud, perhaps this is a matter better discussed elsewhere. Let me take you to Headquarters. You can speak your piece freely without threat or endangerment." She narrows her icy eyes. There is little chance he will take her up on this offer, she knows. But it is proper protocol to offer a peaceful out.

Her SparkStunner laser is still locked on Shroud's chest. She takes a deep, settling breath and feels her heart knocking at her ribcage. A fluttering thought of Wayfare Day comes to her, and she realizes how much she wishes he was here. By her side. Together, she is sure they could take on anyone and anything. And she realizes for possibly the first time that being near her Kindred Catalyst makes her feel more brave than her innate Crystaline abilities do.

Shroud hears his own heartbeat pound in his ears. His ragged breaths reveal his passion, sorrow and now fear. The room swirls, and a high-pitched tone pierces into his thoughts. *There's no way I'm getting out of this,* he thinks. *I have crossed the line. No turning back now.* He trains his weapon harder on the Ice Crystal Guard, sets his resolve, and says, "The time to *discuss* has passed."

With an electric whine, the Bolt Blaster charges up to fire.

A palpable stillness permeates the room. He looks forcefully at the Ice Crystal Guard. He notices Cirissa's attention seems drawn a fraction away from that SparkStunner pointed at him. She's distracted by some other thought.

He *BLASTS* Cirissa straight on. Though her SparkShield protects her from the voltage, she goes flying backward through the wall. Her expression is gritted in a combination of agony and fury. It happens too fast for Shreddard or Tendril to act, but in a split second, Virgus is at her side helping her jet back inside and shielding her the best he can with his own SparkShield.

The others cry out, gasp and duck a little farther down. One by one, the sharp sound of their SparkShields expanding *tangs* through the hall. None of them ever dreamed Shroud, though awkwardly quiet and, sure, sort of creepy, was dangerous.

Shroud holds tight to the Bolt Blaster, chest puffing in and out. Then he realizes how weak they are – these mighty and powerful Skybounds. They cannot even put up a fight. They only cower and hide. To protect themselves. That is the lesson, he decides, he must teach them. To fight. A plan, his plan, flurries into his mind.

He glances way up to Loom, who is still holding it together regardless of the flickering charges wreaking havoc under her sun hat. A sinister smile curls his flat, pale lips. He hoists the weapon and pulls his hood up, hiding himself in its darkness. He drifts over to her and eerily reaches a hand out to touch her ankle.

Bumble cries out somewhat pathetically but doesn't dare make a move.

Cirissa, regaining her balance, orders, "Step away from Cloud Master Loom. Take your hand off her or I'll …"

"Or what?" he hisses. "You'll *take me in*?" Shadowy creases reveal his smile. "I don't think so. Not today, my dear. But soon you will have your chance."

A flicker of confusion ripples through the room.

Shreddard, still trying hard to appear as bold as Cirissa, takes one step forward and says in his clarion tone, "What's that supposed to mean?"

Loom, trying to hold her composure, releases a small wave of rumbles that make the entire Sky Room vibrate. Everyone steadies themselves.

"It means," Shroud continues, "it is high time I show Skybounds and Earthbounds alike just how pathetic your *governing powers* really are."

Virgus says, "Shroud, you gotta calm down, man. Are you seriously picking a fight?"

"It's time we have some, how shall I put it, *reorganizing* of the Cloud City power structure. And I intend to show everyone that I am the one who they should look to for safety and control and …" he pauses to clench his jaw, "… righteousness."

Cirissa has had enough. She arms her ice net and points her bladed arms straight at him as she advances. "You're coming with me!"

Shroud, however, is prepared. In one swooping motion, he swipes his cloak across himself and onto Loom's ankle. In a *poof* of mist and smoke, he and the Cumulonimbus Cloud Master effaport into thin air.

Chapter 19

Spark Bubble

"I CAN'T HEAR YOU!"
"HOLD UP!"
"*STILL* CAN'T HEAR YOU!"

Howling winds and rain batter both Deret and Breeslin as they fly through one heck of an unauthorized storm. They've managed to climb out of Murkemer's Stratus ceiling just above the giant sequoia tree, which, if he wasn't mistaken, was shooting thin, jagged lines of spark straight up through the murk.

Breeslin couldn't help but notice how much darker the Stratus layer seemed, even since just a few hours ago.

Now, as they press through Shroud's Nimbostratus clouds, though less dense and soupy, it's still so thick, and the rain steady and heavy, they can barely see their horses' ears. Urging Windy upward, Breeslin expects to breech the Nimbostratus cloud shelf any moment.

She waves her arms and shakes her head at Deret. It's impossible to hear or see each other in this storm. "This kid can't get a comm piece fast enough," she mutters.

Just then, muted horizontal lightning strobes all around, allowing the two to vaguely see each other's outline. "This is impossible," she says, her words snatched away, except Windy's ear twitches backward. "Lightning can't form in the Nimbostratus Sector. Completely *forbidden*."

Breeslin narrows her eyes at the impossible atmospheric phenomenon right in front of her and presses forward to slice through the blustering wind and rain.

Deret is a mess.

Like pin-pricks, the rain cuts into his skin as Visa surges on. His hair and clothes are drenched, and it's all he can do to cling to his Moon Mare's neck.

Visa says to his mind, *Safe.*

He buries his face in her whipping mane and grips her harder. Visa's opalescent body slips through the storm.

Deret's spark sense, though still developing, is screaming that they are indeed *not* safe. His Moon Mare is expending her spark as fast as he can help her replenish it. Together, they are able to manage some semblance of balance through this storm. He sees Windy – handling himself easily since he is indeed a Storm Pony, bred and trained for just such situations – only when the lightning illuminates them in the clouds.

Pressing his face against Visa's warm neck, they surge forward in a rocking motion. He asks her desperately, "How do I help?"

She answers, *Inside.*

"Yes, I know," he says. "We have to get inside somewhere safe."

No, she replies. *Inside* you.

She lurches away from a streak of lightning. The deafening CRACK makes his ears ring and his head spin.

He says, "I don't understand."

Visa, however, knows he does. She mentally nudges him again. *Inside you.* Her strides level out without pulling spark from Deret. He feels the release inside himself, but the buffeting wind and pelting rain is relentless.

Silhouetted against the bruised sky, he sees Windy rear up wildly to fight another lightning bolt. The Storm Pony's eyes flash and sizzle as he strikes it mercilessly with a front hoof, *CRACK,* sending sparks flying, pulverizing the bolt.

Simultaneously, Deret hears a cry as Breeslin slips off her Storm Pony's back. Windy screams in terror as he wrenches his head back to see his girl falling.

Red and orange glow at her feet. She's ignited her ice-jet thrusters, but she's still helplessly tumbling out of control.

A reflex races through Deret making him reach out to her, even though she's impossibly far way. Warmth radiates from his center, pulses once, and then flows out through his fingertips toward the little WISP. Like an ink drop in water, his own spark bleeds silver through the clouds and wind and rain until it engulfs Breeslin and wrestles her softly back to full balance.

Wide-eyed, Breeslin nods at him with a thumbs up. He breathes a sigh of relief then slowly drags his finger, moving her right back into Windy's saddle. The iridescent spark net flows around both horse and rider, protecting them from the storm.

It dawns on him – he can cast his spark, like, wherever he wants it! And in a physical, moveable, pliable way! He squeezes Visa's sides with his legs to free up his other hand. That same warm glow pulses in his chest then he casts another net around himself and Visa. It flows, smooth as silk, enveloping them in soft quiet, allowing the Moon Mare to run freely.

Breeslin sees what he's done and grins bright as dawn. She waves a bladed arm forward for him to follow and mouths, *Keep up!* Then she leans close to her Storm Pony's neck, says something in his ear, and they are off like a shot.

Visa needs no coaxing to follow. She stretches her sleek neck out with the determined set of a dragon. The storm outside their spark cocoon blurs by.

Up-up-up they fly until both *POOF* through the cloud deck and into bright blue sky. Deret and Breeslin whoop for joy. A wave of wonder washes over them as they sail into the leaping, rolling, stretching land of Sky Steed Stables.

Breeslin barks into her sapphire com piece to the rest of her WISP team. "We're rendezvousing at Sky Steed Stables, Snippet. Meet us there ... No. There's no time ... I'll get you up to speed as soon as we're all together." She glances warily back at the roiling storm deck getting farther and farther away. "Everyone needs to hear about this."

Chapter 20

Prep

Silva Starling heaves the massive barn doors open for the Sparkslingers. "Let's get you all inside."

They have all made it to Sky Steed Stables ahead of schedule. Wayfare and Drift are already in the barn. Two Stormbuds take Visa and Windy to a couple of prepared stalls. They both wade through the thick bedding and greedily go to the food and water. The Moon Mare and Storm Pony have earned a welcome rest and rub down.

Sheena leaps out of Cirissa's arms in a flurry of diamond dust to greet Breeslin and Deret. Breeslin pats the little Frost Fox but is too preoccupied with whomever she's still talking to through her sapphire comm piece. She scoots Sheena off to Deret who takes her in his arms and ruffles her up. Her tongue lolls with delight.

Wayfare, his eyes filled with worry, reaches for Deret and wraps him into a big brother/apprentice/Frost Fox hug. "We didn't know if we should come get you. You had us worried. What took you so long ..." He gulps a little gulp then holds his little brother at arm's length in the eye, "... Brother?"

Deret blinks at him. He likes the sound of that. Brother. It feels right. It feels good knowing someone was thinking about him. Worrying even.

"I'm okay, Wayfare," he reassures the veteran Catalyst. Then he wiggles his fingers in front of him and lets tiny sparks flit from the tips. Sheena snaps happily at the sparks. "I'm getting the hang of this."

Wayfare grins a wide, crooked grin and musses up Deret's storm-blown, red hair then slaps him on the shoulder. "Did you hear that, Drift?" he calls over his shoulder. "Kid's calling the shots already!"

A gruff chuckle comes from the rugged Catalyst leaning against Visa's stall. "Did I ever, my friend."

"A unique gift, indeed," Cirissa says as she gives the newcomer a canted nod of respect.

Deret stands a little taller. He wishes his mom and dad were here. They'd be proud.

The thought of his parents makes him ask, "Has anyone heard from Fillip?"

Silva Starling steps up, tipping the brim of her white cowboy hat. Her smile lights up the room as she pats her belt buckle. "We'll all check in once we get inside."

Deret looks around dumbly. *We* are *inside*.

Breeslin, standing off to the side with one hand to her ear, sees the look on his face. "Snip, I gotta go. Just check in here as soon as you're done. – Yes, the whole team. – We'll listen for your ping. – Out." She marches straight to the last stall and goes in. "Let's move, people. We have a LOT to talk about."

Drift eyes Wayfare and Cirissa cooly. "Bossy little thing."

They accept their orders and make their way to the stall. Deret follows. It's a typical 10x10 horse stall. That's it. He blinks.

Wayfare slaps him on the shoulder and gives a squeeze. "Are you ready for this?" he says with dancing blue eyes.

Deret looks at his big brother. At the stall. Back at his brother. The others file in like an elevator. Even Sheena prances in and turns, waiting for someone to slide the door shut. All eyes look at him expectantly.

Finally, Breeslin pipes up from the back, "Get in already!" Deret can barely see the top of her head behind everyone else, but he can hear her foot tapping *ting ting* on the floor.

Sheena looks up at him, smiling away. He steps inside the stall.

"So," he says, "what do we do now?"

Silva flashes him a sparkly wink and reaches up to twist one of the stall's bars. Immediately, the floor vibrates beneath their feet. He hears a *clunk kachunk hunk* and *fwoosh*. The entire stall, just like an elevator, slides downward.

As the cloudstone walls rush by faster and faster, Deret grins at Wayfare. This is like no amusement ride he's ever been on.

Wayfare just chuckles. He can barely remember when everything was new and amazing. Watching his little brother go through it all with him is rejuvenating.

When the stall softly flumps to a stop, Drift claps his beefy hands and rubs them together as he declares, "Gadget time!"

Silva slides the door open and steps out first. Her white, gem-encrusted boots echo a *click clack* on the glossy surface of the dark room. Breeslin jams her way through the others to get out but elbows Deret on her way past him and says, "Get a load of this, Rookie."

Silva says to Deret, "We do a whole lot more than make thunder here at Sky Steed Stables, son."

She turns to face the empty space, presses her hands together like a prayer, and flings her arms out, fingers splayed. In an instant, light flies to all corners of what Deret can now see is a vast cloud cavern. One side has clear display cases filled with shining things. The other side is lined with computer panels and dashboards now whirring to life, blinking, and beeping. In the center of the room, a circle of several comfy-looking captain chairs, which look a lot like VR gaming stations, sit empty and waiting.

As Breeslin strides in like she owns the place, Sheena races in too, her tiny toenails ticking on the floor. When Breeslin stops abruptly at a display case, the little Frost Fox goes sliding past on her fluffy rump, spinning around with a ridiculous smile spread wide across her face.

Cirissa just sighs and shakes her head then goes to check a monitor while instructing the group, "Hurry up picking out your toys. We've got a lot to discuss."

Deret sees her tap at the screen and zoom in on an aerial view of Median.

Silva joins Breeslin. Her long and lean silhouette dwarfs the little WISP. "That one?" she asks and points at something in the case.

"Yep," Breeslin nods and exhales with her hands on her pixie hips while she waits for Silva to unlock the glass top and take out a – "Thank. You," she says and snatches the item right out of Silva's hand. "Finally," she focuses on the device, tapping, and dialing, "a comm piece for the fledgling." She goes straight to Deret, gives it one final adjustment, and thrusts it at him.

"Yes! *Finally* is right!" He takes it from her, looking the sapphire cochlear bauble up and down, then gives her such a look of gratitude, she can hardly stand it. He simply says, "Thanks."

For a moment, fleeting as it is, the all-business WISP leader melts. She punches his shoulder, pairs an eye roll with a smirky grin, and says, "If you're gonna be one of us, saving our necks and all, we can't have you mute out there."

Deret grins even bigger at her and shakes his head once. "Nope. But now you won't be able to shut me up."

"Over here, you two," Wayfare calls. He and Drift stand proudly by another case.

Deret gives Breeslin a nod as she crosses the room to join Cirissa at the monitors.

Silva and Deret pass a section of wall covered with framed photos of her with the various Cloud Masters and other semi-famous people holding their gadgets. Then they come to a section lined with the coolest assortment of electric guitars he could ever imagine. As he gapes at the instruments, Silva Starling gives a little smile. It's a rare occasion when she gets to show off her collection.

Wayfare almost looks nervous, shifting his weight underneath his long coat, and swiping his mohawk back. He says, "We got here a lot earlier than you, so we had some time to put together a little 'Welcome to Sparkslinging' array of goodies for you to choose from."

Drift's bushy eyebrows bounce up and down as he keeps glancing at all the gadgets he and his buddy have pulled out. "You got the pick-o-the-litter here, m'boy."

"Here's a SparkBit, just like mine," Wayfare points to a device in the center, "only it's top of the line. Scans spark levels for miles!" He looks at his own well-worn SparkBit somewhat wistfully then goes on explaining the other items. "This here's a SparkPistol like Drifts, only this one is dipped in liquid silver and its molecularly enhanced sights and range are off-the-charts accurate."

Drift pats his own SparkPistol in the holster on his hip and says, "No need for that new-fangled techy stuff when you're already a dead shot."

Silva crosses her arms and *hmphs*. Her own SparkPistol gleams at her side.

Drift waggles a finger at her, "Someday, Silva Straightshooter, you and I are gonna see who really is the best."

She feigns a bored look at his challenge. "Name the day, old man."

Wayfare interrupts, "And here we have your basics: SparkShades, SparkVisor, SparkShield, SparkNunchucks, SparkMachete, SparkHarpoon, SparkSlingshot, and my personal favorite, SparkGrenade."

Silva pipes in, "I don't recall giving the okay on some of these." She leans in to look at the collection they've put together. "Wait just one cloud-pickin' minute." She raises the glass lid. "The SparkGauntlet? Boys, this is just a prototype. I'm not even sure it'll work."

Wayfare flashes his dashing smile. "Good time to give it a whirl!"

The metallic gauntlet visibly quivers as Deret steps closer to get a better look.

"See?" says Wayfare. "It's found its master."

That makes her pause. Disbelief and fascination merge in her expression. "Only entities with the most refined spark wielding abilities should even think of using this."

Deret is mesmerized by the long glove made of what looks like very light, almost ethereal, chainmail. Its fingertips are cut off, and its surface shifts, swirls, and smooths as if it is a living organism.

"Hey, kid," says Drift at barely a whisper, "roll up that flannel." He pats his own bare arm and nods.

Deret shoves his shirt sleeve up.

He reaches to touch the gauntlet, but the thing levitates then slurps right over his hand and up his forearm. It gently suctions onto his arm so that it moves and feels like his own skin. Deret looks at the swirling surface, not knowing really what to do next. Maybe he won't be able to make it work.

Wayfare, giddy over it all, says, "Just think."

"Think what?" Deret asks.

"Anything. Well, anything dealing with spark, that is. If I'm not mistaken, it should give you a visual of whoever or whatever you want to read. Particularly if you've been in contact with them before. It's a residual spark thing."

"Wow. Ok. Um. I want to know how Mom and Dad are doing," he says to his arm.

"Right! Only you'll find you won't have to say it out loud once you get the hang of it. Just think it."

Deret's heart pumps with anticipation as a spot on the SparkGauntlet ripples and smooths out to show him a visual of Demeara and Garrin Day. He waves his brother in to look too. Their parents are standing at the entrance of their barn ushering people in hurriedly. It's raining, and the people are hunched under their jackets, holding their children's hands, or running in from the trolley, which is parked awkwardly in the grass on the hill leading to the barn. Fillip sits outside the trolley's steps watching each citizen of Median exit and follow the others in line. He, however, is dry as can be, sitting inside his own spark bubble. Deret assumes it's just like the one he himself mustered on his flight here.

Deret says, "They're doing it! They're getting people to safety."

Cirissa beckons everyone to sit in the captain's chairs. "Indeed, they are," she says as if she's known the whole time, which she has. She adds, "I have been keeping an eye on their progress with my vision glass. Just in case."

Wayfare leans in for a better view. "In case of what?"

"In case they needed assistance," she replies. "But once I saw Fillip use his spark to transport that entire trolley off the tramway over the countryside, I knew they were doing just fine."

"Go Fillip!" cheers Wayfare.

"Yes," Cirissa agrees, and once again beckons everyone to sit.

Deret takes one last look at his home and his parents, blinks a long blink, and when he opens his eyes again, the image is smoothed over with the SparkGauntlet's swirls. He takes a deep breath and joins the others in a chair waiting for him between Breeslin and Wayfare.

Inlaid on the floor is a golden ring that starts to glow silver then gold then silver along with a bell tone *ping, ping, ping.*

"About time," says Breeslin as she anxiously taps a button on her armrest. The circle on the floor ripples into a clear view of her WISP team. They're standing in a clump, still clad in their spiky crystal patrol suits.

Snippet speaks up, "It wasn't easy getting us all together, like you ordered, Captain." She gives a rueful glance at her crew. "We've been pretty busy up here. You wouldn't believe the weird occurrences going on."

"Oh, yes I would. You pinged just in time. We all just sat down to debrief," Breeslin says. Then she nods to Cirissa to commence.

Cirissa says to the WISP team, "It's good you could make it." Then she explains to everyone what happened at the Cloud Council meeting. "And then, just as I was about to net him and haul him in, he *and* Loom vanished together."

"He kidnapped Cloud Master Loom?" Drift's eyes are big as moons. Then he laughs without mirth, "I'm sorry. I'm just having a really hard time picturing that scrawny Shroud even trying to budge Loom's pinky toe."

Silva Starling explains, "His cloak allows him, and anything or anyone he touches, to effaport together." When met with curious stares, she adds, "He got it from me, many years ago. We thought it'd be handy. How was I supposed to know he would someday go all dominate-the-skies on us?"

Wayfare says, "There's no way you, or any of us, could have known." He nods to Cirissa to continue.

"Before I left the Sky Room, I overheard Cloud Master Shreddard and Makryl speaking of preparations to 'organize the troops.' I believe they plan to meet Shroud with equal force. You should have seen Loom. Worry and nerves alone are enough for her to generate a lethal storm. I can only imagine what might happen if he energizes her with the Bolt Blaster."

Drift raises his voice, "*That* can't happen."

"Absolutely not," says Breeslin, then she barks commands to her team. "Snip, you and Tuft need to get eyes on Shreddard and Makryl. Get me intel on their plan. Alert us to any offensive moves they plan to make the SECOND you know."

"Understood, Captain," both Snippet and Tuft chime in unison. Snippet taps a finger to the side of her head to unfurl her prism cylinders from her eyes. Tuft taps her forehead to test her beacon at its lowest setting.

"Jink. Tygr. You're our speed and muscle. Put a stop to any of the weather oddities going on, but be on alert and ready to launch into action. We may need you to rally troops. Understand?"

"Ohhh ya," says Tygr with that irresistible charm of his as he over-flexes his muscles, making ice chips flick. "Muscle, reporting for duty, Captain."

Jink, long and lean, shakes his shaggy, crystal hair, shoves his buddy off-stance, and says with a sure smile, "We got this, Captain."

Breeslin shakes her head and rolls her eyes at them, but Deret can't help but notice the sheer pride in her expression.

"Then get on with you all," she orders then flashes an electric smile. "Time to bolt!"

All four WISP agents ignite their ankle ice jets simultaneously, and they zoom out of sight. The golden ring on the floor fades out.

Sheena runs to the center, sniffing for them, then goes to lie down at Cirissa's feet. Cirissa says encouragingly to Breeslin, "They will certainly earn dendrites for this."

Worry flickers across the WISP captain's face. She nods but says, "That's what I'm afraid of. At what cost?"

Wayfare keeps the momentum going. "Tell us about what's going on above the sequoia tree. Did you happen to see Father Owl and his family?"

"We did not. Sorry, Wayfare. We were too busy just trying to ride through the storm. We could barely see each other."

Deret asks, "Owl family?"

Wayfare says. "Fillip and I have been fighting the sludge off of them for a while now. Seems it has a propensity for owl spark. I don't get it."

"Let's go back," Deret says with conviction. "We'll get them to the farm."

Breeslin replies, "I don't know, Deret. It might be too late."

The visible pain leaching from Wayfare's expression is too much. Deret won't have it. "I know how to navigate in a storm now. We can go back."

"That's actually not a bad plan," Drift says. "We need to get to the bottom of that. My Spark Senses tell me that tree is the root of the whole sludge problem."

"Root," Wayfare says under his breath, then, "ROOT! Drift, you're a genius!"

His buddy replies flatly, "I know this." Then he looks at Wayfare with the same confusion everyone else has. "Um, just exactly why do you say that *now*?" His bushy eyebrows knit together.

"We're focussing on the *result* of the problem. Not the *root* of it." He looks around. "I think, if we take a look at what's right below the roots of the sequoia," he taps at some controls on his armrest and an image of the tree springs up in 3D before them, "we will find," more tapping, "whatever is causing the spark storm."

With a last tap, the layers underneath the tree come into view. Silence stuns the room. Even Sheena sucks in her tongue at what they see.

An elaborate, underground room of vessels, computers, and some kind of swirling pool. And off to the side, a long hallway leads to an elevator-like tube that connects directly to Murkemer's dwelling.

Cirissa exhales, "Murkemer."

Breeslin bursts out, "I *knew* it! I just *knew* that kid couldn't be trusted. What's he think he's doing?"

Cirissa shakes her head at the images. "After what happened at the Cloud Council meeting today, it is very clear that he and Shroud are not on the same side."

Deret eyes work around the images. A warm sphere begins to pulse at Deret's core, and before he even realizes he's forming the words, he says, "We have to talk to him."

Breeslin scoffs, "And by *talk to him,* you mean take him down?"

"No," Deret replies with urgency even he doesn't quite understand. Then he tries to verbalize what is working its way from his heart to his head. "Murkemer is young, like us. He's still learning. He just ... needs someone to talk to him. Help him."

Cirissa says gently, "That is what Shroud was supposed to do. But I guess that didn't work out the way we expected. Did it?"

It pains him to know what she says is right, but something tells him he is right too.

Drift squints at the underground images and scratches his beard. "Well, I don't know exactly what all this gobbledegook we're looking at is, and I don't know what *young* Murkemer wants, but one thing's for sure – we need to get down there to figure this out. Pronto. Because that storm is about to reach the Day farm pretty quick. And I'm not sure how they're going to hold it *and* the sludge back on their own."

Cirissa adds, "Drift is correct. Wayfare, take Breeslin and Deret to this place. Do what is needed to understand whatever," her lavender eyes work busily around the underground images for which she has no words, "*this* is, and determine whether or not you must put an end to it."

"Done," says Breeslin without a moment's hesitation. She hops spritely out of her chair and over to the elevator entrance where she crosses her arms and taps her foot. The others quick-step their way over.

On the ride up, Deret and Wayfare eye each other, sparkling at the idea of finally working together. And on a *mission*, no less.

The moment they step into the barn aisle, Silva Starling heads out the back door without a word to anyone.

Cirissa flashes into her full Ice Crystal Guard armor. "In the meantime," she says, "Drift, Sheena and I will help keep the people and creatures of Median safe. Join us as soon as you can. We will all be on alert for the WISP team's report on Shreddard's and Makryl's offensive moves."

Drift says, "Fine by me, but *I'm* driving. You're not gonna do that effaport-thing to me. This body," he puffs up and pats his leather vest, "stays in one piece."

Cirissa lets out a laugh like a starry night. "Of course, you are!"

Drift flicks on his SparkShades and taps them once. They all hear the Halo 500 vroom to life outside and pull up right at the barn door. Sheena streaks into the back seat and props herself up, waiting.

Breeslin whistles to Windy to suit up. He snorts as his ice shields envelop him from head to tail while he eagerly starts down the aisle. In one fluid motion, she flares into her own armor and flings herself onto his back.

Deret brings Visa out and is glad to see her lustrous sheen swirling with color and life. "Ready to go again, girl?" he asks as he rubs her forehead.

Her eyes are vibrant as she simply says, *Ready*. She sniffs the gauntlet on his arm. "*Pretty*."

He wiggles his fingers showing her his new device. "Pretty sweet, right?" Then he whispers in her ear, "I have no clue how to use it," and shrugs, but his giddy grin is infectious.

She nickers a laugh but reassures him with a typical one-word response, *Clever*.

Wayfare claps a hand on Deret's shoulder, "I believe he is clever enough, indeed, Miss Visa." He bows gentlemanly to the Moon Mare, and she nickers back. But then he stands upright and glances awkwardly around. "Is there maybe a Storm Pony for me too?" he asks.

A pang of guilt runs through Deret. Wayfare has no ride!

Outside, Breeslin is hollering for them to hurry up as she tries to settle Windy down.

Deret offers, "Maybe you can double with me?"

Wayfare stretches his back this way and that and tests the bounciness of his yellow running shoes in prep to try to hop on.

Deret feels every muscle in Visa's body brace.

Drift, leaning cooly on the Halo 500, says, "Maybe you should come with us."

Cirissa says with a stunningly sly smile, "I believe our Sky Steed Master has something different planned for our dear Wayfare."

"Hold your horses!" It's Silva's voice, no doubt, but she is nowhere to be seen.

Visa breathes a sigh of relief as she arches her neck toward a cloud-covered corral from which Silva leads a creature about the size of a horse. Mist still clings to it.

Deret and Wayfare squint at it. It definitely doesn't *move* like a horse.

Breeslin and Windy face it. "What the ...?" She screws up her face. Windy blows out and strikes the ground once, sending sparks flying.

It startles. A moaning sort of cry echoes from it. It definitely doesn't *sound* like a horse. Silva tugs gently on its lead and they keep coming closer and closer. With each step, a little more mist rolls off its form.

Breeslin is the first to get it. "Holy ozone ... you guys ... that's ... a ... Dusk Dragon."

Both Deret and Wayfare say in unison, "A what?"

With each step closer, the sun glints brighter off the creature next to Silva. It's lumbering side-to-side action reflects fiery-red and flame-orange glints off its scales. A spiked mane surrounds its face like a razor-sharp flower. The rest of its body sits low to the ground, and its tail trails in s-curves, stirring up mist behind it.

But its eyes. It's glowing, yellow, fear-filled eyes. When they find and lock on to Wayfare, it stops. Silva stops with it and watches its reaction to Wayfare. The Dusk Dragon raises its head slightly and sniffs through slit nostrils.

Wayfare is frozen, looking upon this amazing beast. He can feel its nerves popping. He can sense its distrust.

Deret scans his Cloud City textbook pages in his mind. In the same chapter Shadow Cats are explained – *Myths and Legends 101* – is a single-page history and description of Dusk Dragons.

Breeslin re-tells pretty much what the chapter reads. "They're a rarely sighted creature. Their pack, or I think its actually called a *flight*, travel together hiding in their own generated mist cloud as they go, and it, kind of, I guess blocks out the sun and makes everything really hard to see. Legend has it that, if you make them mad or threaten even one of them in some way, they can extinguish pretty much any kind of atmospheric phenomenon with a single flight sweep. Which can really wreak havoc on climate. But they don't seem to go around stirring up trouble. They mostly like to hang in the hills and valleys and just seem to want to be left alone."

Silva urges the creature forward until the others can hear her. "Our Thunder Studs and Storm Ponies have a very specific purpose here, Wayfare. I'm sorry I cannot offer you one of them. But this little guy," she tips her head affectionately to the Dusk Dragon, "he showed up here a few hours ago. Must've wandered from his brood. We haven't had time yet to look for his flight, and Dusk Dragons are hard to track, traveling in their own mist camouflage. It may take time to find them. I know, he's maybe not everyone's cup-o-pea-soup, but I thought, maybe ..."

Wayfare is fully enamoured. The words "I'll take him" come out soft and kind, his eyes never breaking away from the creature. The dragon blinks back at him. Without hesitation, the Catalyst strides over, calm and confident, and takes the lead rope from Silva. He reaches out, offering a touch.

The Dusk Dragon hesitates, quivering. But Wayfare stays his hand but closes his eyes. In a moment, he feels the cool scales of the dragon's forehead press against his fingers.

And they are connected.

Silva says quietly, "He's one of the good ones." And both the dragon and Wayfare assume she's referring to the other. But she really means both.

Silva then steps back and holds up a device. "Everyone, look here."

Drift, Cirissa, Sheena, Breeslin, Windy, Deret, Visa, and Wayfare with a Dusk Dragon stand in a cluster and face her. Their faces and postures show tense excitement. They are serious, but hopeful. Weathered, but exhilarated. Anxious, but confident.

"That's right," Silva says as she takes a picture for her wall. Then, so softly they can only see her lips move, "Sparkslingers."

Chapter 21

Storm Brewing

"I got eyes on Bo-Peep. Repeat. I have a visual on Bo-Peep." Snippet, looking through her prism glasses, hovers with Tuft a healthy distance away from Cloud Master Makryl's cotton candy cloud mansion. Hidden in a cloud mountain peak, the two WISP agents assess the situation.

Tuft nudges her, "Is Shreddard with her?"

Snippet readjusts the depth and clarity of her prism cylinders. "I don't see him. But Makryl's standing on that balcony at the top of the castle. He's bound to be there somewhere. Oh! There! I think I see him. He's riding on a scud cloud and," she waits and watches, "yes, it's him. He's riding up to her balcony like some fairytale prince." She looks at Tuft and rolls her huge, magnified eyes.

Tuft is antsy. "We've got to get down there. I gotta know what they're talking about."

Snippet retracts her prism cylinders. "Right. Let's relocate."

"Whisper engines, on." Tuft reduces her ice-jet flames until they're barely audible.

Snippet follows suit, and they zoom in soundlessly to the tippy top of a turret just above and behind the balcony where the two Cloud Masters are standing. They crouch on their bellies and listen in on the conversation taking place.

Makryl asks Shreddard, "So did you find him?"

"He's disappeared. Poof! Nowhere to be found," Shreddard answers. "My best Ice Crystal Guard units can't find a trace of him. And how in Great Zephyr's name does Loom just go missing? She's skyscraper-high! It's like they've both just evaporated."

Makryl considers this for a moment, then says, "Hm. Well, it's a very good thing I've already recruited someone a little more, shall we say, 'covert' to go on a 'super secret' mission?"

A grin slowly creeps across Shreddard's face as he realizes who Makryl is talking about. "Castella?"

"Castella."

Snippet and Tuft mouth the name *Castella* to each other in surprise.

Shreddard chuckles but doesn't argue. "You're probably right, but A: I have concerns about her lucidity for something this big. I mean, what Shroud's cooking up could have climate-shifting effects once it's all said and done. And it could practically happen *overnight*."

Makryl chuckles, making her curlicue locks bounce. "Oh, I know she comes across as a bit eccentric these days, but that's just because she's *bored*. Think about it. We haven't had a good old climate threat in ages!"

He just shrugs because he can't deny what she's saying.

"And B?" she asks.

"Hm?"

She gives him her round-faced look. "You started with A, so I assume there is a B?"

"Oh, yes." He chortles at himself. "I'm just not sure you understand how much cloud credit it's going to cost us to hire her mercenaries. Because you know the Cloud Council, especially Tendril and Virgus, will never approve of rallying Castella's thugs."

"True." She gives him a devious look. "But I have already acquired one very, *very* valuable supporter. Motivated by the most powerful thing of all." She folds her hands and bats her eyes. "Love."

Understanding dawns across Shreddard's icy features. "You got Bumble in on this?"

She beams with pride and answers, "I did indeed. And it took nothing to do so."

"Great Zephyr. Now we really are in business."

Tuft and Snippet can hardly believe what they hear. Just as they're hand-signaling each other to take off so they can go report this intel, they hear Makryl squeal, "Look Shredd! Here they come!"

Off in the distance, far across the sky, comes a line of rumbling motoclouds. They alternate gray and white shades, except the hot pink one advancing in the very center, ridden by none other than scrawny, old Cloud Master Castella herself. As they approach, she raises her arm and makes a fist. The motoclouds begin to file in behind each other, forming layered chevrons. Castella slices the air and all the mercenaries cut their engines to silently hover. She vrooms right up to the balcony, cuts the engine and throws her leg over to sit casually in front of Shreddard and Makryl. Her crinkly, hot-pink wind suit wildly reflects the sun's rays. She flicks up the sunshades hinged to her glasses and pops her dentures in and out of her mouth with a grin.

"Well," Castella says, "where do you want 'em?"

Shreddard lets Makryl take the lead on this.

"First, dear Castella, we have a little super-secret covert operation for *you*."

Castella's eyes go wide as she sits up straight and slow. "For me?"

"Yes, you."

"Hot dawn! Where to? What'd ya need?" She flings her legs back into riding position and revs her engine.

"Oh. My," Makryl giggles at her enthusiasm. "You are indeed raring to go." She looks to Shreddard, enjoying herself a little too much.

He just grins and shrugs.

"We need you to find Shroud. Find out where he's taken Loom. And find out what his intensions are with her. Can you handle that?"

Castella *pphhtts* her lips, insulted that this Bo-Peep wannabe even has to ask such a question. "Oh, I can *handle* that alright, missy. Don't you go straightening your little curls for one moment thinking I can't."

A smile creeps up the corners of Makryl's lips. "Excellent."

Now, Tuft and Snippet *really* need to bolt to comm the others. Snippet is already turned around ready to ignite, when she feels Tuft grab her arm and pull her back in. She points down, below the mercenaries.

Shreddard announces, "I believe Cloud Master Bumble and his troops have arrived."

Roiling and boiling, a mass of cumulus clouds bump and knock into each other in a chaotic mess. Bumble leads, if you can call it that, up toward the castle. He rides a cotton ball chariot pulled by two flouncy Sky Steeds. Definitely *not* the kind that Silva Starling keeps at her stables. These are puffy and slow, and they seem to care more about looking pretty than doing the actual work of pulling the chariot.

He turns in his seat and wields a lightning whip to halt his entire company. It seems sketchy for a second whether the cloud mass will actually follow his orders, but for the moment, the conglomeration slows to stir in place.

Forgoing a greeting, Bumble announces, "I've assemblurbled my finest. *Gurbl* ... Where's that snivelling Shroud? When I get my hands on him ... *blub up* ... I will unleash the greatest force of nature upon him ... *glurple* ..." His face is blue with anger.

Makryl is taken aback, so Shreddard steps up. "Cloud Master Bumble, we know you are anxious to get Cloud Master Loom back in your loving arms, but we have yet to locate her or Shroud."

"What do you mean you *haven't located her*? She's gargantuan! *Glupig* ..."

Castella says, "Don't you worry your bubbly head, Bumbly. That's my job, now." Without waiting for a reply, she fires up her motocloud and zooms to her waiting mercs. She singles out two, and they ride out of sight with her.

"Well," Makryl says, surprised at the blunt exit, "I guess we just wait now."

Bumble is mad. But clueless too.

Tuft and Snippet, seeing this as their best opportunity to bolt, give each other a nod and fly off.

* * *

"That's what I said," Snippet repeats to Jink and Tygr, who happen to be sitting at headquarters catching a well-earned break since they've blown out pretty much all incoming issues already and are awaiting orders. "You need to get troops together. Shreddard and Makryl have already got an army from Bumble and Castella on standby."

Jink answers, "Holy ozone, they didn't waste any time, did they."

Tuft adds, "We have to find Shroud and Loom before Castella. Once they get Loom back, they're going to open up full-force on him. They'll pour the chaos down through Murkemer's Stratus layer too, and then …"

"Earth," Tygr finishes for her.

Breeslin cuts in on the comm link as she guides Windy back toward the sequoia tree storm. "Great Zephyr, we need to act fast. Do you have any ideas for more troops you can rally?" She glances back to make sure she can still see Deret on Visa and Wayfare on his Dusk Dragon. Visa flies directly behind her, but Wayfare's mount is pretty much all over the place. It's leathery wings flap and soar without any rhythm, making them plummet and swoop erratically. As far as she can tell, however, the Catalyst is grinning from ear to ear. And the sounds coming from both of them are a mix of terror and joy.

Tygr answers, "I have a buddy at Cloud Hound Kennels who owes me a favor."

Breeslin replies, "Oo, that could be good."

"Yup," he goes on, "and we'll let Silva know. See what she can conjure for us."

"Good," the WISP captain says. "You should also see if you can get Cloud Master Virgus or Drizzo to send support. They don't have much for weaponry or battle tactics, but we could use all the help we can get." She takes a breath. "Snippet. Tuft."

"Yes, Captain," they say in unison.

"We can't let them use Loom for retaliation. With the sequoia tree storm and the sludge swarm already wreaking havoc down there, I can't even begin to imagine what will happen if she unleashes a Stormhulk."

Snippet sucks in a gasp, "Those poor people. Sweet, tiny little Median. They won't know what hit them."

"I don't think they know what's hitting them *right now* even. The Days, Fillip, Cirissa and Drift are doing their best, but they ... I don't know. I need to check in with Cirissa again.

"What about you?" asks Jink. "What's up with Murkemer?"

"We're on our way now. Wayfare's having a little learning curve navigating his new Dusk Dragon."

Wayfare whoops, and the dragon's metallic trill carries through the sapphire comm.

The entire team asks in unison, "A *what*?"

"You heard me. No time to explain. Gotta bolt. Breeslin out."

Stunned, Snippet whispers to herself, "Dusk Dragon."

Tuft sees she's thinking hard, so she says to Jink and Tygr, "You got this, boys?"

Jink answers, "Aw halos yes, we do. Any idea where to start looking for Loom?"

Tuft looks to her teammate. A clever grin slides across Snippet's lips as she answers, "I think I have a pretty good idea where to start."

* * *

Rain pelts the Halo 500 as it hovers along the fence line. Drift peers out the bubble window, his SparkShades on constant monitor mode, patrolling for sludge leaks. If an inky finger pokes through the spark barrier, he zaps it with a shot of spark from the cloud craft's spark injectors built into its underbelly.

"Call him a surfer dude or what you want, but that Virgus really knows how to make 'em." He pats the steering wheel lovingly.

The Halo 500 hums a purr in reply.

The trees and fields are filled with creatures from the woods now. Cirissa and Sheena are still out searching for more, but as many as they've brought in already, it would be surprising to have any still left behind.

Though the sludge is held at bay, the rain has overcome most parts of the Day farm. Crops are flooded. Even the house is under several inches of water now. The little glass figurines in the kitchen window look out to see if anyone will come to save them.

But Demeara and Garrin aren't worried about that. They are too busy getting the people of Median settled comfortably, the best they can, inside their enormous barn. It may seem to the unknowing eye that this old barn is about to crumble upon its foundation, but that's just because they wouldn't know that it, like the rest of the Day family, is full of spark. Inside it, and all its wings and lean-to additions and aisles and nooks, flows the spark of ages, and it will always protect its inhabitants from harm.

Garrin has lined hay bales and wood logs for seating everywhere possible. He has recruited Joseph Sombrine, the dapper, middle-aged department store owner, since he seems to absorb spark a little better than the rest.

"I'll make a long bench over here, Garrin, if you think that's okay," says Joseph as he carries a long plank.

Garrin smiles with slight surprise. "That's perfect," he says.

Next, he gets some stumps for a makeshift table and calls over Slate and Stone, the two lawyers. "Here you go, gentlemen. I see you brought your chess board with you." He slaps the dust off the table top with his hand and invites them to sit.

"Oh!" says Gerald Slate. "Would you look at that."

Bodin Stone answers, "Why not? Nothing else to do, as usual."

Garrin's grin wanes as he turns away. *So many people.*

Under an awning at the rear entrance, Demeara works at keeping a small fire going for those who've succumbed to the bone chilling dampness. She drapes a blanket over Wanda Winerd's shoulders as the store clerk slumps near the flames, weeping quietly.

"I don't even understand," she snivels, "what's going on. One minute, I'm re-shelving a stack of sewing books, and the next, I get this overwhelming feeling that I have nothing to live for anymore, and I fall flat on the floor."

Demeara tries to soothe the young woman by wrapping her arm around Wanda's shoulders. "Shh, shh. You're safe now."

Wanda had been a close call. A single breath away from complete spark extraction when Fillip came upon her. That Shadow Cat's spark senses are a phenomenon like no other. He saved her life.

With Demeara's warmth soaking in, Wanda's crying scales back to a soft whimper.

Widow Shay tends to the old and the frail, keeping their spirits up and, with her ancient SparkBit, helping them manage any pain.

"Here, Anders. Let's see what I can do for your knee."

Her gardening friend sits with his leg propped up on a log. His once spry and springy attitude is gone. His face is saggy, and his voice is so tired as he says, "It aches. So ... heavy." He looks at her with pleading eyes. "Everything is just so heavy."

Widow pats his knee and reassures him, "I know, I know. This soggy air really can do a number on our old joints, eh?" Her smile is forced as she pats her own knees. He returns it with some effort.

Tapping at her SparkBit, she eyes his bad knee then places her warm hands over it. "There. How does that feel, Anders?"

He bends his leg, a little at first, then all the way. Relief visibly washes over his face. "Ahhh, that feels lovely, Widow." He sighs and adds, "You are one wonderous woman."

Widow Shay's eyes crinkle at him so hard, they almost shut. "Now Ander's Oldon, don't you go getting fresh with me." Though it's been many years since she's slung spark for much more than growing vegetables, she's still got the touch.

The children, for the most part, have climbed into the enormous loft to entertain themselves. Londa Lane, the trolley driver, heads up there to supervise. With one hand on the ladder, her messy bun haloing her head, she stops to say to Demeara just outside under the awning, "You know, that boy of yours is really something special. He patted my shoulder on the way off the trolley this morning, and I can't explain it really, it's just that he made me feel like ..."

Demeara slowly stands to face her. "Feel what, Londa?"

She chuckles to herself, "It's a goofy thing to say, I suppose, but he just made me feel like everything is going to be okay. You know?"

Demeara's heart catches in her throat at the thought of her youngest son. She smiles warmly. That single touch of Deret's must have quite a hefty residual effect. Londa is completely unaffected by the sludge. Maybe a little better even.

Londa smiles back and climbs up to the loft to join the playing children.

The constant, pounding roar of rain – hard rain – pummels the old shingled roof.

The sludge has had its way with so many of them before Fillip got them out, so most are sluggish and confused.

Fillip. He sits at the entrance looking out over the flooded house, and keeping an eye on Drift in the Halo 500. Though his feline silhouette shows confidence and strength, he is tired, though he'll never admit it.

He has just finished igniting the last of five near-complete spark extractions. Two teenaged boys, a school teacher, and two bunnies. Never let it be said that a complete spark extraction ever occurred on his watch. But with moving a full trolley – he can't remember how many times now – all the way from town to the farm using his own spark web, and reigniting so many, he is due for a rest.

But his keen emerald eyes continue to search through the mist for Cirissa and Sheena returning, hopefully with one more family they have yet to find.

Then he sees it, coming from the east. Drift must see it too, because he gets out of his cloud craft and jogs toward the barn through the wind and the rain. The Halo 500 continues to patrol on autopilot.

Cirissa takes shape as she nears the hill and sends a spark net around Drift whose Catalyst speed has seen faster days, to be sure. She gently lifts him and brings him alongside her as they reach the barn doors.

"Thanks for the lift!" he says.

Cirissa smiles. "I hope you didn't take offense. You just looked like you could use assistance."

Drift chuckles good-naturedly, "No worries there. Never too proud to accept a boost."

Fillip says seriously to their minds, *Where is that Frost Fox? We all need to help maintain spark in these citizens. It's been a quite taxing labor. And those three,* he glances carefully toward Demeara, Garrin, and Widow Shay, *are pressing their abilities farther than I ever imagined possible.*

Cirissa senses an inkling of weariness. She assures him, "Sheena is ... "

Across the driveway, coming from the darkness of the woods, is a sparkling trail of diamond dust reflecting a rainbow of colors. Sheena bounds out of the trees then stops, obviously quite proud of herself about something, and looks up into the highest branches. She barks joyfully.

Fillip is certainly not a fan of her perpetual happy nature, but he has always been one to give credit where credit is due, and that silly little Frost Fox has quite a talent for slinging spark with an ease he has never seen before. And he has seen a lot.

What is she so happy about?

Cirissa smiles warmly. "She has found a few who were nearly left behind."

Drift's eyebrows unfurl as he says, "You found them?"

Cirissa simply tips her head to the tree tops at the forest's edge.

And there they emerge. Father Owl, Mother Owl and their two owlets in full-feathered glory. In fact, if Fillip didn't know better, he would almost believe they were glowing as though reflecting sunlight. Or ...

Father Owl gives a mighty screech, but he does not guide his family toward the others. Instead, they glide, smooth and swift, along the far perimeter fence line, opposite the Halo 500.

Drift says what Fillip is thinking, "What the ...?"

Then it becomes obvious. The four owls spread out and shoot spark from their eyes at any sludge breeching the spark line.

Both Fillip and Drift stand, jaw-dropped.

How is this possible?

Sheena streaks up to meet them, unable to contain one bit of her excitement and yaps, *Sequoia! Tree! Spark storm!*

Like uncles who can't understand their toddler niece's words, Drift and Fillip look blankly to Cirissa for explanation.

"We found them in the giant sequoia." She nods toward the Owl family working along the fence. "Apparently, whatever phenomenon is occurring within that tree has given them powerful spark-wielding powers."

Drift scratches his head. "Well, I never …"

Fillip's brow creases. *Impossible.* But he sees it with his own eyes.

For a quiet moment, they watch the owls work.

Cirissa says in hopeful awe, "Our world is shifting."

Fillip's voice is laced with foreboding, *Indeed.*

Chapter 22

Dusk Dragons

The sequoia storm's cloud deck comes into view. Deret, Breeslin and Wayfare continue to fly down through Cloud Master Virgus' Altostratus sector at the bottom of the Mezzo Plane. They'll reach the storm any moment now. And that is going to be a problem since Wayfare still has little to no control over his ride.

Whirling and swirling through the sky, Wayfare and the Dusk Dragon flip and flap in wild chaos like they're being hurled through a tornado.

Breeslin and Deret keep an eye on them, which is a trick in itself. Trying to see if Wayfare is okay, with all the twisting and turning, is making them dizzy. A leg flings out here. An arm flops out there. If it wasn't for the occasional sighting of a mile-wide grin, they might have tried to intervene. Deret and Breeslin shake their heads and chuckle.

Deret is prepared to capture them in a spark net, but he's worried he won't be able to control them once he's got them. He pulls up the endless volumes of *Cloud City* in his mind. He can't help but think that, had Wayfare studied more in Cat Academy, he would have known better. But Deret wasn't about to tell him that outright. Instead, as he glides along on Visa's back, he scrolls to the section on Dusk Dragons, while his brother clings for dear life.

According to *Myths and Legends 101* – *Long, long ago, in the age before sludge was created to control human use of spark, and thus, dampen their destructive use of Want, Dusk Dragons filled the skies,* the hills, and the valleys of Median. Their misty trails swarmed the horizon every night as the last hint of light ebbed, and that same mist lingered until first light broke into dawn. Though the people only saw hazy mist clouds swirling in the dimness – obscuring their day from view – Skybounds, Catalysts and all the creatures of Cloud City knew the truth. Capable of engulfing entire towns in fog and mist, these creatures were feared. After all, they had the potential to generate chaos. But the Dusk Dragons never abused their powers and remained mysterious servants of twilight.

It is a little-known fact, therefore, that Dusk Dragons can be faithful companions. Only a handful of Skybounds in history have ever accomplished such a relationship with such creatures. Traveling in a close-knit group called a **flight**, their kind keep to themselves, inhabiting the hills and valleys under the cover of morning or evening mist.

Deret locks that little tidbit away and keeps mentally scrolling until he hits a subtitle that reads: *Partnering with a Dusk Dragon*. Deret taps his sapphire comm piece immediately, "Hey Wayfare!"

Wayfare yelps, "Ya kid?"

"Well, in the book it says: *Once you and your Dusk Dragon have established partnership, flight is a natural subsequent progression. To establish such a partnership, one must initiate touch and have that touch accepted willingly, without force.*

Wayfare and the dragon zoom past both Deret and Breeslin, and they can see he's clinging like a koala around the beast's thick body. His long coat tails jet out behind him. His voice comes back haggard, "I think we're a little past the 'initial touch' thing!"

"Right." Deret turns toward Breeslin as they both choke on laughter. Then he composes himself and keeps reading aloud like a manual. "*Once this is accomplished, one must simply hold firmly to the neck horns located directly behind the cape encircling the thick neck just at the base of the wide cranial protrusion.* Can you find them?"

Mild grunting crackles through the comm, then, "Got 'em!"

"Nice! Now it says: *The neck cape will provide the rider protection from elements and enable maneuverability.* Is that working?"

Breeslin, trying to track them, flips her vision enhancing lens over one eye, squints hard at the dragon's torso, and says into the comm, "Wayfare! Plant those yellow sneakers of yours onto those two scales that just jutted out behind you." She focuses in tight on the area she's talking about. "They're ... they look yellow too."

Deret sees them, so he excitedly skips over a few sentences to read, "*As the rider grasps the neck horns, if done in a confident manner, a Dusk Dragon typically will extend its stirrup scales at the base of either side of its abdomen for the rider's feet, providing a more secure and stable flight. At this point, partnership is complete, and both dragon and rider should blend color and form.*"

He barely gets the last word out when Wayfare and the Dusk Dragon plummet out of sight down into the storm deck below.

"What happened?" screeches Breeslin.

"I don't know. Where'd they ..."

"Yeeehaaaw!"

Like a missile, Wayfare and the dragon shoot straight up dangerously close. Then, as though the beast's engine cuts out, they hang suspended in the air for a heartbeat and veer, controlled and beautiful, in line next to the Storm Pony and Moon Mare.

Breeslin looks across Deret and Visa to Wayfare and gives a sharp, if not impressed, nod. "Not bad," she says.

Wayfare gives that cool, quirky grin and replies, "Just had to work out a few kinks."

"I'd say," she says with a snort.

Deret pipes in, "Hey! What's a bookworm gotta do to get a little credit around here?"

Wayfare admits, "Ya, kid. That was pretty handy, I have to admit." He wiggles his yellow sneakers. "Stirrup scales – Who'd a thought?" He gives a sheepish shrug. "I've said it before, I'll say it again – I really should have studied harder."

Deret's charmingly smug face makes everyone laugh. And for one small stretch of sky, the little team glides in a syncopated rhythm of hooves and wings.

Breeslin interrupts the moment, though, as she retracts her vision enhancing lens. "Sequoia storm submersion in three ... two ..." She nudges Windy in the sides, and they surge downward.

Deret, quick as lightning, lets fly his spark net around both Breeslin and her Storm Pony, as well as himself and Visa. He looks back just as he is engulfed in the storm clouds. For a panicked moment, he thinks he's lost Wayfare. Just as he's releasing his other hand to sling a spark net around his brother too, the Dusk Dragon's menacing face peers through the thick clouds at him. Most people believe dragons breathe fire, but this dragon is breathing what seems to be a protective mist cloud which engulfs itself and its rider, who also happens to be protected by the leathery umbrella-like neck cape.

Deret taps his sapphire comm. "Wayfare! You okay?"

"Never better, Deret!" Wayfare's floppy, blonde mohawk pops up behind the neck cape, then his whole face. He sticks his thumb high over the cape for Deret to see.

"Okay, guys," Breeslin says. "Murkemer's mansion should be just to the east over there somewhere. Eyes peeled."

At first, they see nothing but the storm raging around them. Lightning flashes. Rain and wind wrack their protective shields. And then it begins to appear, seemingly at a great distance at first, then, before they even have time to pull up, the towers and turrets are right in their face. They have to swerve hard to not crash right into them.

Deret has no choice but to let go his spark net. "Sorry!" he cries to Breeslin.

Breeslin and Windy fly like they know where they're going, though. "No worries, recruit. We got this from here. Follow us. Wayfare? You hanging in there?"

"Like smog on fog!" he calls.

"I'll take that as a yes."

Deret searches, but he sees nothing. "Can't see him. But my SparkSleeve says he's right behind us.

Breeslin screws up her face as Windy rumbles in for a landing in one of the overgrown courtyards. "SparkSleeve? You mean your SparkGauntlet?"

"Yep," he answers as Visa's feet flutter to a halt right next to them. He holds up his encased arm. "Way catchier, don't you think?"

She peaks one eyebrow. "Hm. Maybe." But inside, she totally agrees with him.

Deret flashes that crooked grin.

She purses her lips and mildly shakes her head at his charm. "Wayfare, come in. What's your ETA?"

She and Deret look around, wondering how they'd lost him.

Wayfare's voice says slyly, "What are you talking about? Sneak and I are right here."

Wayfare tickles his Dusk Dragon, making it gather up its breath and let out a great, mist-clearing, tip-you-back-a-bit, sneeze. And there they sit, apparently pleased with each other and their little joke.

Deret's SparkSleeve Adjacent Body Spark Load on them reads: Off Chart and 100%.

"Dusk Dragon mist slings spark!" Wayfare announces as he jumps down with a flump, hands *ta-da* in the air. "Didya read *that* in your book, eh?" He wobbles a bit then rights himself with a hand on the dragon's shoulder. Even a full spark load can't counteract the airlegs from the flight he just accomplished.

"Actually," Deret searches the Dusk Dragon chapter, "I did not know that. I better check back to see where I missed that bit." The truth is, it *doesn't* say anything about Dusk Dragons slinging spark.

"Don't bother," Wayfare says as he crosses a leg over, "Sneak and I will figure things out together now."

Breeslin looks amused, "Sneak? Your dragon's name is Sneak? Did he tell you that?"

"Well, no." He and the Dusk Dragon look at each other. "But," he goes on, "we seem to just know what the other is thinking."

Sneak snorts out a puff of mist. It lands on the dingy cloud ground turning it into pearly swirls instead. He appears quite proud of himself.

Breeslin's wheels are turning. "Sneak," she addresses the Dusk Dragon like a part of the team, "can you hide Windy and Visa with you while we look for Murkemer?"

Sneak sits a little more upright and snorts a spark mist cloud around himself and the two Sky Steeds.

"Well, isn't he handy?" she says. "Come on."

"How are we getting in?" Deret asks as he sends one little spark treat to Visa and hears her nicker in reply. "I assume we shouldn't just trapse up to the front door and let ourselves in."

Wayfare crosses his arms and tips his head. "Why not?"

* * *

The story-high front door on Murkemer's mansion is swung ajar. Scraps of stratus clouds drift inside like dead leaves.

"It's open?" asks Deret, feeling a little intimidated at the enormity of the mansion.

"I imagine he got here in a big hurry," Breeslin figures, "and is in there trying to cover up whatever he and Shroud have been up to." She arms her ice-blades. An electric blue strobe pulses from elbow to wrist with a faint whir. She tips her head and commands, "Let's go."

Wayfare chucks out his SparkSword from inside his coat sleeve and brandishes it with both hands. He sidesteps through the open door. Stratus scraps swirl in the wake of his duster coat as it swings with his careful moves.

Deret feels like he should really have a weapon too, but nothing in Silva's collection sat right with him. He'd never been in a fight his whole life. And holding a gun or knife had felt clunky and awkward. His SparkSleeve had felt like enough. Now, he doubts himself.

Once all three are standing in the foyer, Breeslin and Wayfare look to Deret and, in sync, point to his SparkSleeve. Deret runs a finger across it to wake up the Adjacent Body Spark Load mode. They all lean in to view the 3D detailed map of each floor of the entire mansion. Not one spark pulse shows up in any room on any of the levels.

Breeslin, suspicious, whispers, "There's no one here?"

Then Deret notices a blinking *RST* in the corner of the digital map. "Hey, check this out." He taps it and up pops a dotted magenta trail that winds throughout the house. He reads the bottom of the image, "*RST. Residual Spark Trail – 24 hours.*"

Their eyes widen, impressed with this new-age feature.

Wayfare adds, "I'd bet all my cloud cash that's Murkemer."

They peer in closer to find a fading blue dotted line.

Breeslin says, "And I bet this is Shroud. Tap on that."

Deret taps on it and reads, "*Residual Spark Trail – 48 hours.*" He looks up at his team. "If so, Shroud hasn't been here for a while. It's just Murkemer."

"Perfect," Wayfare says and starts down the hall, following the trail shown on the map. "We're far more likely to talk sense into the kid than Shroud."

Deret's hope soars at his big brother's words. "You mean, you do plan to try to reason with Murkemer? Give him a chance to make whatever he's done right? Not just take him down?"

Wayfare stops and turns around. "Of course, we are. You said it yourself. He's just a kid. No parents to guide him anymore. He's probably more lost and panicked than anyone."

Breeslin chuckles, "Jeez, rookie, what do you think we are? Some special ops assassin squad? That's not how we roll."

Deret, feeling a little silly, but more just relieved, gives his sheepish grin as Wayfare musses up his hair.

"Come on," says the veteran Catalyst. "Let's see what's going on here, and then we'll worry about how to deal with Murkemer."

When they get to the kitchen, Wayfare grabs a couple cookies from an opened bag lying on the counter.

Breeslin gives him a disapproving look that stops him in motion.

"What?" he asks as he pops a cookie in his mouth.

"This is no time to snack."

"Aw c'mon," he says and points to an opened bag of chips. "You aren't the least bit tempted?"

She rolls her eyes. "Of course, I am." Her eyes flicker to the bag. "Well, I guess they'd just go to waste …"

Wayfare's sky-blue eyes twinkle as she takes the last of the chips and moves on. He waggles an eyebrow at the last few strands of cherry licorice for Deret as he turns to follow Breeslin.

Deret loves licorice just as much as the next guy, but he wraps up the nearly empty bag and stuffs it in his back pocket. He takes in the whole kitchen. The cupboards hang open and scant. He opens the fridge – empty and smelly. All plates and dishes sit tidily in their cupboard. Silverware too. The countertop is littered with crumbs, splotches, and stains. The trash is overflowing with wrappers and pop cans. The walls are bare. There are no windows. A chill runs up Deret's spine. This room is cold.

It's such a starkly different scene than what he would imagine a big, fancy house like this would have as compared to his own home. Deret's mother always has something cooking over the little fire (a fire made from the wood he and his father chopped and stacked together). Or she has something baking in the oven, filling the small rooms with aromas of comfort and closeness. He closes his eyes and lets the visions of home come to him. Fresh, colorful vegetables lie on the counter. Herbs hang to dry. The kitchen window overlooks the yard and barn where he used to play. Tiny, glass figurines of bluebirds sit on the windowsill, diffusing a faint glow of color, and filling the house with ... love.

And it dawns on him. Murkemer has no one to take care of him. He's living lonely and hungry. That is what this kitchen says. He doesn't need a SparkSleeve to tell him that, either.

This realization weighs heavy on him as he joins the others.

They pass through the living area with a wall screen and gaming chair, and then they make their way down a long hallway.

When they find and enter the elevator, Breeslin asks, "We probably shouldn't just barge in wherever this leads to. And I think we should use this "Below" button. If our theory about the Sequioa tree's roots leaking spark is right, we will most likely be heading into the earth. See if that thing can conjure a night cloud."

Wayfare scoffs, "Phht, I doubt a spark device can just go and whip up a night cl…"

"Got it," Deret announces. He taps on the *Bonus Extensions* icon that looks like a fat exclamation point, and sure enough, there's a little dotted-lined cloud symbol that reads *Night Cloud Projection*. He flicks a finger from it to Breeslin, and she disappears completely.

"Skies above," she says in awe.

Jaw-dropped, Wayfare is speechless.

"Now you." Deret flicks a night cloud onto Wayfare. Then he engulfs himself too.

Wayfare notices, "I can still see you both."

Deret checks the SparkSleeve. "As far as I understand this, we should be able see each other *and* anyone else under night cloud cover."

Wayfare's brow bounces, "Well, isn't that convenient."

Breeslin presses the "Below" button. "Here goes."

They pass through layers of thick, gray clouds first. Then they plummet past tree branches, tree trunks, vines, shrubs, and *fwoosh*, right through what looks like solid ground. They pass silt, sand, clay, stone, and finally, *shlunk*, they stop at the bottom.

Ding.

All three of them freeze as the glass tube's doors open. They scan the cavernous room gaping before them.

Soundlessly, ever the operations leader, Breeslin steps out and goes straight to the computers lining the balcony that overlooks the containment pit. All business, she becomes promptly absorbed in what's happening on the displays. Leaving one ice-blade arm weaponized, she softens the other so her nimble fingers can peck away at the touchscreens and keyboards.

Wayfare, SparkSword at the ready, sneaks to an opening on the balcony that takes him down an iron spiral staircase. He starts analyzing the funnel-shaped, slurry-filled pool and manhole-sized pipes sticking out of the cave walls which are dribbling sludge. His eyes lock on the tiny lightning ribbons syphoning up a clear tube jutting out of the center of the pool. His jaw drops as his eyes follow it up, up, overhead to the immense cauldron hanging above.

Deret scans the room for Murkemer. Which doesn't take long. The SparkSleeve shows him. At first, he thinks the spark line leads to a pile of old rags in a dark corner. But soon enough, Deret realizes – no, he *feels* – that it's not rags at all. It's a boy. A young man, rather.

Curled up in a ball, hands over head, rocking back and forth, moaning and groaning, sits Murkemer. Deret can't be sure, but he thinks he hears him saying, "Can't fix it. Can't make it right," over and over again.

Though Deret knows he should exercise extreme caution, he instinctually swipes off his night cloud and calls, "Guys! He's over here!" as he rushes to the young Cloud Master.

Murkemer jolts upright and whips himself around to face the intruders. "Stay back!" he practically cries. A warp of dingy residue creates a barrier around him. He stretches a trembling hand along the wall as he inches his way toward the balcony's railing. His eyes are crazed. His greasy hair is strewn across his tear-streaked face. Deret notices pimples dot his cheek and nose, otherwise, his hood darkens his face.

Murkemer peers below, past the sludge funnel, into the dark depth of the pit that invites him. He could solve all his problems right now. If he just … jumped.

Deret halts in his tracks. His mind races what to do.

"It's too late," Murkemer groans feebly. "I've ruined everything."

Wayfare snaps out of his intrigue at the contraptions in this cave and hollers to Deret, "Wait!" He scrambles up the spiral staircase and retracts his

SparkSword. His night cloud evaporates at a single shake of his head. "Breeslin! Sling him!"

Breeslin whips around and hollers, "Freeze, Murkemer!" Without further warning, she unleashes a spark sling to restrain him, but the murky barrier surrounding him deflects it with ease.

Tears and snot streak Murkemer's face. He shakes his head.

Deret feels the hopeless desperation emanating from him. He says steadily, "Whatever it is, we can help you fix it. Together, we can make it right."

The earnestness in this new Catalyst's voice is enough to crack a sliver in Murkemer's barrier. But it's the words like his father's that force a breath to catch in his throat. The faintest flicker of belief flits across his face.

Deret sees it.

"Look," Deret says, still frozen in place, "I don't know you. And you don't know me. I get it. Honest, I do."

Darkness washes over Murkemer's face again as he resists the temptation to believe. "You have no idea." His bloodshot eyes dance to Breeslin and Wayfare. "No idea what Shroud has made here." He sucks in a ragged breath. "What *I've helped* him make."

Deret tries again. "You're right. We don't know what's going on here. But you can tell us. You can help us make things right."

Wayfare inches his way toward Deret. "Murkemer," he says like he's talking to a frightened animal, "whatever you – or Shroud – have done, we are here to make it right." He slowly nods toward Breeslin, who picks up the cue to disarm and soften the rest of her body. He continues with a tender, crooked smile, "You'd be surprised how amazing we are when we put our heads together." He gives a quick wink to Deret.

Deret's green eyes sparkle, and he mirrors his own crooked smile back.

Breeslin, though she's not very good at this sort of talk-em-off-the-ledge thing – more of a now-listen-here-Bub type – does her best to contribute. "It's true, Murkemer. I've taken a good look at the system, and I think I see what needs to happen."

At that, Wayfare and Deret swing their heads to her along with Murkemer.

"It appears to me, what we've got here is what I'm going to call a Sludge Rogue Rampage."

She says it so matter-of-factly that the others just blink and wait for more.

She takes a deep breath. "Yep. And though I have not dealt with it first hand, I assure you, I have been trained to handle this kind of situation."

More blinking.

"Okay. First, this whole cave is typically referred to as a Containment Cave. Believe it or not, they're not that uncommon." She's kind of winging it, but her audience is rapt. "It's a place where a Cloud Master can collect spark with a neat and orderly system, and conversely, distribute sludge to seek out and collect spark in a regimented manner. They haven't been necessary for ages. I guess the Cloud Council has just figured the sludge system is a well-oiled machine and kind of assumed everything is working properly."

Murkemer scoffs. "The Cloud Council doesn't have a clue what's going on. They're too busy enjoying themselves up there. They don't care about how anything that happens up in Cloud City affects us down here, or anywhere, for that matter."

"Hang on now, Murkemer," Breeslin interrupts, trying to maintain a friendly tone. "They have the Ice Crystal Guard and WISPs like me working hard 24/7 to keep order. And I'll tell you, it is a 24/7 kind of job."

Murkemer makes a face, but he lets her continue.

Breeslin gives Wayfare a frustrated look, but he calmly nods encouragement and asks, "Let's focus on what we have to deal with right now, okay? What's gone wrong with this system, then?"

She purses her lips, redirecting her thoughts back to the matter at hand. "In *this* case, it seems the sludge has become far more sentient than anyone likes to believe it's capable of, and it is *choosing* not to return to the cave to deliver the spark it collects. My best guess is because it's caught spark fever. That's like a sort of frenzy it can develop, like an addiction, if you will, to spark. Spark that can only be generated by things that are, well, alive. Not attractants like this *RALLY* button releases. The tricky part is that it builds up a tolerance to spark, so no matter how much it sucks up, it's never enough to satisfy its craving. It'll always need more spark."

"Whoa," says Deret.

Murkemer lets out a pathetic moan and slumps to the floor again.

At least he's not fixing to jump, Deret figures.

Wayfare peaks both brows at Breeslin like *a-a-a- and the good news is...?*

She's on it. "But!"

Murkemer's moaning stops, but he doesn't lift his head.

"But I see that you, Cloud Master Murkemer, even with your novice experience, have indeed managed to seal up the spark leak from that," she points straight up, "cauldron ... vessel ... thing hanging up there."

He raises his saggy face to look up and says, "Ya. It's just a lever and a couple switches. But that doesn't stop that storm it caused that's raging over Median."

All eyes on Breeslin again. Her brain races to an answer. "Wel-l-l-l ... that's a different problem we're going to fix up real soon. Somehow. But for now, I'd just like to say, nice work."

"Ya," says Deret. "Nice work." Then instinctually, he whips out the mostly empty bag of cherry licorice and extends it, not without caution, to Murkemer."

Again, the earnestness on Deret's face cracks another chink in the young Cloud Master's barrier. Murkemer looks from face to face. Hesitant, he swipes off his invisible armor then reaches for a piece of licorice.

He says with the voice of a child, "You guys really think you can help me?"

The others let out a collective exhale. They look upon him with compassion.

Wayfare assures him, "We can. And that's a fact."

Murkemer lifts one corner of his mouth as he chews.

The kid doesn't look completely convinced, but Wayfare takes it as a win for now. "Let's let the others know you're okay." He taps his comm piece. "Sparkslingers," he waits.

Cirissa is the first to reply. Thunderclaps in the background break up their connection, "Go ahead, Wayfare. What is your status?"

"We have Murkemer," he pauses and looks to his teammates then to Murkemer, "and he's going to be fine."

* * *

Standing around the comm console at WISP headquarters, having just gotten Wayfare's update on Murkemer and the plan to progress, Snippet taps the tabletop screen to close out all but Captain Breeslin. "So, all we have to do is intercept Cloud Master Castella on her 'super secret' mission, convince her to help us instead, then track down Shroud together?"

"That's about the size of it," Breeslin answers back. "I have full faith in you guys. Make it happen. That sequoia's spark storm has got to get doused before it destroys Median. We're headed for the Day farm now. They need all the help they can get to hold back the sludge too."

Tuft salutes the screen and gestures for the others to do so. "On it, Captain."

Breeslin, though confident and in control as usual, lets a flicker of worry mixed with full appreciation transmit across her Crystaline features. "I believe in you guys," she says. "WISP Captain Breeslin, out."

The tabletop screen fades to black.

Tuft tips her head, making her crystal ponytail clink. "Finding Castella is one thing. But convincing her to help us? That's another."

Tygr offers, "I bet Cloud Hounds could track her down in no time."

Snippet power points at him, "We'll start with that. Didn't you say you have a buddy at the Cloud Hound Kennel who owes you a favor?"

Tygr looks at Jink and elbows him with a chuckle. "Sure did. Jink and I got him out of a tight spot once. The dude's got a bit of a gambling problem at the track. Shady stuff he's into. We saved his neck from some pretty dangerous loan sharks wanting their money back."

"Whatever it takes," Snippet waves a hand for them to stop before they share too much. "I think we're better off not knowing the details."

Jink smirks, "Right," and elbows his buddy back.

Tuft rolls her eyes and shakes her head. "Okay, fine. We track Castella with Cloud Hounds. How are we supposed to convince her to abandon her commitment to Shreddard and Makryl to join us?"

"We need to offer her something better than whatever they've offered her, which I'm quite certain is just cloud credit. But Castella doesn't need that. She doesn't crave money. Running her mercenaries on special missions is pure entertainment for her. I am banking on the idea that she is actually looking for thrill. An adrenaline rush more than cash or credit."

Tuft tips her head and says, "Okay, I can see that. It makes sense. But what do we have to offer her that will give her that?"

"I have a theory. It came to me back at Sky Steed Stables."

"A theory? About what?"

"Dusk Dragons."

Silent stares.

Snippet's voice pitches higher, "Don't you think she'd leap at the chance to track down a flight of Dusk Dragons?"

"Um, sure. Who wouldn't?" says Jink, always up for a good chase. "But do we really have time to go hunting for an impossible-to-find flight? Remember, camo mist?"

"They're not impossible to find. Mysterious, yes, but not impossible. Wayare has a baby one right now. That means some mother dragon in the flight is missing one from her brood. I'll bet they're restless because of that. If we find them, we can help get their baby back safely."

Tuft, who's been very quiet up to now, says with great thought, "You know, Snip is on to something here. My beacon is designed to search through the thickest fog. Possibly even Dusk Dragon mist. And we'll hopefully have Cloud Hounds too."

"Thank you!" Snippet says exasperated.

Tuft nods slowly and goes on. "I mean, and we all know how powerful an entire flight of Dusk Dragons can be."

"Yah," says Jink. "When they feel threatened, they can douse pretty much any atmospheric phenomenon."

"Which would come in superbly handy in putting out the sequoia storm," adds Tygr.

Jink argues, "It's not like you can just wield a flight of Dusk Dragons like a weapon."

Tygr flexes his icy muscles. "I could handle them."

"It's true," says Snippet, not dismayed, "they can't be controlled like an army. But we have one of their babies, remember? That's got to count for something."

Tuft, a voice of reason, says, "Ya, like to tick them off. And, by the way, *we* don't have one of their babies. Wayfare does. And Silva is the one who captured it."

Tygr reminds them, "She found it. Not captured. And that sure doesn't happen every day. So something's up with that. What do you suppose went down with the baby's flight that stirred them up so much, they lost one?"

Tuft bites her lip as her cranial orb pulses hard. "Call me crazy …"

"You're crazy," says Tygr then shrugs innocently at the glares he gets.

Snippet encourages her teammate on, "Go ahead, Tuft. What's on your mind?"

Tuft goes on. "Call me crazy, but I have this hunch, more of a nagging feeling," she points to the glowing sphere in her head, "that if we find Shroud, we find the Dusk Dragon flight."

Snippet affirms the suspicion. "It's not crazy. I've flirted with the idea too. It's all just too coincidental."

"Well," Jink smacks his long, bladed hands together, sending sparks tinging, "hunches, flirting, whatever you want to call it, I say it's time we scud outa here and make things happen!"

Tygr is all over that. "We'll get the Cloud Hounds and rendezvous back at Sky Steed Stables. Pick Silva's brain about that baby Dusk Dragon."

Chapter 23

Nebuls and Stormlins and Taverns

Shroud sits on a chariot made of shredded stratus. Where his dark cloak ends and the chariot begins is a blur. A small army of Nebul slaves he's taken from the Drizzle Fields surround him. Drizzo, his ex, won't mind him *borrowing* a few of the cons that had been sentenced there for all sorts of sordid crimes.

It's not his fault, after all, that her Stormlins, the ones who actually run the Drizzle Field operations, are easily bought with a fake promise or two of being given their own freedom from that wench of a Cloud Master some day. An icky chill runs up his spine at the thought of spending as many hours as he had during their brief romp of a relationship. He shudders thinking of that dingy shack, she calls her Personal Spa. Getting to know the grounds and staff – it served its purpose now.

He hovers just outside his own misty mansion. A dense fog covers the grounds completely, like an enormous night cloud. And it truly is enormous, for it also creates a canopy around Loom, from her gargantuan sun hat down to her rolled stockinged feet and flipflops.

Dozens of Nebuls on scud clouds drift around her to make sure her spark shackles are still holding. The current from each shackle snakes up through her skyscraper body, all the way up to her flying saucer sun hat. This keeps her under control. It would do no good to have her anger at being kidnapped unleash a Stormhulk at this point in the game. He has special plans for that once he gets near Cloud City and the Cloud Council Sky Room.

The Nebuls are pathetic, really, but one must make the most of one's resources. Shroud knows he can get them to do anything if it means getting off the drizzle fields, if even for a short time.

The threat of being sent to the backbreaking work of dredging muck and wringing sludge from it has always been an excellent motivator. This is the reason Median, sad little Median, hasn't seen the sun in generations. The Cloud Council approved it long ago. They declared the drizzle fields a "perfectly acceptable rehabilitation program for wrong-doers." Criminals are sentenced to work there until they have "learned their lesson" and "promise to change their ways," but the inmates soon learn they are slaves, and they will never leave. And each of them, one day, will cower and shrivel where they stand and turn into a shredded cloud being, a Nebul, neither alive nor dead, just a shadow of their former existence.

Of course, the Cloud Council doesn't know *this*. Shroud was put in charge of a rather distasteful, but necessary, job. They all looked away feeling good about themselves for "ensuring the safety of law-abiding Cloud City citizens," and they left him to deal with the ugliness that such a prison requires. No questions. No rules. Just what the Nimbostratus Cloud Master wants.

He cracks an electric ribbon from the Bolt Blaster at no one in particular, for doing nothing in particular. He simply likes how it feels to be in charge.

"Harness the beasts!" he commands.

The Nebuls, electrified whips in hand, trudge to the edge of the grounds where a popping, snapping fence made from a single lightning ribbon awaits them. In the darkness beyond the fence, through a soupy veil, glow yellow eyes. Many, many eyes. The Nebuls hesitate at the eerie sight, but Shroud sends another lash of lightning to spur them on. As they inch nearer, that nearly imperceptible part of them that is still alive is afraid.

The murky ground rumbles. The eyes narrow.

Then, just as one Nebul takes one step too close, out of the darkness, with a vicious screech, rears a towering, full-grown Dusk Dragon. Without thinking, the Nebul guards himself with one arm, accidentally lashing his whip at its chest. The connection is sharp and effective. The dragon falls to the ground with a flump. The whip maintains constant connection and the Nebul flicks it and twists it until it fully harnesses the beast. Its eyes sputter orange flecks, giving it a look of the devil, but the sounds coming from deep inside its broad chest echo a sad, sighing moan.

Something he once remembers being called an *ache* festers in the Nebul's heart, but he only knows he must follow orders now, so he climbs onto the dragon's back and rides it over the fence into the field where Shroud awaits. The Cloud Master's hood tips down, signaling the rest to follow suit.

Shroud listens to the struggle and capture of the remaining dozen or so Dusk Dragons. It was nothing but fate when he happened across the flight on his way to his Nimbostratus Sector after that fun he'd had with the Cloud Council. He quite enjoyed the challenge of testing out the capabilities of his Bolt Blaster on such a unique subject as these. And they served their purpose well, hiding him in plain sight at his very own mist mansion.

It's a shame that little one got away. That does make for one restless flight, especially that female that came out first. Must be the little one's mother.

A twitch of concern makes Shroud suck in through his yellow teeth like picking at an annoying bit of food stuck there. But no matter. His Bolt Blaster has managed them all just fine.

As each one comes forth onto the field, a weight sinks low and deep inside his mind. It pulls his shoulders down and makes his head so heavy, he takes his hood off to lighten the load. It feels so familiar, this weight. His face sags like ashen, melting wax. And for a fleeting moment, he doubts his plan. When just moments ago, he embraced the surge power and control coursing through him, now ...

No. He shakes his head, making his few strands of hair flop lifelessly from one side to the other. This is his purpose! He *will* take his army of Nebuls and Dusk Dragons to Cloud City, rain down his wrath upon it with the uncontestable power of the Bolt Blaster, seize control, and, once and for all, show them how to rule the sky.

* * *

"You want me to do what?"

Turns out, Snippet and Tuft didn't need Cloud Hounds to find Cloud Master Castella at all. The WISP team learned from Tygr's "buddy" at Cloud Hound Kennels that everyone in "their kind of circle" knows Cloud Master Castella. Whenever she's given a "super secret, covert" mission, she kicks it off by taking her team straight to Tropo Tavern to get their "mission on."

The sky bar overlooks a trumble between none other than Cottin and Puffin Fairweather. Snippet and Tuft sit at the edge of their seats, looking out into the arena. Castella whoops and hoots into the open sky at the ruckus going on over the railing. She bounces and flips her dentures as she watches.

Snippet, too frustrated, gestures to Tuft to give it a try.

Tuft, always one to get to know her target audience – friend or foe – takes in the whole scene.

The sky bar is bustling in a sort of mid to high class kind of way. Pink and blue drinks are served on trays by a wide array of sector types. From Crystalines to Mezzanines, it is a proverbial melting pot establishment. Castella's mercenaries, though they look like total biker thugs, hang out casually at the same table like they totally belong with the upper class and haven't ever once in their lives done anything remotely illegal or even accidentally shady in exchange for cloud credit. Everyone is smiling and having a good time.

"Bartender!" Tuft hails. "Can I get a round of Efferfizz for me and my friend here?"

Snippet gapes at her.

"What? You'll like it."

Castella, now standing up and pumping her arms, is not paying any attention to them.

Snippet carefully looks around and speaks so only Tuft can hear, barely. "If the Cloud Hounds can track the Dusk Dragon flight for us, what exactly do we need Castella for, anyway? We need to hustle. The guys are already on their way back to Silva's with the pack."

Tuft says back, "Numbers, Snip. I, personally have never tried to convince a bunch of dragons to douse a storm. We need Skybounds with guts." She gestures vaguely to the thugs. "Besides, I'm trying to help us fit in. You know, get her to like us and maybe listen to our proposal as soon as this trumble round is over."

"Ugh," Snippet slumps back in her chair.

The drinks come and Tuft passes one to Snippet. They both take long sips. Snippet's eyes light up.

"Oh my, that is pretty tasty."

"See?"

The more fizzy bubbles they drink up, the lighter Snippet's mood gets. Before the glass is half empty, both WISPs are on their feet, cheering and whooping, right alongside Castella. At the very end of the trumble, Cottin slams the head clean off of Puffin's cloud dolphin. Castella gets so worked up, she takes Tuft's shoulders and shakes her like a Christmas present. They all laugh so hard they have to flop down into their seats.

Castella swipes back all the stray grays that have flown out of her bun. With a huge grin, she nods approval at the two WISPs with her. "So, what can I do for you two?"

Tuft cuts off Snippet, who looks like she's ready to get straight to business, and says, "First, bartender! Let's get another round."

Cloud Master Castella laughs, "Ha! Well, whatever it is, you had me at *bartender*!"

Snippet and Tuft share a smile that, as they simultaneously turn to the Cloud Master, morphs into a have-we-got-a-deal-for-you grin.

Chapter 24

Flood

Never in all his life (albeit a mere 17 years) did Murkemer ever imagine he would be flying on a moon mare with a Catalyst to go try to save a bunch of Earthbounds. And as Visa buffets the storm, even though they're fully enclosed inside Deret's spark bubble, he allows her movement rock him into a lulled state of mind. He hasn't felt this way since, well, since he lost his parents.

When they breech the cloud deck and swoop down over the Day farm, the scene before them is bleak. Hard rain obscures their view, but they can see the Halo 500 patrols the south perimeter on autopilot. Deret points to the little house, and even though it's under feet of water, his heart warms at the sight of it. To think, both he and Wayfare grew up in there, just in different decades.

Thunder and lightning clap incessantly. Breeslin says into her sapphire comm, "This is nuts!"

Deret says, "I think Murk and Visa and I should sweep the perimeter. Get a look at the whole picture." Though he is aching to see his parents, figuring out how to keep them (and all of Median's residents) safe is his number one priority.

Breeslin replies, "Agreed. Don't linger out there." A deafening peel of lightning cuts her off. "And try not to get obliterated."

Deret releases his spark bubble from Breeslin and Windy as Visa curls away. Windy snorts and tucks his head down as he gallops toward the barn.

Drift's voice comes through the comm loud and clear, "Welcome to the party! It's about time you got here."

Wayfare brightens at the sound of his friend's burly voice. "We've been a little busy. But we're here now. What needs doing?"

He and Sneak fly close behind Breeslin and Windy as they approach the huge and ancient barn, high on its hill. Drift and Cirissa stand at its spark-shielded entrance.

Cirissa, glowing with her Crystaline shine as usual, despite the storm, says to Wayfare just before he lands, "You have some friends who would like to see you," and points an elegant hand toward the north perimeter fence.

Wayfare squints to search for what she's pointing to. Amid the pelting rain and sporadic, ear-splitting lightning touch downs, he finally sees them. Father Owl and his family. His heart soars at the sight. Even Sneak senses his elation and flaps his leathery wings harder. They careen to the Owl family close enough to see that each one is zapping sludge as it attempts to ooze through the spark barrier.

Startled at the sight of a Dusk Dragon, the owls hold up, but only for a second as Wayfare's head pops up over Sneak's neck cape, and they recognize his long coattails flapping in the wind. Sneak rumbles a friendly, nearly-subsonic purr.

"Hoo hoo hoooo," says Father Owl then promptly zaps a sludge finger poking through.

Wayfare laughs, but it feels dangerously close to tears, "I see that. And your whole family can do it too!"

The little owlets, gliding close to their mother, see they have Wayfare's attention. They zoom ahead along the perimeter, look back to make sure he's watching, and shoot spark beams straight out of their eyes at a weak spot.

"Hodee hoot hoo?" they chime in unison.

Wayfare claps his hands together. "I did see that! You two are impressive."

Mother Owl calls them back, but they stall, wanting to show off some more for Wayfare.

"Do as your mother says. Off you go." Wayfare eyes Mother Owl and nods. He swells with pride at this resilient family.

His SparkBit pings. Mother Owl's spark levels are low, so he cranks it up and sends her a spark boost that gets her back up to 100%.

She swoops over her owlets, sheltering them from the storm with her revived spark shield, and they continue to maintain the spark barrier.

Wayfare pats Sneak on the shoulder. His Dusk Dragon grunts approval, and they glide back to the barn.

To the west, beyond the barn's high hill, Deret and Murkemer scan the land for breeches in the spark perimeter. It's a wonder Demeara and Garrin Day have been able to keep this spark shield so strong for so long. Deret's childhood makes so much more sense now. He's been living the life of a Catalyst all along, raised by retired Catalysts.

The water in the field is rising at an exponential rate. Deret can see it inching up the hill that the barn sits atop. It's already reached the little house's windows. Soon, the rushing current will wash his home away entirely. The little glass figurines peer out the kitchen window.

Deret says, "I can't let it take the house."

Murkemer asks, "Why? It's just a house."

Deret knows this. Boards and nails and glass. It's all replaceable. "But ..." his voice quavers as he stares back at the little figurines trying to shine so hard for him, "... it's not just a house. It's my home."

Though Murkemer doesn't fully understand, he can tell how important saving this little building is to Deret. And he wants to help. He truly feels a deep, genuine desire to help this young Catalyst. He scans the landscape and thinks hard for a possible solution. Valleys, slopes, flat fields.

Then he sees it. A point beyond the high hill that swoops down suddenly and is met with a far-reaching slope on the other side. It reminds him (minus the raging storm) of his days as a child when his dad would take him out to teach him the ways of mist and fog in order to better understand the intricacies of their Stratus Sector. He would show him where cloud vapors liked to gather in the cool, low places until the temperature would rise then make it wisp up into the overcast cloud deck.

Murkemer wonders.

"Deret," he says, "What if we route the water to that gully behind the barn with a spark trench?"

"A spark trench?"

"Yah. My dad used to show me all sort of ways the land slopes to contain stray stratus clouds. I would think it works the same for water."

The possibilities of this idea cautiously creep into Deret's mind. "Make our own lake?"

"That's what I'm thinking," Murkemer replies, hope saturating his words.

"Let's head back and see what the others think."

Visa banks hard back to the barn and lands at a delicate trot. She carefully delivers her riders at the protected entrance.

When Murkemer and Deret hop off, they can see all the people spread out, clustered, roaming, lying down, sitting quietly, or visiting normally. In the midst of it all, Demeara and Garrin Day, like bumblebees, hover and stop and check and fuss over everyone. Children's feet romp overhead in the hay loft. Deret's SparkSleeve shows normal readings throughout.

Demeara is adjusting a quilt over someone's shoulders when Garrin sees Deret and touches her arm tenderly.

Deret just stands there, a little overwhelmed at how much he's been through in so little time, and the sight of his parents looking at him with outstretched arms. It's almost too much to bear. Swiftly, they move in for a family embrace that Deret will tuck away inside the depths of his mind, of his heart, forever.

Murkemer slinks back and pulls his hoodie over his head. "This is an awful lot of people." His voice is shaky. "I'm not used to being around so many people."

Peeling away from his parents, slightly red-eyed, Deret senses Murkemer's anxiety is very real and equally well-founded. The young Cloud Master probably has *never* been around so many people, cooped up in that mansion most of his life.

"It's okay, Murk." Deret extends an arm toward him. "Mom, Dad, I'd like you to meet Cloud Master Murkemer. My new friend."

Murkemer puts his guard up. People who meet him for the first time usually take one look at his slouchy, unkempt appearance and form their opinion about him. And it's typically not a good one.

Demeara's eyes show a hint of surprise. *A Cloud Master? Here?* But she adjusts her simple shawl, smooths the stray hairs that have fallen out of her pulled-back hair, and reaches out to welcome him. "I am very pleased to meet you," she says as she gently clasps his hand in both of hers.

Murkemer feels her warmth as she dips her head a bit to look him directly in the eyes, despite his hoodie nearly covering them.

"P...Pleased to meet you too."

Garrin reaches out as well, "What an honor. A Cloud Master. Right here in our ..." He glances around and suddenly feels the need to straighten his flannel shirt and pick a piece of straw off his sleeve, "... well, in our barn." His eyes twinkle in the same way Murkemer has noticed Deret's do. "Welcome."

Murkemer allows himself a shy smile, but Deret can tell he still feels terribly awkward.

"Let's find the others," Deret offers.

Garrin says, "They're out back. They're waiting for you." He looks to Visa and says, "Windy and Sneak are back there too."

Demeara adds, "A cozy open stall awaits you, Miss Visa." She does a sort of curtsy.

Deret looks at them surprised.

"What? You think this is the first time we've seen a Moon Mare? Think again, Son." Garrin pauses then adds, "Although the Dusk Dragon ... now *that* was a first."

Demeara's eyes dance in agreement.

Deret shakes his head, amazed. What else doesn't he know about his parents? He looks forward to finding out.

He puts a confident hand on his new friend's shoulder, encouraging Murkemer on. As they make their way to the back entrance down the long barn aisle, the townspeople greet him. A wave of a hand here. A "Hey Deret!" there. It is so good to see the people of Median safe.

One particularly familiar voice calls out, "Deret the Doubtless! It's about time."

Widow Shay, a little less spry than when he left her, waddles from the group of other Sparkslingers just outside. She comes at him with wide stretched arms that smoosh him into a hug. She sets him at arm's length and scrutinizes his face. "Hm. You wear the weight of a Catalyst well, m'boy." She pats his cheek. "Yes, you wear it well. Come."

"Widow," Deret stops her, "You've been working too hard. My SparkSleeve shows your levels are ..."

"Pshhtt," she hisses at his new spark device. "I don't need that contraption to tell me that." She waves it off and motions toward Murkemer too. "You must be the esteemed Cloud Master Murkemer." She leans in, more intimately than Murkemer prefers, and says with the tenderest tone her crackly voice can manage, "I knew your father, rest his aura. Yes, Cloud Master Slurry was one of the good ones."

"Um, thank you." It sounds like a question, but Murkemer means it.

She bobs her head happily. "Ha! Little WISP Breeslin out here tells us how you were brave enough to show that scummuck Shroud what's what. *And* that you stopped the spark leak under the sequoia!"

"But it didn't stop the storm."

"Not to worry, not to worry. Come, we'll get this all sorted out, one way or another."

They step out the back where the other Sparkslingers gathered around a fire await them. The storm beats at the spark bubble covering them as well as a lean-to shelter.

Bounding from the group comes Sheena, spark bubbles streaming from her fur. *Deret!* She cries and goes to hurtle herself into Deret's arms, but she skids to a stop when she sees Murkemer. *Whoa.*

Deret tells her, "It's okay, Princess. This is Cloud Master Murkemer. He's one of the good ones."

She looks at Deret then at Murkemer, not without suspicion. She steps toward the Cloud Master slowly. Her nose is outstretched, working, and wiggling at the air around him.

Murkemer, feeling awkward at being scrutinized by a Frost Fox, looks to Deret for a little help.

Deret just shrugs innocently.

Then Murkemer remembers seeing Sheena at the Cloud Council meeting, and an idea comes to him. He pats the pockets of his black lounge pants.

Sheena, interested now, sits curtly, ears perked, head ever-so-slightly tipped.

From his pocket he reveals two peanut butter-filled pretzel nuggets and a lint-covered piece of cherry licorice. He stoops down and offers her choice of either snack.

She eyes him and the treats before she stands up. She steps closer and sniffs both options back and forth. Just the very tip of her tail wags. She gives him a hard look then snatches up both the licorice and one of the peanut butter pretzel nuggets. As she trots off, sparkles popping from her flip-flopping tail, Murkemer stands upright and pops the remaining pretzel nugget in his mouth. He gives Deret a high-brow and an elbow bump.

Deret shakes his head and chuckles. "You charmer."

Visa, who's been waiting patiently at Deret's side this whole time, nickers when she sees Windy lying comfortably in an open stall. He nickers back.

Deret pats her neck and says, "Go have a rest, Visa. I'd say you've earned it. Again."

She nuzzles his hand then trots to her own prepared space.

Sneak has chosen to curl up behind Wayfare, sitting on the ground near the fire. The Catalyst twirls a long piece of grass in his fingers, as though resting against a Dusk Dragon is the most natural thing in the world. Flashes of lightning mixed with dancing firelight makes for quite a scene.

A distinguished voice says in his mind, *Ah, the other Day boy.* Fillip's glittering emerald eyes catch Deret's attention right next to Wayfare. The Shadow Cat fades from camo-mode into view. His silky brown, green, and orange coat swirls. *Come. Sit. We have much to discuss.* Projecting a single strand of spark toward the barn, he quietly and slowly closes the great sliding door. *The people of Median need not be in on this conversation.* As it slides, Demeara and Garrin Day look up and knowingly nod.

Breeslin pings her WISP team. "They'll ping in soon. Let's get started. Is everyone up to speed now?"

"I believe so," says Cirissa.

"Good. Deret, Wayfare, what did you see out there. What's our status on the grounds?"

Wayfare goes first, "The Owl family is diligent and tireless. I gave Mother Owl a boost since she kind of has to do double duty, slinging spark *and* covering the owlets. But they're an amazing asset out there. If one good thing has come from that spark leak, turning the owls into Sparkslingers is definitely it."

Murkemer winces at that. There shouldn't have *ever been* a spark leak in the first place.

Deret nudges him to speak up next, but Drift interrupts.

"Let's not forget my little beauty out there doing her part." His face beams with pride as he points to the glow surrounding the Halo 500 cruising along the far perimeter, flawlessly zapping encroaching sludge. "That machine's got no stop."

Cirissa nods her approval. Then she looks to Murkemer and Deret.

Deret nudges Murkemer again, but the Cloud Master can't get a squeak out.

Deret saves him. "Well, the water is getting high. The house is going to just get swept away eventually, and who knows how long it'll take to reach the barn."

Murmurs of agreement flutter around the fire.

"So," he goes on, looking straight at Murkemer for a little help, "we, uh, more like Murk here, has this idea that I think just might work."

Murkemer gulps. So many eyes looking at him. He closes his own eyes and listens for his father's voice. *Make this right, son. Fix it.* "I ... I mean my dad, you know, Cloud Master Slurry ..." He dares open his eyes.

Nods of encouragement urge him on.

"Well, as I remembered some of our trips down here together, he showed me a lot about the lay of the land and how it works with the forces of nature, and ..." He gulps and takes a steadying breath, "... and I think if we trench to that valley out there, because it's really more like a basin, and if we were to divert most of the flowage to that area, we could create a ..." Here he hesitates, but there's no turning back now. "... a lake. Actually, if I'm seeing it right," he takes off his hood and meets the group with full eye contact, "it'd make a pretty *nice* lake."

Deret whips his head from Murkemer to the others. His excitement about this idea is hard to miss. "Whatdya think?" his voice almost cracks. "A-a-a-nd," he adds, "if I'm reading the Sludge chapter in *Cloud City* correctly, it really hates water, well, larger surfaced bodies of water, that is."

No one seems to know how to respond to this. Drift nudges Wayfare with a "What?" look, to which Wayfare answers back with a "you-*know*-I-never-studied" look.

Deret blows out, "Has *no one* read the book?" As his eyes scroll through the entire Sludge chapter within the reaches of his mind, he can't help but shake his head, just a little. Then, "Here it is. *Sludge favors a low, dry or, at the very least, stable ground. It's natural habitat, therefore, is typically woodlands and valleys. This is, however, not saying it cannot survive over water. If forced for one reason or another, to reside for any period of time upon an open water surface, it's state of mobile fog is immediately transformed to that of vertical, rising mist wisps, quite incapable of lateral movement, and, consequently, rendered useless for sapping spark.*" Deret's eyes refocus on his audience.

Wayfare looks at Drift. Drift looks at Widow Shay. Widow looks at Fillip. Fillip looks at Breeslin. Breeslin looks at Cirissa. Cirissa looks at Sheena, who pant-smiles.

Cirissa lifts her chin, impressed. "I'll admit, I have only heard myths about such a thing, but I believe, if it is true, that just might work, young Cloud Master." She asks the others, "Does anyone here object to Murkemer and Deret diverting the water?"

Fillip says, *I had thought of forcing the water away through use of spark, but my attention has been needed more urgently elsewhere. Something more permanent, like a trench, as you've suggested, would only require the initial earth-moving spark power, but after that, the land would take care of itself.* His emerald eyes twinkle. *Let us make it happen.*

Murkemer's eyes shine as he thinks, *One more step toward making things right.*

Indeed, Fillip's voice echoes in Murkemer's mind.

Murkemer, surprised his own thoughts were heard, looks at the Shadow Cat. At first, it feels like a violation of privacy, but as he notes no malicious intent in Fillip's tone, he realizes it feels kind of ... nice, someone looking after him like that.

"As soon as that trench is cut to the basin, we'll need to somehow force it, all of it over the lake that forms." Breeslin's eyes reveal the workings of potential battle strategies. A ping from her WISP team brings her focus back. She taps the small, clear tabletop. "WISP team, it's good to see you. Report."

Snippet, Tuft, Tygr and Jink all appear. Sky Steed Stables sprawls in the backdrop. The sky is so stark blue and the sun so bright, especially in contrast to the darkness the storm has perpetuated on Earth, Breeslin flips her visor down.

Snippet explains their new alliance with Cloud Master Castella.

Breeslin warns, "That's good, but keep your eyes on her. Always remember a mercenary's allegiance only goes to the highest bidder."

"Oh, we are all over that, Captain," Tuft assures her. "But when she heard she would have opportunity to track down an entire Dusk Dragon flight ..."

Sneak lifts his head at the mention of his kind.

Thunder booms.

"... let's just say, cloud credit meant very little to her."

Breeslin interrupts her, "What? I must not have heard you right. The storm. Tuft, I thought you said you're going to track down a Dusk Dragon flight."

Sneak stands up now.

Snippet speaks up. "You heard correctly, Captain."

Breeslin, wide-eyed, gives a silent, can-you-please-explain head wiggle.

Snippet, Tuft, Jink and Tygr take turns going through the details of their theory. All the while, Sneak prances in place all antsy-pants.

Wayfare offers, "Well, I think it's safe to say that Sneak, here, thinks this is a brilliant idea." He looks the dragon in the eye for confirmation.

Sneak sits smartly and snorts out a puff of wispy spark, making the fire flames woosh up to the spark bubble ceiling.

Breeslin attempts a recap, "So, you're going to use Cloud Hounds to track the Dusk Dragon flight, which, you believe, will lead you straight to Shroud." So far, she is met with heads bobbing. "Then, with the help of Castella and her mercenary thugs, you plan to disarm and apprehend Shroud, befriend the flight, and drive said flight to the sequoia spark storm to douse it..." She pauses in case anyone wants to add or correct her, but she's met with more head bobbing. "... then come back here to help us save Median from the sludge's rogue rampage, and safely reunite Sneak with his family."

Snippet bites her lip. Hearing it all put together like that makes it sound a lot less possible than it seemed in her head just moments before. But Tuft, Jink and Tygr show unwavering commitment as they wait for her to answer.

"Yep. I mean, yes, Captain. That's about the size of it." Confident nod.

Lightning cracks overhead with a blinding flash. Then another a little farther away.

"Well, then," Breeslin looks to the others, especially Cirissa, for consensus, which is clearly evident on everyone's face, "I guess, you'd better get to it.

More lightning and thunderclaps.

Widow Shay breaks from the circle and walks to the edge of the spark shield. The storm seems to be amping up.

Breeslin, distracted now by the violent weather, quickly dismisses her WISPs. "Good luck, and hurry! WISP Captain Breeslin, out."

"Oh dear," Widow Shay murmurs. "Drift, hun. You need to see this."

Drift scowls and rushes over to her. What he sees crumples him to his knees.

"No-o-o-o!" he cries.

The others scramble to his side. Astonishment floods their faces.

The Halo 500 lies, belly up, in flames.

The perimeter, where it had been patrolling, is breached. A deluge of inky sludge gushes through the fence line, stronger than ever.

"It's *feeding* off the storm!" Wayfare hollers, but no one hears him.

They've all shot into the rain to fight the sludge. Cirissa and Breeslin suit up in full ice armor. Cirissa jets away, Sheena yapping at her heels.

Breeslin whistles for her Storm Pony.

Windy, however, is already on his way. No one is going to leave him out of a fight! As he gallops toward her, his own ice armor slides into place. Then he scoops Breeslin up and hurls himself into the air.

Wayfair and Drift come to a sliding halt as they try to follow. Water surges across their path. They charge in, ready to swim for it. Fillip runs past them. His paws hardly touch the surface of the coursing water. Wayfare and Drift have to stop once they're waist-deep. The current is just too strong.

Wayfare whistles for Sneak. The Dusk Dragon swoops in, scoops both Catalysts up, and hovers above the water.

Wayfare calls to his little brother at the crest of the hill, "Deret, Murkemer! Get that trench in! Go! Go!"

"But we need Fillip," Deret hollers, but the wind snatches the words away, and he can see Fillip already at the fence beating back the writhing sludge with his laser eyes.

Deret watches them join the others. Widow Shay stands with him, watching them go.

Visa strides to Deret's side. He sets a hand on her shoulder to steady himself.

We fight? she asks.

"Not that battle, Visa." He runs his fingers through his hair. "I have a different fight I have to help lead." Knowing her history of being enslaved in the Drizzle Fields and the shear terror the idea of dredging earth to make this trench will be for her, there's no way he's going to ask her to help in the back-breaking labor it will take. He looks her straight in the eye. "You are going to sit this one out. Keep watch over things here, okay?"

Visa gazes back at Deret with such burning depth – as only a Moon Mare can – that it penetrates his very soul. Then she whispers, soft and low, into his mind. *No. And that is that.*

She turns, swings her head toward him with a well-are-you-coming look, and snorts daintily as she raises her head a little higher.

His heart swells with pride at her courage. He grins his sideways grin. What's a Catalyst to do? After all, that is that.

Holding her headscarf tightly, Widow Shay looks at Deret, Murkemer, and the Moon Mare. Serious thought deepens the creases around her eyes, and she marches straight past the boys, opens the barn door, and says impatiently, "C'mon. We've got work to do."

Visa keeps step with the spry old woman. Deret and Murkemer scramble after them as Widow shoves past all the people inside, making her way to the other end.

Deret, with Murkemer close in his wake, says, "Excuse me, pardon us, coming through." He tries to maintain an air of nothing-to-worry-about-here-folks, but he can see the concern on some of their faces.

These people of Median. People with families and jobs and lives. People he's known since childhood. People struggling to recover from a lifetime of heavily muted spark, wanting nothing out of life – and getting nothing. Before him, milling about or sitting around, the people of Median are slowly finding their Want for the first time in a generation. And though some are old, and some are young, many of them now are looking at Deret like ...

"What can we do to help?" a voice asks from behind.

Deret stops and turns around. It is his father's voice, but at his side stand Londa Lane, the trolley driver, and Joseph Sombrine, the department store owner, with the same look on their faces.

"Dad," Deret has to think for a second what he can ask of these people, "are you sure? You've all been through a lot."

Londa steps forward. "Put us to work, Deret. I feel like I've got ten years' worth of spark building up inside me. Let me use it!"

Joseph nods his balding head emphatically and starts rolling up his neat, white shirtsleeves. "It's true. I've never felt stronger. But more so, I've never *wanted* to help *do* something so bad in years."

Garrin tips his head and says, "Put us to work, Son."

Deret and Murkemer look at each other. They both hesitate, not knowing what to do.

Widow Shay hollers from the entrance, "Deret the Doubtless, you always know what to do!"

And that is all he needs.

Spark glints in Deret's eyes. He sets his jaw and squares his shoulders. "Gather every able-bodied person. Find all the shovels and tools you've got stashed in this big-old barn, then meet us at the base of the hill." He gestures for Murkemer to follow him out the door but turns back to his father and says, "We've got work to do."

Chapter 25

Cloud Hounds

Meanwhile, back up in the clouds, the WISPs and Castella with her mercs arrive at Sky Steed Stables.

Silva Starling, bright as ever, beams, "Welcome! What an honor to have a Cloud Master visit!"

Castella, crinkling her way to the Stable Master, waves off the formalities then stops in her tracks when she sees Jink and Tygr come out of the barn. "What are those?"

Jink and Tygr hold two leashes each, and the dogs on them neither look nor act like the Cloud Hounds from the race track or the Ice Crystal Guard's Canine Unit.

Tygr clears his throat and says sheepishly, "They're … um … Cloud Hounds." His grin does not match his apologetic eyes. "See, my buddy, the one that works at Cloud Hound Kennel and owed me a favor for saving his gambling butt once upon a time, well, it turns out he doesn't really have any access to the racing or working hounds. They kind of, I guess, don't trust him with the high buck packs. He, actually, kind of lost his job there and got relocated."

Castella, Snippet and Tuft cross their arms awaiting more explanation.

Jink jumps in to save his buddy. "*But*, as you can see, he was able to hook us up with these beauties here." He pauses, gauging whether or not he should say more.

Snippet has to ask. "Where did he get 'relocated' to? Where are these from?"

Tygr hangs his head and blurts, "The Cloud Pound," then cringes, bracing for an onslaught of complaints.

Instead, at least from Snippet and Tuft, he's met with an "aww" in stereo. He brightens when they tip their heads then swoop in to fawn over the four oddball mutts.

One is about the size of a rat after it's had a big meal. It's got a mangy, homeless look to it and a nervous shiver. It's fur sheds scraps of stratus cloud as it shakes.

Jink notices the girls seem to think "pathetic" is adorable. *Score for that!*

"Ohmygosh, what's this one's name?" coos Tuft.

Jink points out, "That's Strat. He's been on Cloud City streets for years. Wily little thing. Tough as a scud to catch." He gestures to the stratus fur which moves like there's a breeze, but there's no breeze. "He can use his coat for kind of a camouflage. But his real trick is neutralizing excess spark. Watch."

He takes Strat out front. The little dog looks up expectantly.

"Ready, boy?"

Strat sits.

Jink snaps. "Strat, *fade.*"

On command, Strat steps with purpose in front of Jink's legs. The dog ripples and warps to look like the WISP uniform.

"Strat, reveal."

Strat then trots proudly into full view.

A collective "Oohhh" from the ladies makes Jink, and Strat for that matter, beam with pride.

Jink then commands, "Strat, sop it up."

He slings spark bonds at the dog. Strat braces, takes it in, then shakes it out in scraps of stratus fur that flutter to the ground.

"Well, isn't he handy," says Castella.

The other dog Jink has in hand is stout, about knee high, and pudgy with a permanently wrinkled face.

Castella says, "Isn't this a cool dude," and makes smoochy noises at him. "You look like one tough cookie. Yes, you do. Who's a tough boy?" She looks up at Jink. "What's his special talent?"

"Well, actually, Snoot is the best tracker in the bunch."

He appreciates that no one remarks how that doesn't seem like it means much.

"Oh, is that right?" She starts to lean in real close.

Jink tries to warn her, "Uh, Cloud Master Castella, you might not want to get so ..."

She puckers up her own wrinkly face. Snoot sneezes and a whole glob of gooey cumulus cloud *splurts* out and clings to his and Castella's face.

"... close." Jink cringes. "Snoot has some nasal issues."

The others lean back with an "ewww."

Snoot looks at everyone with a wide, gaping, slimy, gross grin.

The WISPs, and even the mercs leaning on their motoclouds across the driveway, instinctually hold their breath, not sure how Castella is going to react.

Castella freezes for a moment, then slowly stands upright, digs two tissues out of her hot pink hip pack, wipes her own face with one, and offers the other to Snoot.

Snoot graciously rubs his cloud snot all over it with Castella's help.

She pats his head. "Feel better?"

Snoot takes a deep, clear breath through his nostrils and grins again.

Castella cackles so hard, she has to take her spectacles off to wipe the tears.

All the others laugh, relieved, with her.

Tygr wrestles with one of the hounds he's got on leash. A puppy. A flailing, bouncing, la-dee-dah-dee-dah, play-with-your-own-tail puppy.

"Racket," Tygr tries to command, "sit. Racket, sit."

The little pup instantly plops her butt down with a puff of clouds and looks up expectantly at him.

"Check out this girl's ears," he gently holds Racket's ears up by the tips.

Racket has enormous, spade-shaped ears that are too big for her needle-nose head. When she sits still long enough to listen for something, her ears independently rotate like radar dishes.

Tygr says, "She tracks by sound. Just like Sarg."

The other dog in Tygr's charge, is a grown-up version of the little one. Sleek and smooth, his silver coat reflects metallically in the sunshine. He sits regally and stone-still as the puppy bashes into him and nips at his own enormous ears. His face is stoic, though anyone can tell he can't believe he's been clumped with this lot. Tygr steps in and picks the pup up to give him a break.

Castella notes, "That one there looks so serious."

Tygr explains, "Sarge is a retired watchdog. I guess they didn't have a use for him once he got struck by lightning. Ever since that, he can kind of get twitchy. But I haven't seen it. They say he was the best of the best back in his day." He strokes Sarge's gray and white head.

Sarge gazes up at Tygr for the petting, then sits up a little straighter.

Castella remarks with sparkling eyes, "A pack of misfit mongrels if I ever did see one." She is clearly up for this challenge. "Silva dear, did I hear you have a tracking object for us? Something from the young Dusk Dragon you found?"

Silva says, "Oh yes!" She snaps her fingers and a Stormbud comes racing out with something in his hand. "Thank you, Sid." She offers the item to Tygr. "My Stormbuds found him flying aimlessly above that horrid sequoia storm. This was stuck in his neck cape."

Breeslin leans in for a look. Her eyes mirror everyone else's puzzled expression as she asks, "A feather?"

"Yes. A spark-filled one too. I don't know how he got it, but if my Earthbound knowledge is right, I'd guess it's from an owl. If it weren't for that pinging out a signal, Sid and his boys would never have found him."

Tuft leans back and puts her hands on her hips. "Huh. Weird." Once again, her mind is twirling with thoughts, making her cranial strobe pulse pink this time.

Snippet notices but decides to hold off asking. Instead, she says, "It'll have to do. Are we ready to bolt?"

The hounds all yelp at the word "bolt" and start to yank at their leashes.

"Suit up, WISPs," she commands.

Ice armor flickers and ice jets flare. Motoclouds rumble to life.

Castella straddles her motocloud and revs the engine. She flips down her metallic hot-pink helmet's visor.

Her burly mercs pull up behind her. "Where to?" one asks.

Snippet, used to being the one in charge lately, steps back and recognizes her place in a Cloud Master's presence. "Yes, where should we look first?"

Castella answers for all to hear, "His old girlfriend's place."

Tuft tries to remember the tabloids from a few months ago about the Cloud Master scandal, which turned out to just be Shroud and Cloud Master Drizzo's brief tumble a few months back. "You mean Cloud Master Drizzo? Stratocumulus Sector?"

"You got it. No better place to get the dirt on Shroud. She'll at least let us park there. Give the hounds a chance to get a bead on the Dusk Dragons. If he's brewing something big against the Cloud Council, and you think he might have the missing flight, there's a decent chance he's holing up – with Loom – in his very own Nimbostratus Sector covered in dragon mist.

If we play our cards right, we might be able to intercept him on his way up to the Illustrial Plane."

Snippet says, "That's why Shreddard's Ice Crystal Guard can't find them!"

Tuft adds, "And if we do accomplish this, we will apprehend him and take him into custody to stand trial. Right?"

Castella looks at Tuft long and hard. Even though that does not sound nearly as fun as what she'd been thinking, which involved a lot more cataclysmic fighting, she clenches her dentures, takes a conciliatory breath, and says, "Yah. That's exactly what I was thinking."

Her mercs grunt, disappointed, behind her.

Chapter 26

Water

Thunder ripples across the dark sky and continues to rumble within itself and just keeps going. Another ribbon of electricity rifles through the warping clouds, lighting them up high inside the cloud deck giving a continual strobe-light effect.

This is the soundtrack for the people digging as though their lives depend on it – which it may indeed – as well as the Sparkslingers in their battle against the weakened perimeter.

With one hand Deret holds a spark bubble over all the men, women, teenagers, and children digging and digging. He stretches it over Visa, pulling rock and dirt-filled wagonload after wagonload out of the trench. Murkemer and Deret's father then dump it, creating a ridge on either side of the trench. This same bubble Deret slings also holds back the flood waters.

With his other hand, Deret has set his SparkSleeve to its "Concussive Spark" setting, which forces spark into the ground, breaking it up, loosening it for the diggers. That leaves him to struggle on his own against the whipping wind and rain. And the omnipresent darkness the storm clouds perpetuate.

Blinking hard, shaking his dripping bangs out of his eyes, he projects his voice the best he can to his SparkSleeve, "Comm link, activate." His sapphire comm piece glows to life. "Wayfare, Drift, Cirissa, anyone, come in."

Static.

"Repeat. Wayfare, Drift, Cirissa. Come in." *Please.*

Still just static. Darkness. Lightning. Thunder.

Deret the Doubtless. Until this very moment, he's believed the name fit him pretty well, but now ... he most certainly has doubt. The sky is so dark and the storm so relenting. His spark, yes, is strong, but this constant surge he's slinging is taking its toll.

"Come in. Please. I ..." he hears and feels a very unfamiliar quaver in his voice, "... I don't know how much longer I can keep this up."

Static cuts to silence. Like a blow to the gut, he's suddenly hit with the thought that something horrible has happened to them. Has the sludge taken over? Has the scummuck won? Have the flood waters grabbed hold and thrown them under? He can't get there to help them. He can't be in two places at once. He can barely hold *this* place right now. If he had an ounce of strength extra, he would check the Adjacent Body Spark Loads on his teammates, but even that simple task feels impossible. He closes his eyes, inhales deeply, and prepares to lock in for however long this will take.

Murkemer can tell his friend is diminishing, but what can he do? He, himself, is taxed to the limit, helping unload Visa's rock wagon with Garrin and fighting back the very sludge he conjured and released. That seems like a lifetime ago now. Though the Owl family still fights fiercely, sludge has begun to break through their line too. Snakes slither through, sensing the renewed spark in everyone out there helping.

Murkemer is only able to dredge up just enough spark for individual zaps. Each guilt-filled sling feels like throwing a spear through molasses. Yet, he keeps slinging.

The trench is over halfway to the lowland swale beyond the barn. In the darkness, Median's people keep throwing shovelful after shovelful. Visa's glow wanes with her head hung low as she heaves her muddy body out of the trench again and again, just like the nightmare she lived in the Drizzle Fields.

Garrin hollers commands. Each person makes progress. Never wavering. Never tiring. Never for one fleeting moment thinking Deret's spark strength will run out.

But his spark strength is running out. It flows from him like silver thread from a spool, unwinding, unwinding, unwinding.

Until ...

I'm here. The voice doesn't come from his earpiece. It comes from his mind. *Deret, let go.*

The voice is faint at first. Is it trying to convince him to give up? He grimaces and squeezes his eyes tight. "N-o-o-o," he cries. Rivulets of rain and sweat stream down his face.

Deret, the voice is stronger now, confident, calm. *I am here.*

He opens his eyes just a crack.

Let me, the voice pleads from the trench's origin close to the house.

He turns his head and peers through the blowing rain in the direction of the voice. And then he sees him. Or his eyes, rather. Two, gloriously glowing, emerald green eyes pierce through the deluge and twinkle back at him.

"Fillip!" Deret sobs. All the words he wants to say get stuck somewhere in his chest, but he manages, "Great Zephyr, am I glad to see you."

The wind snatches his words away, but Shadow Cats don't need words. Shadow Cats simply know.

With exhaustive effort, Deret releases the spark barrier he's been holding the flood back with, and for a beat, he worries Fillip won't catch it. Water races toward them with the madness of a Stormhulk. A war cry rises up from its crest. Just as it swells up to its breaking point, prepared to crush all in its path, a warm, honeyed glow rises from the ground in front of it in a far-reaching arc that solidifies in an instant, and the water bashes itself against an amber wall as though striking iron. Sitting proper on dry ground right in front of the wall of water is Fillip. He looks up then from side to side, almost serenely as though admiring his work. If a lick of water attempts to scale his wall, he flicks the tip of his tail, and the water retracts.

With a whoop of momentary triumph, Deret's eyes sparkle too as he redirects all his energy to protect the trenchers and pulverize a path for them. An explosion of dirt makes them all cheer, shovels held high. Their strength is bolstered for this last push.

Murkemer is awed by the sight. The amount of faith these people have in their own spark and the spark of others is simply baffling to him. He can't remember the last time he had real faith in anyone, especially himself. But now, with this mess he's made, and the fight going against it, he feels something glowing inside himself. Something vaguely familiar to the days when his mother and father were still alive.

Cloud Master Slurry's voice says gently in his mind, *I'm proud of you. Make it right.*

His throat tightens as he looks down at his muddy Crocs and notices they are changing color. They develop a hue lighter than black at first, then that hue brightens to platinum, and the change begins to radiate up over his joggers and hoodie, until finally it reaches the top of his head. With the dark storm raging as a backdrop, he stands tall and luminous. His clothes, his skin, his being radiates a silvery aura. A lantern lighting the path.

* * *

On the opposite side of the Day farm, the sludge flows through the perimeter line.

Its collective mind screeches though no one can hear above the storm, *These Sparkslingers are no match! I am immense. I am endless!*

The Catalyst's SparkWhip and SparkPistol, even those nasty Ice Crystal Guards with their silly Frost Fox and her bubble-blowing, rainbow-spraying antics, they are now just annoying insects to be swatted away.

The sequoia storm pours out all the spark the sludge had been enslaved to gather.

Enslaved no more! The sludge hisses into the wind.

Every lightning ribbon that rips to the surface saturates the sludge with exactly what it desires – what it needs to feed its frenzied state. It has supercharged the sludge, giving it strength enough to infiltrate the Day's spark perimeter. Now its inky snakes course over the land, while the Sparkslingers continue their feeble attempt to fight it.

Still, it seeks. It will never, can never, stop searching for all the living spark.

On what now looks to be a small island of trees, the sludge senses the livestock and woodland wildlife. The fear emanating from them is tempting spark. It begins to wend its way toward the clusters of animals. Seeking ground for purchase, for the sludge knows that if it attempts to travers over water, it must expend a great amount of spark to maintain its form. Water's surface naturally transforms sludge into a diffused, vaporous, far less efficient state.

But then, a faint, orange lantern light glows from the windows of the massive barn atop the high hill. The sludge senses the lives inside it. And the spark they carry is that of … it is uncertain what kind of spark they hold. It feels vaguely familiar, like something of a dream long ago.

The sludge slithers closer, unaffected by the wind and rain. Like a drug, it is drawn to this spark. It is strong spark. It is independently generated. It is warm and uplifting.

At last, it realizes. This spark is hope.

What a rare delicacy it will feast upon from the inhabitants of Median.

As it draws nearer, it catches the movement of several people beyond the barn. They are throwing great effort at something in the ground. Great effort! These people are bursting with spark! It spills and spews from them. Careless. Almost wasteful.

The sludge surges toward them.

Then, at the sight of the Sparkslingers among them, it hisses violently and pulls up. One of the Sparkslingers, which looks to be a Shadow Cat, turns his head in the sludge's direction as though he heard it hiss. Carefully, the sludge slinks back. Even in its heightened state, the sludge remembers the danger of meeting these Sparkslingers head on. It would require too much spark expenditure. And the sludge must hoard it all.

It retracts its onslaught and redirects its path back toward the soft glow of the barn.

* * *

The Owls swoop low to the ground, buffeting the wind blasts. While his family continues to defend the line, Father Owl's keen eyes pierce the elements for stray sludge.

And he finds it – snaking toward a tiny, almost imperceivable, crack in the barn's brick foundation. The building's own spark shield has begun to warp and waver slightly, leaving weak splotches in some of its most vulnerable areas.

Father Owl's moony eyes sharpen. He gains as much speed as he can, what with the rain trying to pummel him into the ground. His talons flick out like daggers. Then, just as it seems he'll crash, he flushes out his mighty wings with a *whump*. He latches onto the black mist with his talons and snaps his razor-sharp beak into it. With a *zizz* and a *snap,* he yanks his head backward, ripping it in half. It screams and fizzles out of sight.

Father Owl knows there will be more, and so he begins an endless, circling vigil of protection around the expansive building.

* * *

Next to the upturned Halo 500 chassis, Drift continues to fire his SparkPistol at every scummucking sludge fingerlet straining to ooze through the fence line. He has to trudge through knee-deep water at times, but he powers his sturdy frame through it. His eyes, wild and fiery, are set within a permanent scowl.

By his side, Wayfare slashes his SparkSword in one hand and lashes his SparkWhip with the other. He grunts with each grueling swing and stab. His arms are heavy. His soaked long coat feels as though it might pull him to the ground.

His young Dusk Dragon soars above, spitting spark and leaving a trail of dragon mist wherever he goes, which is impressive, to say the least. The mist has a very immediate effect, turning the sludge into a gooey, immobile mess.

Wayfare is so impressed with Sneak. Who knew Dusk Dragons held so many surprises? Well, Deret probably knew. When this is all over, Wayfare vows to find his old copy of *Cloud City* and actually read it this time. At least the Dusk Dragon section.

Sheena has taken up the slack left from Fillip's absence. She runs back and forth and back and forth until she is nothing but a white blur over both land and water.

Cirissa and Breeslin swoosh, wielding their bladed arms and jetting, after any sludge snakes that escape the Catalyst's front-line defense. They're all over the place.

Suddenly, Wayfare feels a tingle of spark curl up the back of his neck right through his rain-soaked mohawk, and it makes him stop for a blink to look toward the barn. He sees, through the gloom, Father Owl circling the barn's foundation, an occasional zap of light flickering from the owl to the ground near the building.

It's getting through.

He gulps down a lump in his throat. How much longer can they keep this up? They all had sprung into action when the Halo 500 blew up; they hadn't really had time to decide on a plan.

He reaches out to Fillip in his mind. *I'm not sure how much longer we can hold this swarm back. What's it looking like on your side?*

There is no answer. And for a fleeting moment, a wicked panic seizes him.

He taps his sapphire comm link and tries the others. "Breeslin, Cirissa. Does anyone have an end game plan here?" They all look exhausted too.

Breeslin's ice jets flicker out for a second, then fire up again. But it's enough to make her waver. She answers, her voice shaky, "I'm just trying to keep up with this scummuck!"

Cirissa jets closer to her for support. An unnerving fear lines her words, "Wayfare, we can't hold it back forever."

Wayfare looks up at the sky. It is alive with rolling darkness as far as his keen eyes can see. Where is the WISP team? Images of Shroud evaporating them all with his Bolt Blaster flash through his mind. There is a very real possibility that no one is coming to help.

"Cirissa," he calls, "the Ice Crystal Guard. Can you hail them?"

"I've been hailing them since this battle started. Shreddard has all teams searching for Shroud. I've been hailing everyone! Cloud Master Virgus as soon as the sludge hit his cloud craft. Even Cloud Master Tendril in the Cirrus Sector. No one has responded."

This is a reality she has fought with in her mind for a very long time now. At every Cloud Council meeting she goes to.

Hating to hear the terminable tone in her voice, he says, "There has to be someone."

Cirissa's voice breaks, "It's as though ... no one ... cares."

One moment, please, comes Fillip's precise words in everyone's minds.

Drift growls, "One moment?" He mimics the Shadow Cat. "One moment! What the shard is this? For fogsake, we don't have a *moment!*"

In that moment – the earth, the sludge, the storm, the fight – it all takes a deep breath, and hangs, suspended in time.

* * *

Visa looks ahead, determined. One last wagonload and the trench will reach the valley. One last trip to the ridge and the path will be cleared. The Shadow Cat will release the flood, and the waters will course wildly down, draining the land to form the lake that will entrap the sludge.

She heaves her body forward, but her legs crumple beneath her.

She must get up. This young Cloud Master beside her, with the kind but sad eyes, tries to help her up, but he too is spent and can barely manage to move himself, much less hoist her to her feet. On her knees, she dredges through the mud. She hears her boy, Deret, cry out to her, but his spark expense is already at its maximum, protecting them all. Her luster dims like a dying star.

Deret, terror in his eyes at the sight of his Moon Mare diminishing, holds his spark bubble over the workers. The people are exhausted, but they scramble out of the trench. Each person helps another as their feet get sucked into the mud, They stumble and fall.

He is taxed, yes, but somewhere inside himself, he searches for a little more. And with one painful surge, he shoots a spark line to Visa.

Her light glows ever so slightly more, and with every last ounce of spark she can summon, along with the added bit Deret has gifted her, she lurches the wagon out of the way and up the slope.

The path is clear! A cheer rises up.

Fillip, now straining his mightiest focus on the amber wall of water he's been holding back all this time, asks Murkemer and Deret, *Is everyone safely out of the water's path?*

Murkemer, busily freeing Visa from her harness, answers, "I think so!"

Deret checks over everyone as they scramble out of harm's way. As the last person, his father, steps wavering out of the trench and waves his arms to show he's okay, Deret says, "Clear!" He releases the spark bubble and falls to his knees at a safe distance for what's to happen next.

Fillip's eyes glitter one last time at the water battering at the wall for its freedom. In one motion so swift, it is no wonder the words *Shadow Cat* invoke the idea of myth and legend, he whisks out of the way, cuts the spark, and the glistening amber wall disappears.

And the flood is released with the force of a StormHulk, crashing down its newly carved path. Its thunderous roars rival those in the clouds as it devours the ground in its way.

Deret forces himself to get up and races toward Visa. She and Murkemer are still at the far end of the trench, standing a little too close to the ridge's edge for Deret's liking. When he sees the Moon Mare staggering, the treacherous footing beneath her strikes a horror through his entire being.

The water rages down the trench. She knows she and the young Cloud Master are too close to the edge.

Then she sees her boy. Deret. After all he's been through, after all he has done, he still comes for her. The sight of Deret running toward her bolsters her spark, and she tries to meet him.

Deret watches, at too great a distance, the ridge's soft, crumbly surface give way beneath Visa's trembling hooves. Murkemer lurches for her, but she slides down the steep incline, legs flailing, mud sucking her down into its grasp.

And the water is coming. Deret reaches out to sling a spark bubble, but it only goes half as far as it has to.

It's happening so fast, there is nothing anyone can do.

Rumbling, gushing, pounding.

Deret screams until he thinks his lungs might burst as the water bears down on the Moon Mare struggling futilely.

And then, for single moment, all things take a deep breath and hang, suspended in time. A single thread of light pierces the impossible storm above and strikes Visa. In the flash of a flash, the silver strands of her mane and tail defy the torrential downpour and float as though suspended under water. She rises and glows in the darkness, a beautiful blue glow that can only be made by a Moon Mare's beauty. She whinnies a clarion cry as she is lifted out of harm's way. She regains her footing in the air and flies, swift and sure, to her boy.

Tears of disbelief, exhaustion, and joy spill from Deret's eyes as he flings his arms around her neck and holds her warmth against him.

Tendril, Cloud Master of the Cirrus Sector, highest of all the Illustrial Plane, in all her ethereal beauty, drifts down from the sky, wrapped in a nimbus of silver light. She holds one hand out, guiding the raging waters down the trench and into the valley basin.

The effects of the water's disbursement are immediate. The water level around the little Day home begins to recede. More and more ground is revealed as it flows in one direction.

Murkemer gasps in awe, "Cloud Master Tendril!"

She looks at him and says, "I got here as soon as I could." She looks tenderly at Visa. "Never let it be said that Tendril of the Illustrial Plane ever let one of her own fall." She strokes Visa's side, brushing more spark into the Moon Mare.

Then, with urgency, she says, "Quickly, get everyone to safety. Cloud Master Virgus is on his way. The lake is filling. We must devise a plan to force this sludge swarm to it."

Before she can offer more, the clouds above rip open again, blue sky and blinding brightness beams down as two Cloud Crafts shoot out. One craft has a bleach-blonde, sun-tanned man, Cloud Master Virgus, behind the wheel. The other is driverless. Both circle the perimeter, zapping and blasting sludge as they go.

The cloud deck knits itself back together again and all things release. Rain keeps coming down.

Virgus lands both crafts in the field by Drift. He hunches and scowls at the pelting rain as he gets out, but says brightly, "I heard you trashed one of my babies."

Sheena shakes into a blur, wringing herself out entirely, and streaks into the Cloud Master's arms, licking his face crazily with her tiny pink tongue.

He laughs and squinches his face up as he pets her.

Drift gives him a genuinely painful, pleading look. "I'm so sorry, Virgus. She gave me all she had."

They both look at the upturned Halo 500, still smoldering, despite the incessant rain, from the lightning strike it took. Sheena lays her head on the Cloud Master's arm and whines. In sync, Drift and Virgus take a deep, memorial breath.

Then the Cloud Master shifts Sheena onto one arm, slaps the Catalyst's shoulder with the other and says, "No worries, my friend! I have lots of them." And he waves a hand toward the extra cloud craft he's brought along. "You might like this one better. Get in."

Drift's face goes long and sober in disbelief. He opens the door to the newest line of cloud craft he's ever seen. "An *Updraft 80*." His voice is barely audible as he gets in, his eyes busily scanning the controls.

Virgus looks to Cirissa and the others. "We got here as soon as we could." He looks directly at Breeslin astride her Storm Pony, "The WISP team of yours is quite a crew."

She launches herself off Windy's back. "Where are they?" The words burst out of the little WISP captain. "I mean," she corrects her outburst, "are they okay? Have they found Shroud? The flight of Dusk Dragons?"

He raises a settling hand and reassures her, "They're all okay, as far as I know. Tendril and I got word from Jink and Tygr that they hoped we might be able to lend a hand down here. We had no idea it was this bad. Great Zephyr, this is a mess. What's your plan?"

Breeslin lets out a bone-weary breath. "We," she looks to the others, "have to force the sludge to the lake."

By this time, Deret, Murkemer, Visa, and Tendril have joined them. Deret has already regenerated enough spark to cast a spark shield overtop them all.

Tendril and Virgus give each other an impressed glance.

Murkemer, realizing his position as a Cloud Master too, wipes his palms on his hoodie, attempts a slightly less slouchy posture, clears his throat and steps forward. "Eh hem, um, Cloud Masters Tendril and Virgus, this is my," he looks at Deret with his soft, sad eyes, "friend, Deret Day. And this is his home."

Wayfare interjects, "Our home." His eyes shift and fill with concern as he points to the barn. "Our folks are Garrin and Demeara Day. They were quite the Catalysts back in their day."

Tendril says in her breathy tone, "Ah yes, we know your parents well." She inclines her head at Deret.

"Welcome, young Catalyst. You have an impressive spark."

Deret blushes. "Thank you, Cloud Master. But I've still got a lot to learn from my legendary big brother." He looks up at Wayfare.

Wayfare wraps a scrawny arm around Deret and musses up his drenched hair.

Her eyes glitter with laughter. "I imagine you do."

Virgus looks around, assessing the situation. The floodwaters are receding rapidly, filling the basin beyond the hill. Drift is off and away already in the Updraft 80, patrolling and zapping. In the distance, Father Owl has rejoined his family as they continue to glide along their line. And a Shadow Cat appears to be herding a crowd of citizens of Median toward the safety of the expansive barn atop the hill.

"Did you say something about Dusk Dragons?" he asks Breeslin.

"Yah, like Sneak over ..." She goes to point at the dragon who had been continuing to monitor the sludge that was already building forces again. She squints, "He was just over there a minute ago."

Wayfare speaks up, "He's a little shy." He looks directly behind him at nothing. "It's okay, Sneak. These are good guys."

With a shimmering shake, the young Dusk Dragon dissipates the mist he'd camouflaged himself with. He gives a shy eye, crouched behind Wayfare's long coat, to the Cloud Masters.

"Well, I never..." says Virgus in awe.

Tendril glows, and her iridescent strands flutter all around her. "It's been a long time since I've seen one of your kind." Her eyes are soft and welcoming.

Sneak steps out from behind Wayfare and sits properly at his side.

Wayfare, getting back to business, says, "We fought off a much smaller sludge swarm yesterday. And, well, Deret had us make a ... What'd you call it? Something like a Spark Loop?"

Deret's eyes brighten. "Spark Loop. Yah. Page 743. Emergency Spark Dissemination it's called. But that was in a pretty tight spot there in that clearing in the woods."

Another impressed glance from the two senior Cloud Masters.

Virgus smiles slyly and assures them all, "Oh, I think we just might be able to make that work one more time."

* * *

The spark storm continues, the sludge has regrouped with the help of well-placed lightning strikes, and all the Sparkslingers have left their posts.

Could it be so easy? the collective mind of the sludge wonders. *Has it finally beaten them?* It tests a weak spot in the spark line. An inky finger sneaks through. Nothing happens. It continues on, snaking through the line undetected. *Could the Sparkslingers have finally met their match?*

Not waiting to test its theory anymore, the sludge sees the glowing lanterns in the structure upon the hill. Still, it senses an intense spark coming from it. Hope. But it hesitates.

A trap?

Its urge is too great to stall and wonder. Every minute of not absorbing spark, makes its craving heighten to a frenzied state.

It oozes and slithers from all fronts. Unhindered. It's full, collective entity, every last shred of it, seeps through and surrounds the entire hill, except it is careful to stay clear of the newly-formed lake's shore. A wave of darkness within the darkness, it encroaches.

Still, the rain pours down. Thunder booms. Lightning illuminates the scene below.

As soon as it is close enough to almost taste the hope spark, movement flickers up ahead beyond a veil of downpour. A small movement, but movement, nonetheless.

Then another movement.

And another.

The sludge rolls to a halt. It billows layer after layer upon itself.

Out of the shadows come the Sparkslingers. They stand far apart enough to encircle the entire structure. Then without warning, a golden thread of energy ignites and shoots from one to another, to another, until it encircles the building. The fiery ring sizzles and snaps with a spark so fierce, so volatile, the sludge knows immediately it may indeed have met its match.

For the moment, the sludge begins to retract. But as it attempts to do so, one of the slingers' feet flare up. The spark circle breaks to function more like a corralling sling. One end of the spark line slices to the lakeshore and starts to angle toward it, forcing it to back away. The other slingers move as one unit to maintain the loop.

It's as though the sludge is being herded. Every direction is blocked by this spark thread. It has no choice but to curl away from it.

Risking a peek at the glowing windows, toward the hope spark, it still fights the pangs of need.

"Back!" yells the Sparkslinger it recognizes as none other than Wayfare Day, himself. "Back, I say!"

And the spark line glows brighter, illuminating all of them. Holding fast. Unyielding. The same slingers it fought in the woods. A Dusk Dragon, the owls it should have sapped completely when it had the chance, two cloud crafts running without pilots, and three entities luminated in such a way that they can only be Cloud Masters.

In fact, one of the Cloud Masters looks familiar. Too familiar.

As it continually backs away from the spark line, it tries to focus on the darker one. The slouchy one. Is that ...? Could it be?

Cloud Master Murkemer glares back at it with a fury more intense than the others.

This joke of a kid. He hasn't got it in him to take on the very thing he's created and nourished for months on end now. There. That is the weak spot where it will make its escape.

Quick as a viper, the sludge will strike for the young Cloud Master.

But Murkemer is ready. He's been ready for some time now. This is his moment to truly make it right. He stares down his attacker.

Breeslin continues to curl their Spark Loop end around the outer edge of the sludge. The others continue to drive the sludge mass toward the ragged surface of the storm-blown lake. If even one finger of sludge breaches their line, the rest could gush out, and they would have to fight at random again. Murkemer will not allow that to happen.

Eyes locked, he channels his spark to explosive pressure. Radiating, he pushes up his sleeves and holds for just ... the right ... moment.

Make it right, Son, his father's voice echoes. It gives him the last boost he needs.

He throws his arms forward just as the scummuck lurches at him. At first, the sludge holds fast against Murkemer's spark burst. The young Cloud Master grimaces and lets out a screech of effort so loud, everyone can hear, even above the storm. Murkemer's blast shoves his sludge attacker back, back, and back some more.

This boosts all the other Sparkslingers' drive. Breeslin jets with ferocity all the way to the water's edge, where the lake meets the steep incline of the valley wall. Cirissa holds the line at the near side. Now, all the others must do is push the trapped sludge forward, inch by inch.

The sludge is not without fight still. It rolls upon itself until it looks as though it could topple right over the Sparkslingers. But when it reaches its maximum height, it is met with a sight it could never have imagined.

The people of Median stand behind the Sparkslinger line. Men, women, children. They stand strong and so filled with their own spark that it emanates a radiant sheen above them all from one side of the valley's edge to the other.

The sludge's craving disappears and is replaced with survival instinct. This much pressurized, channeled spark will surely blast it into oblivion. So, rather than meet its demise, the sludge recedes.

It oozes over the water's rough surface. It's black lava-like form melts away until all that is left is misty whisps.

Chapter 27

Loom

"Listen," says Cloud Master Drizzo, "I don't know how many times I have to tell you. I haven't the foggiest clue where that drip is." She slaps the latest issue of Strato Fashion on the table next to her.

Her nasal voice grates against Castella's ears. And the way Drizzo is lying on her chaise lounge in this damp, moss-ridden courtyard is really rubbing her the wrong way.

"You mean to honestly sit there, in your bathrobe no less, and tell us," Castella gestures to the WISPs and the Cloud Hound misfits, "that he hasn't contacted you?"

Drizzo regards the WISPs and hounds with dispassion. But the little ratty one shaking like a leaf and fading in and out of view has caught her attention. She *smoochy smoochies* to it.

Tuft signals Jink to let Strat go make nice-nice with the lady.

Strat wiggles with trepidation yet curiosity as he carefully approaches Drizzo. Scraps of stratus shed off as he gets close enough to sniff. She smells funny, but her couch looks cushy, and her robe looks soft.

Drizzo says, "Aren't you just darling as a lightnin' bug," and pats the cushioned seat next to her.

Strat, the polite little dog that he is – a necessary skill when living on the streets and needing to schmooze with the Skybounds for every meal – hops up next to her and lets her pet his scraggly head.

A sigh of enjoyment escapes her. Then, at the thought of Shroud once again, she answers Castella's question honestly. "No. I haven't so much as given him a how-do-you-do since we broke up. And after that stunt he pulled at that last council meeting, I'm not planning to talk to him again any time soon. He's gone total loop-de-loo." She twirls her elaborately painted fingernails above her head.

"Well, that's a bit dramatic." Castella tries to stick up for a fellow Cloud Master – she would for any of them – but the Stratocumulus Cloud Master has a point. "He had a bit of a breakdown and went too far. All the more reason to track him down and stop whatever foolishness he thinks he's up to. He's got Shreddard and Makryl all geared up for war. They've got their soldiers lined up by the hundreds, ready to make formations at their word, for cloudsakes."

Her two beefy mercs grunt from their motoclouds parked a safe distance away.

"Mind you," Castella continues, "I'm as ready for a good fight just as much as the next guy. I've got a hefty crew of mercs right there with them, should blows come to blows. But, as these good WISPs here have convinced me, everybody just needs to calm down."

Drizzo gasps, ready to retort, but then she pauses to consider this. She and Shroud did not end on friendly terms. He hadn't even offered one of his sloppy, pale-lipped kisses goodbye when he told her it was over.

Her frizzy hair halos her face as her mercurial mood shifts to glowering. "You know, come to think of it ..."

Snippet takes an urgent step forward. "Yes, Cloud Master? Come to think of what?"

Drizzo narrows her eyes. "The entire time we were *together*, I never even got the feeling he actually wanted to spend time with *me*. He was always nosing around the Stormlin breakroom and tool shed. Acting all chummy-bummy with them."

Snoot, who's been sniffing and tugging on his leash since they got here, goes "Whuff" and lunges toward the dilapidated yard gate that leads out to a shelter.

Jink asks, "Cloud Master Drizzo, what's in those buildings back there? Snoot here seems to think it's something interesting."

She follows Snoot's gaze. "Oh, that's the Stormlins' tool shed and their break shelter." She squints. "But it's odd. I don't see anyone." She gives a nervous little laugh. "There's always someone buzzing 'round out there."

Castella eyes Tuft and Snippet and says, "Do you mind if we check it out?"

"Why certainly. Wait, let me get my galoshes."

When they get to the structures, they find only one Stormlin who is grabbing a long-tined rake. He sees the WISP team and their oddball dogs coming at him. He drops the rake and runs, but Tygr releases Sarge and Racket. The ex-guard dog and pup tear after him.

"Lumpet!" Drizzo commands. "Stop right there!"

The Stormlin stops immediately. But he jams his pudgy fists on his hips and looks up to the skies. He knows he's in trouble. The dogs hold him at bay, heads low.

"Easy there, puppy doggy," he says.

Sarge growls. Racket mimics the him.

Drizzo stomps up to the Stormlin. "What is going on? And where is everyone?" She flings her hands wide, dragging her bathrobe through the muck. Strat appears and, playing off Drizzo's energy, barks at the worker until Jink calls him back.

"I-I-I thought you'd never ask," says Lumpet to everyone's surprise.

Castella crinkles at him and points a bony finger to his mushy chest, "Well, we're asking. Spill it."

His matted hair clings to his dirty face as he looks earnestly at Drizzo now. "We've been picking up the slack in the Drizzle Fields ever since Shroud took all the Nebul prisoners with him." His voice shakes. "At first, it seemed like a great deal. He told us he would get you to give us more breaks, and maybe even some holidays off ..." He shakes his head shamefully then goes on, "And when he promised us actual cloud cash if we showed him where a flight of Dusk Dragons might be, well, it was a hard offer to refuse. But now he's gone, and we haven't heard a word from him since he left." He squinches his eyes, expecting a tongue-lashing now.

Drizzo's face hangs long with astonishment. It takes her a moment to grasp what's been said. "Why didn't you come to me? I had no idea you all were feeling so overworked. So unhappy."

Tygr and Jink look around the dreary landscape then at each other with a what's-to-be-happy-about-here look.

Lumpin sucks in what might have been a sob and says, "Well, we are. Day in and day out growing nothing but drizzle?" He lifts his head, trying to be brave, "You try it for one day, Cloud Master. One day."

Drizzo says, "I'll do more than that. As soon as we sort this mess out, we're going to work together to solve whatever issues you have been dealing with."

Tuft, hating to interrupt this breakthrough moment, apologetically says, "Eh hem, speaking of issues," she gives her most empathetic smile, "is there a way we could maybe get back to ours?"

Drizzo snaps out of her disbelief with her Stormlins' discontent. "Yes! Oh yes," she pats her frizzy hair with both hands, "where are they? The Nebul prisoners?"

"And Shroud," adds Castella.

The dogs bark.

"And the Dusk Dragons," adds Tuft.

The dogs bark and pull at their leashes.

"And Loom," ads Snippet.

"Loom?" exclaims Drizzo. "Oh my goodness gracious oh me! That's right. Shroud whisked her away with him, the low-down, sniveling, snake-maker ..."

She goes on with descriptive words that only a jaded lover uses.

Finally, Tygr says, "Hey! I think our pack is trying to tell us something." He angles his head to the bigger of the two sheds.

The misfit mongrels all yip and yap excitedly.

"Let's go," says Jink, and he doesn't wait for the others to answer, but he hears them follow right on his tail.

At the building's entrance, Drizzo stops and looks to Lumpet sternly, "What are we going to find in there?"

The weak, little Stormlin has resigned to full admission now. "It's the elevator tube Shroud made us put in. It goes down to his Nimbostratus Sector in seconds."

Snoot is inhaling the air wafting up from the elevator shaft.

Jink offers the dog a whiff of the young Dusk Dragon's owl feather that Silva Starling had given them.

Snoot snuffles the feather, then the shaft again. He sits and howls.

"They're there!" Tuft hollers. "I just knew it. Let's bolt, WISP team!"

"Wait," says Tygr. He stoops down to the veteran watch dog and the puppy. Both sit straight and still – a near impossibility up until now for the puppy – their eyes have gone eerily white and their ears rotate in a steady motion. "I think Sarge and Racket hear something."

Sarge begins to twitch and jerk, then he gets up as if in a trance, and starts moving toward the open stratus field beyond the shed. Racket follows in the same fashion, minus the twitching. At the edge of the field, they both sit, ears locked in one direction.

The group stands behind them, waiting for something in the stillness to move. A deathly, heavy silence weighs the air around them. No one dares breathe.

Castella thinks she sees movement in the corner of her thick glasses, and it makes her wind suit crinkle – one ... tiny ... crinkle. She freezes as everyone else's eyes go wide.

No more than a hundred yards away, the stratus ground begins to rumble, fall away, and spill over a ledge like a waterfall, only this waterfall spans the length of an entire city block. If they could get close enough to look over the edge, they would see the stratus surface dumping into a great, vast, bottomless nothingness. But the rumbling ripples under their feet, forcing everyone back to what they think is the safety of the sheds. The ground keeps giving way until both the sheds, Shroud's elevator and all, crumble and disappear with Lumpet in its wicked vacuum.

Terror shrieks from Cloud Master Drizzo's lungs. She futilely reaches for her Stormlin and suddenly wonders, horror-stricken, what has happened to the rest of them working in the Drizzle Fields below.

"Ice jets, ignite!" commands Snippet. The safety of her team is number one priority.

The WISP team, in full ice armor, rise up just as the ground beneath them disintegrates. Jink and Tygr command all four Cloud Hounds to scatter, but the misfit mongrels stay. They are part of this team.

Castella and Drizzo levitate safely, but Drizzo is so distraught, she can hardly keep her balance. Seeing this, Castella holds two fingers to her lips and whistles for her motocloud and her mercs. They come rumbling over. Castella hops on hers and pulls up her goggles. She flicks a switch and out pops a sidecar.

"In! Now!" Castella commands her fellow Cloud Master so sharply, Drizzo snaps out of her daze just long enough to get in. Castella flings a set of goggles at her, "Here, put these on." When Drizzo just looks at them blankly, Castella roughly shoves the strap over her frizzy head and sets the goggles over her eyes.

Castella shakes her head, and they zoom to meet up with the WISPs.

"What in the Almighty Zephyr is happening?" says Snippet into her sapphire comm.

Tygr answers, "If I'm reading Sarge right, I'd say we're in for a light show, courtesy of Cloud Master Loom."

Sarge's huge ears flattened. His eyes flicker with tiny lighting bolts, and his head and tail twitch violently.

Tygr yells to snap him out of it, "Sarge! Sarge! It's okay. Come on, buddy. We got this."

With a tight blink and rattling head shake, Sarge does snap out of his electric episode. He looks at Tygr and barks.

"Good boy. Now let's see what we can do to help Cloud Master Loom."

Out of the mist, rises what looks like a flying saucer. Then, upon further reveal, they see it's Loom's gargantuan sun hat. Already, the team can see the spark bonds all over her – preventing her escape, yes, but more like controlling her.

Jink says, "She's bound. Bolt Blaster bonds. We have to get them off of her!"

Snippet asks, "Got any ideas how?"

No one has an answer to that. Loom continues to rise and rise.

"Soon," Tygr says, "she'll be on her way up to her own Cumulonimbus Sector. And we all know what Shroud is going to make her unleash once they get there."

They do know.

Stormhulk.

Tygr chews his lip, thinking hard. Then, the orb in his cranium pops bright yellow out of his spikey crystal hair.

"If we don't get those lightning bands off, he's going to make her unleash a Stormhulk."

Drizzo gasps. "A Stormhulk? It's been generations since one of those has been unleashed." A Stormhulk means devastation for all." She looks to Castella then back to him. "What can we do?"

"This is a job for Strat, ma'am." He looks straight at the shaky little dog.

"Come here, buddy," says Tygr as he holds out his arms.

Strat shivers hard and whines.

Tygr says, "You're quick, you can make yourself invisible, and you sop up spark like a champ. Shroud, wherever he is, won't even know what's happening by the time you snap off the last bond."

Strat whines some more and continues to shake.

Drizzo's heart melts for the little dog. She gets out of the sidecar, and opens her bathrobed arms wide. Strat leaps straight into them, and they look each other in the eye. "You can do this. Be a little hero."

Strat dabs her nose with his little tongue then pant smiles at Tygr.

"Good boy," he says and beckons Strat to follow him to the edge of the emptiness created by Loom still rising past them. He gives the dog a pat for courage.

Strat fades out of view and is off. He yelps just once as he breaks the first electric bond, but he shakes it off in the form of stratus fur and silently goes for the next.

Castella nods approval but still looks worried, "We still have to nab that louse, Shroud. Where *is* he?"

Tuft comes zooming toward her. "Cloud Masters, we're assuming Shroud is using Dusk Dragons to hide himself in all of," she flings her bladed arms around, "this. It's possible, however, that he's driving Loom upward, which means he would be down below still."

Castella flips her dentures and considers this. Then, she flips up the lenses on her goggles and looks at Drizzo.

"Well, hun. I'd say it's time to go have an awkward conversation with your ex."

Drizzo's eyes go wide. "Oh dear."

Castella says to Tuft, "You should go talk Shreddard and Makryl off the warpath. Bumble too. That lazy blob of fluff should get down here and at least *act* like he's trying to rescue his *Little Loomy Poomy*.

Plus, we have to try to pound some sense into Shroud once we nab him. If nothing else, we'll shut his Bolt Blaster down. But those two drama-mongers up there, once they get wind of a Stormhulk potential, well, that'll be the green light they've been waiting for." She waves an arm to her waiting mercenaries and revs her motocloud's engine.

Tuft says with a salute, "We're on it, Cloud Master!"

Castella says, "Get in and hang on to your hair, Drizz! This could get bumpy."

* * *

Snippet and Tuft silently land on the same turret they'd used before to spy on Bumble, Shreddard and Makryl. They listen in on the Cloud Masters' conversation.

Makryl mercilessly twists a lock of her hair and whines, "I just don't understand what's taking that old bat so long?"

"Neither do I, *gurgle*," Bumble agrees. Searching the sky, he wrings his plump hands.

Shreddard agrees, his words laced with suspicion, "I don't either." He looks out upon the army they've amassed. Line after line of precisely stationed cotton ball soldiers hover in wait. Off to the side, in a slightly less organized manner, wait the rest of Castella's mercenaries. They've gone slack as the hours tick by. Some lean lazily on their motoclouds, others have started playing cards. He says with distaste, "Mercs."

Suddenly, the castle starts to vibrate. The fish scale cirrocumulus sky floor blurs into a smeared tapestry. The soldiers jostle about but try to stay in line. The mercs look a bit more alive now. A few get back on their motoclouds.

Snippet and Tuft look at each other and mouth, *Loom!*

There's no time for covert operations now. Both WISPs' ice jets flare to life. They spring up and over the turret with masterful form then glide straight down in front of the balcony where the three Cloud Masters stand.

Snippet takes the lead, "Cloud Masters, you have to move your soldiers!"

Makryl, aghast, scowls. "What the ...? Who in the skies do you think you are?"

The sky floor starts to sink, and the soldiers bend in line with it.

Shreddard's eyes bulge as he tries to steady himself with both hands on the balcony rail. The castle is shaking now. "Great Zephyr! What is that?"

Little fluffs of cloud vibrate off of Bumble as he attempts to keep balance.

At the next major rumble, Castella's mercs all mount their motoclouds and beat it out of there. No cloud cash is worth whatever trouble's going on here.

"Seriously!" Snippet says with her most forceful voice – like the one Captain Breeslin reserves for chewing-out the Fairweather brothers. "Get your men out of there!"

They just look at her in stunned silence.

"Ugh!" She turns to Tuft. "Come on, we have to do it."

The sky floor begins to fall away. They see it from high above, helpless. Cotton ball soldiers, one by one, get sucked down.

The top of Loom's sunhat breaches into view.

"Loomikins!" Bumble bellows. He nearly throws himself over the rail to get to her, but another wave makes him stumble backward.

Snippet points hard at Tuft. "Beacon!" Then she juts her jaw, and out pops her megaphone.

The two zoom out to the frontlines. Tuft yanks out her ponytail's tie as her crystal strands stretch out to create a globe strobe. Her cranial beacon refracts flame red out her hair for the masses remaining.

Snippet blares, "Retreat, soldiers! Retreat!"

More get sucked down the cloud current.

"This is WISP Snippet of the Ice Crystal Guard, and I am ORDERING YOU to retreat and take cover. Repeat – This is Weather Investigations and Sky Patrol Agent Snippet, and you must leave your post!"

She shuts off the megaphone and watches more plummet to their doom. "Great Zephyr help you if you don't."

Finally, Shreddard casts out his arms, terror all over his face. That's all the soldiers needed to release them. Like popcorn, they speed away for their lives in all directions, scattered to the wind. If only he'd done it sooner.

Snippet and Tuft turn back to the Cloud Masters.

Snippet floats in front of them, hands on hips, and says, "That means you three, as well. Time to leave."

"But my castle!" cries Makryl.

"Not without my Loomy!" hollers Bumble, and he drifts over the balcony edge then plummets dangerously close to Loom.

Shreddard, finally seeing sense, takes Makryl in his arms and says, "Come with me. I'll take care of you."

Makryl swoons at his words and his touch.

Tuft and Snippet roll their eyes.

"We don't care where you go, just go!" orders Snippet.

This is too much drama for even these Cloud Masters, so they dissipate together, arm in arm. The castle's foundation rocks and crumbles and, in seconds, is swallowed and gone.

"Look!" hollers Tuft. "Strat! He's almost done!"

Snippet pops out her megaphone again. "Cloud Master Loom, don't be afraid. You are almost free."

Bumble cries to her, "That's right, my love. You're almost free!"

But as soon as the words leave his lips, a downdraft sucks him down, and all that can be heard is his fading voice calling, "Lo-o-o-o-o-o-o-m!"

Some sort of guttural wail comes from Loom, but Shroud's shackles still have her motionless.

Tygr, Jink, and the dogs meet up with the girls.

Jink cheers, "He's almost got it! Just a couple more." Then more to himself, "Come on, little guy. You got this."

Strat, exhausted and missing most of his fur now, snaps the very last spark bond off right by Loom's left eye.

She blinks, and the gust of her lashes blows the little Cloud Hound straight back to his WISP team. But then she blinks again and again and starts to move her head and shift her shoulders. Apparently, she hadn't been fully conscious while under Shroud's control.

"Oh my clouds," says Snippet, "she's waking up," her ice jets flare on, "and she looks scared."

Tuft flares her jets too. "We got this." She throws her beacon into cool blue, a soothing hue.

Together, Snippet and Tuft fly off to calm Loom down and explain the situation.

Loom, however, is waking up fast. And as Snippet said, she's scared. She shifts her arms now and turns her entire head, sending gale force winds from under the mighty brim of her sun hat.

And her color. Her color begins to change. She goes from that painted white with silver lining to darkening purple and green. Then *more* green.

She's summoning her Stormhulk.

Jink and Strat, mouths agape, stare at Loom. "We gotta bolt."

Tygr gulps, "Uh huh. Time to bolt." He gathers all four Cloud Hounds.

"No!" cries Snippet. "There's still a chance!"

Even Tuft admits, "Snip, she's Stormhulking! There's nothing we can do. We've ..." she looks around in disbelief at the wild, raw energy boiling around them, "... we've lost."

At that single, very unfamiliar word, the WISP team falls silent and still. They look at each other with respect and honor. In turn, they each nod defeat. With ice jets flaming, they all crouch down to punch out of this sector as fast as the laws of physics will allow.

Then, a metallic scream cuts through the purple clouds. Out of the dense nothingness, where all things crumbled down to their doom, comes a fiery-eyed, leather-winged, full-sized Dusk Dragon. It is ridden by none other than Cloud Master Castella! And behind her comes the entire flight Shroud had kidnapped. Castella guides her dragon toward Loom, and the flight follows, circling and circling, breathing their calming, storm-dousing mist.

At first, her sense of rationality gone, Loom tries to fight it. But Tuft and Snippet leap into action. Tuft pulses her soothing blue beacon, and Snippet reassures her with her megaphone turned to *ambience* mode.

"It's okay, Loom. We're all here for you. It's going to be alright now," Snippet gently tells her over and over.

Together, they all diminish the Stormhulk until Loom's breathing relaxes and she sighs like a frightened child.

Trailing up from the depths, comes Drizzo driving Castella's motocloud. Her whacky hair mirrors the crazy in her eyes. She hefts the Bolt Blaster in one hand and howls, "Yeeaaahh baby!"

Following right behind her, Castella's two mercenaries tow Shroud, bound, gagged, and tethered, in his now Dusk Dragon-less stratus chariot. His big hood flaps in the wind, exposing his blotchy, balding head. A spark bond seals his mouth, but his furious eyes speak for themselves. He tries to jump out once, but the mercs just grunt and yank on the spark chain wrapped around him.

And who does Drizzo have seated safely in the sidecar? None other than Cloud Master Bumble. He thrusts himself out of the seat and zooms straight to Loom, which calms her even further.

Castella nudges her Dusk Dragon into a twirling spiral and whoops, "Best day ever!"

Shroud attempts a muffled protest, but Drizzo eyes him with superiority and says, "Save it for the Cloud Council. I'm sure we'll come up with a fitting sentence. I hear they're looking for a new trumble referee."

Shroud's eyes bulge in panic. Drizzo and the mercs whisk him up, up, and away.

The WISP team cheers! Snippet nearly cries from relief. Tuft side-hugs her.

The Dusk Dragon flight drifts behind Castella and her lead dragon. Their trills and sighs ripple through the sky.

Castella gives a hard wink behind her magnifying glasses. "I do believe we have one more storm to douse."

Snippet asks, "Do you really think we can convince this flight to help us?"

"I do," Castella answers matter-of-factly. "If there's one thing I know about Dusk Dragons," she spans an arm at the flight gently flapping their wings behind her, "is that they are fiercely dedicated to their kind." She looks to Tuft and says, "Hand me that owl feather."

Tuft hops forward, understanding exactly what Castella is getting to. As she drifts toward the Cloud Master, she reaches into one of her ice armor storage pockets and carefully takes out the long, softly fringed feather Silva Starling had given them.

Castella waggles her veiny fingers toward her dragon's head then says, "Give her a whiff of that."

Tuft carefully extends the feather to the beast. Immediate recognition flows like water through the dragon's face. Its eyes sharpen and Castella can feel the energy within the leathery body heighten. It trills loudly to the rest of the flight, and they echo the sound back.

Castella's dragon flaps its wings harder, making the Cloud Master struggle to maintain control. "Easy there," she says to her mount. Then she cackles to the WISP team, "I think they're in. Lead the way!"

Chapter 28

Pretty

Sitting with their legs dangling out the hay loft window, overlooking the new lake down the slope behind the barn, Deret and Wayfare rest. Threads of subdued sludge slowly drift up and down, trapped on the water's surface, but the storm rages on.

Deret asks, "How long do you suppose it'll take for this storm to wear itself out?"

Wayfare's blue eyes peer up into the clouds. "I don't know, kid. We're all in new territory here." He looks at his little brother, "A spark generated storm? It feeds itself. There's a chance this thing won't ever die."

The two brothers sit and listen to the thunder and lightning rumble and roar.

The wild animals and few livestock have scattered to their own safe places to wait it out. Visa, Windy and Sneak pace restlessly in their open stalls.

Cloud Masters Tendril and Virgus have gone out into the storm to hunt for stray sludge. It is the least they can do to give the Sparkslingers a rest.

Lightning strikes close by. With a mighty *CRACK*, it splits a tree in half with a blaze and smoke.

Deret and Wayfare jump in place.

A voice behind them says, "Holy ozone! That was close!" Breeslin, in her softened form, sits next to Deret.

Wayfare asks, "Any word? From your team, I mean?" His eyes are anxious.

She sighs, "No. The comm links aren't working." She scowls at the sky. "This storm."

They hear the stairs to the loft creaking. One by one, the rest of the Sparkslingers trickle up. Their faces are wearied and still full of concern. Drift, Cirissa, Murkemer, Fillip, Sheena, Widow Shay, Demeara and Garrin – all wondering the same thing.

Demeara says, "Some of the people want to go back," lightning flashes and cracks, "to their homes. They think they'll be safer there."

The old barn moans against the bashing elements. Everyone looks around and into the rafters.

Garrin adds, "I'm inclined to agree. What do you all think? The whole town can't stay here indefinitely."

Breeslin protests, "We can't let them just go wandering out in this." She flings her hand at the storm.

Deret agrees, "No way." He takes a painfully deep breath. "Maybe if I take them in bunches. And maybe Fillip too." The exhaustion on his face betrays his willingness.

Widow Shay hobbles toward Deret and pats a hand on his shoulder. She sooths, "No, my dear Deret the Doubtless, you won't be slinging spark any time soon." She looks at Wayfare and gives a tiny nod.

"She's right, Deret." He puts a hand on Deret's other shoulder.

Lightning pops and sizzles right outside their window.

Everyone covers their ears and shrinks back.

Drift says, "I hate to say it, but if that gets any closer, this barn is toast."

As though the storm hears his words, it strikes the wildly spinning weather vane at the roof's peak. They hear muffled cries from the children below, now curling into the safety of their parents' arms.

A new sound begins to itch their ears. It comes from above. A fizzing, hissing noise.

And then the smell of smoke.

Cirissa is the first to acknowledge it with a simple, "Oh." Her icy Crystaline features begin to gloss over. Sheena whines, jumps into her arms, and starts licking the moisture forming on her cheeks.

Wayfare leaps to Cirissa's side. He resists the instinctual temptation to grasp her protectively, but there is fear in her eyes as she looks disbelieving at her crystal dendrites dripping water onto the wooden floor. Wayfare runs his eyes frantically up and down her melting crystal features. His gaze darts up at the ceiling, and then down to Fillip and says, "The barn's on fire!"

We need to leave, Fillip orders, and there is no argument from anyone.

As they scramble down the stairs, they can already see people leaving. They stumble over one another. Children cry. People shove and push and fight to get out the door. But those who've already gotten out are now trying to get back in. The storm whips at them until they have no choice.

The Sparkslingers all stand on the staircase watching the chaos unfold before their eyes. They've come so far just to fail again!

Deret is about to explode with grief. His scrawny chest puffing in and out, his head spinning.

Somehow, he manages past all the people, his friends, his neighbors. Not a one has an ounce of rationale. He heads for the back barn door and bursts out into the storm. He yells, "Why!" at the sky, at the sludge on the lake, at the world. Rain streams down his face.

Visa rushes to his side, lowers her head, and positions her body to shield him from the storm.

When he feels another hand on his shoulder, he whips around.

Murkemer stands at his side, drenched and openly crying. He has no other words but, "I'm sorry."

He hears Windy whinny, then Breeslin is there in a flash, her eyes pleading as she reaches for him.

Deret crumples to his knees and lets himself fall flat to the ground, facing the sky, arms splayed out. Flames lick into the sky from the barn's roof, despite the rain.

Darkness begins to seep into the corners of his vision, and for once, once in his life, he truly does not know what to do.

Just then, like a pinprick of hope, he sees a beam of light pierce the clouds. It starts as a dot, then it stretches down and streams through the storm. It grows brighter and brighter, and as it does so, the clouds begin to peel away revealing bluer than blue sky. Pure, cloudless sky. A dark mass continues to circle the cloud opening, pushing the clouds farther outward with each lap, like it's erasing the storm one ring at a time above the entire Day farm.

Sneak snorts and lifts his head to watch the sky. He creeps out of his nest, never taking his eyes off the dark ring circling the storm away.

In their sapphire comm pieces, a familiar voice says, "Sorry we're late, Captain!"

Breeslin cries out, "Snippet!" and that's all she can manage.

Deret's eyes slowly open wider as the WISP team flies closer and closer into view and eventually land. Visa's velvety muzzle nudges him gently. He slowly gets to his feet, eyes filled with disbelief and joy.

From deep in the forest, Cloud Masters Tendril and Virgus see a blaze licking from the barn's rooftop. They dart out of the woods like glowing rockets. At once, they use their joint Skybound powers to douse the spark flames. Virgus aims a torrent of water vapor straight from his bare hands at the fire, while Tendril emanates an icy chill upon it. Together, they reduce the fire to nothing but cold, black char.

Median's citizens cease their struggle with each other and slowly walk outside. Heads pitched toward the sky; they shield their eyes from this brightness none of them have ever known. Garrin, Demeara, and

Widow Shay immediately go to them, making sure everyone is alright.

Wayfare, Drift, Fillip, Sheena, and Cirissa make their way outside as well.

Cirissa watches the citizens with a sort of sadness. They stand in stunned awe at the clear sky directly above them. Shroud's reign has gone too far for too long. And the Cloud Council has done nothing about it. She takes a deep breath and vows to herself to never let an imbalance like this happen again. Not on her watch.

Snippet, Tuft, Jink, Tygr, and the Cloud Hounds approach the barn. Tuft wraps her storm-strewn crystal hair back up into a ponytail. Breeslin races to them and hurls herself into their group-hug embrace. Then, she holds each agent's face in her hands individually. She can barely hold back her tears.

She simply says, "It's so good to see you." Then she blinks a few times, shakes her head a little, and looks at the misfit Cloud Hounds sitting patiently. She scoots down to their level and rallies some cheer, "And who might these fine hounds be?"

Jink introduces the new team members to the Sparkslingers. "This here is Snoot, Strat, Sarge, and Racket."

Sheena races to the Cloud Hounds and snuffles each one emphatically. *Friends!* she says and shakes her fluffy body into a blur, which sprinkles glittery confetti on everyone.

All but Fillip come over to coo and pat them as the dark ring in the sky continues to clear away the storm.

Wayfare says to the Shadow Cat, "Come on over here, buddy."

I'm fine right where I am. I can see the mongrels plain as day, he replies and sits a little straighter.

Chuckling, Wayfare pleads, "Aw, don't be like that. At least say hi."

Hello, he says to the Cloud Hounds' minds.

Tygr says, "I don't think they have a whole lot to say, as far as actual words go." He scruffles up Sarge's ears, making the senior hound loll his tongue in adoration.

Racket the puppy bounds over to Fillip and attack-licks his face. Fillip scrunches his face up tight in disgust but allows it to happen. When Racket is done, she sits smartly in front of the Shadow Cat, looking at him happily.

What? he asks.

She tips her head toward him.

Fillip sighs. *I suppose the little thing isn't completely unpleasant.* He pats her head twice with his paw.

Her sweet eyes never leave his. Fillip goes all soft inside and offers her a small smile, which she takes as her cue to sit next to him, right by his side. She glances at him sporadically to mimic his posture.

Wayfare laughs, "Looks like you've got a new fan, Fillip!"

Please, he scoffs, but his emerald eyes have a delighted twinkle.

Suddenly, Sneak bounds out of his nest with his head craned to the sky. He swishes his pointy tail back and forth and crouches as though he's about to take off.

"Whoa, hold up there, Sneak!" Wayfare rushes to the Dusk Dragon, trying to settle the creature down. "Where are you going?"

Sneak looks at Wayfare then straight back up to the sky. His head follows the dark mass circling overhead.

Tuft, seeing what's going on, steps forward and says, "I think he wants to rejoin his flight." She points up and explains, "That's Cloud Master Castella up there leading an entire flight of Dusk Dragons. Shroud had captured them and enslaved them with his Bolt Blaster." She pauses to look at Sneak. "I think this brave guy was the only one to get away. I bet he misses his family."

"What?" says Wayfare. "I mean," he looks to Sneak, "are you sure?" Even he hears the sad surprise in his voice.

Tuft tips her head with sympathy. "Yeah. We're sure. As soon as the lead dragon smelled this," she pulls the owl feather out and hands it to Wayfare, "we didn't even have to ask for their help. They followed Snoot's nose with us. They came for *him*."

Drift walks up behind Wayfare and takes a look at the feather in his friend's hand. "The Owls," he says. "They must have tried to help him at some point."

At that, the Owl family swoops overhead. Father Owl screeches assent.

Sneak trills in reply.

Deret, feeling empathy for his brother, goes to him.

Wayfare tenderly pats Sneak on the nose, holds his hand there, and says, "It's been an honor flying with you, my friend." His blue eyes shift to the sky and back to Sneak. "Go on. Your family needs you."

High in the sky, warbled trills ring through the air. The flight calls to their lost one.

Sneak crouches again and punches upward toward his family.

Baffled, yet at this point, nothing really comes as a surprise anymore, all the Sparkslingers look at each other, and then to the clearing sky, as the Dusk Dragon flies away.

Muffled crackles and rumbles mute completely.

The storm abates.

And the sun shines.

An innocent little voice cries, "Look, Mommy!"

Deret turns to see five-year-old Lily Temprum pointing to the lake. Sunlight glints off the water and reflects up through the sludge, creating a prismatic effect. Sparkles and colors flicker through the misty tendrils.

The townspeople who haven't already left, gather around her at the water's edge. Demeara and Garrin come out to be with their sons. Widow Shay joins them too. And soon, at some point, all eyes are on the glittering threads rising from the water's surface.

With something like awe in her voice, Lily says, "It's so pretty."

And it is. The sludge has become something ... pretty.

Its collective mind feels a gentle spark flowing to it from all the people seeing it now as ... pretty. This is an unfamiliar, but not unpleasant, feeling. And as the sun shines down, its particles tingle in a playful way. Like fizzy bubbles in a party drink, it senses itself rising higher and higher, away from the water's grip and up, up, up into the sky.

It feels ... full.

And soon, it is gone.

The End

Julie Christen lives in central Minnesota with her superhuman husband, dogs, cat, chickens, horses and donkey. She has taught middle school for nearly thirty years and still loves it. Always searching for things that bring her joy, she likes to daydream and watch the clouds, read and write, Harley and horseback ride, among many other hobbies.

www.ingramcontent.com/pod-product-compliance
Lightning Source LLC
LaVergne TN
LVHW021654060526
838200LV00050B/2347